OUT OF THE PAST

To all outward appearances she looks like a
Victorian maiden aunt – but behind the knitting
needles and the lace lurks an acute intelligence
and a pair of scanning eyes which miss
absolutely nothing. Allied to her strong moral
principles, her passion for justice and an innate
understanding of the basest human motivations
Miss Silver is a very formidable detective
indeed.

'Miss Silver is marvellous'

Daily Mail

'You can't go wrong with Miss Maud Silver'
The Observer

Patricia Wentworth's ingenious detective
stories have delighted millions of readers all
over the world and the quality of her writing
has consistently received the highest praise
from reviewers.

'Miss Wentworth is a first-rate storyteller'
Daily Telegraph

'Miss Wentworth's plot is ingenious, her
characterisation acute, her solution satisfying'
The Scotsman

**Also by the same author,
and available in Coronet Books:**

The Alington Inheritance
The Benevant Treasure
The Case of William Smith
Eternity Ring
Ladies' Bane
Latter End
Miss Silver Intervenes
Vanishing Point
Watersplash
Pilgrim's Rest

Out of the Past

Patricia Wentworth

CORONET BOOKS
Hodder and Stoughton

First published in Great Britain by
Hodder & Stoughton Ltd. 1955

Coronet edition 1972
Eighth impression 1987

Printed and bound in Great Britain for
Hodder and Stoughton Paperbacks, a
division of Hodder and Stoughton Ltd.,
Mill Road, Dunton Green, Sevenoaks,
Kent (Editorial Office: 47 Bedford
Square, London WC1 3DP) by
Richard Clay Ltd., Bungay, Suffolk

ISBN 0 340 15952 9

PROLOGUE

THE first time that James Hardwick saw Carmona Leigh was on the evening of her twenty-first birthday. He was in a box with the Trevors at the Royalty, and he looked across the theatre and saw her. She was sitting in the second of the stiff gilt chairs which faced them from the opposite box. She wore a white dress and a little white fur coat which she had slipped off and pushed back. She leaned forward with her elbow on the padded ledge of the box and looked across at him.

She was not really seeing him at all. Her mind was much too full of her twenty-first birthday, the string of pearls which Esther Field had given her, the play she was going to see, and what Alan had whispered as they came up the stairs. She saw nothing except her own thoughts, and she saw them suffused with a wonderful glow of happiness and hope.

James Hardwick saw what he had been waiting for all his life. Love at first sight does happen. It had happened to him. There was a kind of tingling shock, a sense of recognition, of achievement. It wasn't anything he could get into words either then or later. It was something that had happened. He went on looking.

He saw a girl with a delicate, serious face and dark hair, quite young and rather pale. He thought about that, his face hard and serious, his lips compressed. He might have been considering some matter of life and death, bringing everything he had to bear upon it. A girl may be pale because she is tired—sad—ill. The girl he was looking at was not any of these things. Her pallor had a luminous quality. It sprang from some deep intensity of feeling. There was a quiet radiance. Her eyes were dark. Not brown, but a very deep soft grey. But the lashes were black, and it was partly those black lashes which made her look so pale. He was not conscious of any sequence of thought. It was all there

5

in his mind, like a picture seen in a moment of time, but he was never to forget a single detail.

It did not stay. The large, comfortable woman beside her said something, and a man who had been standing behind them came and sat down on the third of the stiff gold chairs. He was tall, fair, and noticeably good-looking. The sleeve of the white fur coat brushed his arm. He pushed it away, laughing. The girl turned. There was a faint colour in her cheeks. They smiled at one another.

Colonel Trevor growled at James' ear,

"See those people over there? The girl's father was the best friend I ever had—George Leigh. Got himself killed in a motor smash—he and his wife. Left me one of Carmona's guardians. Well, she's twenty-one to-day, and I can't stop her making a fool of herself if she wants to."

"I don't know why you should call it making a fool of herself," said Mrs. Trevor in a petulant tone. "I'm sure there are very few girls who wouldn't jump at Alan Field."

Colonel Trevor's voice acquired a military rasp.

"Then they'd be fools, my dear."

James hoped they were not going to have one of their quarrels. Alan Field—now what had he heard about Alan Field? There was an impression that he had heard something—somewhere—and not very long ago. Not a pleasant impression. He couldn't fix it.

Mrs. Trevor was bridling.

"I'm sure I can't see why! It's simply that he's too good-looking."

"Don't like young men who are too good-looking, my dear."

At fifty-five Maisie Trevor could still flutter an eye-lash. She did it now.

"Jealous!" she said, and gave the rippling laugh which had proved so effective with subalterns when she was seventeen.

James, who nevertheless had an affection for her, thought for the thousandth time how silly it sounded, and wondered how the Colonel put up with it. Just as a matter of habit, because his mind was really taken up with the question of Carmona.

Colonel Trevor had snapped at his wife. She was appealing to James.

"I suppose you'll take Tom's side—men always do, don't they? Back each other up, I mean. But what I say is, Carmona may think herself lucky if she gets such a good-looking young man. She's a sweet girl and all that, and she's got quite a nice little income. Tom has been looking after it for her, you know. But you can't say she has got very much in the way of looks—can you? And Alan really is a charmer. Of course he hasn't any money, so it really might do very well. They were brought up together, you know—at least after her parents were killed. Dreadful! That's Esther Field over there in the box with them—Carmona's aunt—a sister of poor George Leigh's. Such a plain woman for a famous painter to have married, but of course she had money, and he wasn't so famous then. Silly, isn't it, how things don't come when you want them. Now, when he's been dead for ten years, everybody knows his name. He was Penderel Field. Ridiculous name, but quite good for advertisement. Esther is Alan's stepmother, so in a way he and Carmona are cousins, only of course not really, if you know what I mean. Such a pity Alan had to leave the Army. I'm sure I don't know why he did, but Esther was very much upset about it, and I expect she would like him to settle down with Carmona."

Colonel Trevor broke in sharply.

"Let's hope she has more sense. And the less said about why he left the Service the better. And you are not to go round coupling his name with Carmona's—do you hear, Maisie?" He turned to James. "All very boring for you, I'm afraid."

Mrs. Trevor produced a late handkerchief and an injured sniff.

"*Really*, Tom!"

James made haste to say that he wasn't bored—people interested him. It was in his mind that it would not be difficult to get the Colonel to take him round in the interval and introduce him to Carmona. A hundred to one he would be going round anyhow to wish her many happy returns of the day. Easy enough to get himself taken along.

Easy enough, but it didn't come off. Mrs. Trevor developed one of her "attacks". The play bored her, and she considered that Tom had been rude. She became faint, threatened a swoon, and said she must go. Since they had come in James' car, he had perforce to drive them home. He had seen Carmona Leigh, and that was all.

He left at cockcrow next morning for the Middle East, and he was away for more than a year.

It was on the day after his return that he saw her again. He was on his way to stay with the Trevors. They would put him up, and he would walk over and see his Aunt Mildred Wotherspoon whose elderly devoted and tyrannical maid no longer allowed her to have anyone to stay in the house. The last time it had been attempted had been so unpleasant for everyone concerned that by tacit consent it was agreed that there should be no repetition, James writing that the Trevors had offered to put him up, and Miss Wotherspoon replying that that would be very nice and that she hoped he would come over to tea.

He sat in the train and thought that it was good to be back. The odd thing about coming home was that you didn't expect anything to have changed. You went away, and things happened to you, but you somehow didn't expect that anything very much would have happened to the people you had left behind. Old Tom Trevor would be growing prize delphiniums, carnations, and dahlias, and Maisie would be finding it dull in the country and giving him no peace about coming up to town for an occasional week to look up old friends and go the round of the theatres. Aunt Mildred would be in the middle of one of her rows with Janet. They had been going on ever since he could remember, and both parties appeared to derive considerable satisfaction from the exercise. Everything in their little world would be just as it had been before he went away.

He began to think about Carmona. The Trevors would be able to tell him where she was and what she was doing. She touched their world, but she did not really belong to it. The years between twenty-one and twenty-three were years in which a good many things might change. He would not admit that they might have set an insurmountable barrier between himself and her. He would not admit that she might have married Alan Field. Or anyone else. Always when he thought of coming home it had been in his mind that he would be coming home to Carmona. He had heard of her once or twice. In a letter from Maisie Trevor—"Carmona has been here to stay. Horribly dull for her. Tom really ought——" From Mary Maxwell, who was an old friend and had stayed in the same house no more than a month ago—"She's some sort of a cousin. Rather an unusual girl. I'm very fond of her. I hope she isn't going to marry that wretched Alan Field. He's a kind of step-cousin of hers, and people are always saying they are engaged, or are going to be——"

No, she hadn't married Alan Field. In some curious way he had been quite sure that she would not. She was going to marry James Hardwick.

They were coming into a station, and as they drew in another train drew out. There was a moment when the two trains passed each other, one just starting, the other slowing to a halt, and in that moment he saw Carmona Leigh. Across the brief space which separated the two trains they looked at one another. She had a window seat, and so had he. It seemed as if he had only to put out his hand and he would be able to touch the glass through which she looked. What he saw jerked at his heart. Her eyes were wide and she was very pale. It was not the pallor which he had seen before. She had been happy then, she was not happy now. There was no time for her to close her face against him. If she was pale now, it was from sorrow of heart. The windows slid away, her face slid away. She was gone.

He found out that the train was going to London.

In between displaying his delphiniums, which were in full bloom, old Tom Trevor told him that Carmona was marrying Alan Field in a week's time.

CHAPTER I

CARMONA HARDWICK came up the zigzag path from the beach. The afternoon was hot and she took her time. She wore a sleeveless linen frock and a big shady hat. Her legs were bare and she had green sandals on her feet. The whole effect was cool and pleasing. She was thinking that Pippa *would* arrive in the middle of a blazing afternoon! All very well to say, "Don't bother to be in, or meet me or anything", because of course you had to. She hadn't seen Pippa Maybury for three years, and there was a time when they had been very fond of each other. These school friendships didn't last. . . . Pippa was always a bit of a goose. . . . Three years was quite a long time. . . . They had both married. . . . A slight shade came over her face.

She reached the top of the cliff, and took the path which led along it to the house which James had inherited from his great-uncle Octavius Hardwick. Much too big for them and it would have to be sold, but meanwhile they could spread themselves, have all their friends to stay, and enjoy James' leave.

In spite of being called Cliff Edge the house stood a little way back. There was a stone wall between it and the cliff path, and a private gate into a bare formal garden where old figureheads of ships stared out to where the horizon met the rim of the sea.

The house was hideous—very flat and bare outside and the rooms full of plush curtains and frightful Victorian furniture. There was a driving-road on the far side and an approach featuring a good deal of stone work. The six urns which flanked the entrance had blazed with scarlet geraniums in great-uncle Octavius' time. They were empty now, and two of them were cracked. Carmona looked at them and thought they had better sell the place as soon as they could, because it really did look very shabby and it would cost the earth to do it up. They would certainly never want to live here.

She had her foot on the bottom step of the half flight leading from the front door, when a sports car whizzed in at the gate and came to an abrupt stop beside her. Pippa, in scarlet slacks and a sleeveless jersey, sprang out and embraced her. When

last seen her hair had been a fair brown. It was now platinum.
She wore dark glasses with scarlet rims which she took off and
snapped away in a startling red and white bag as she brushed
Carmona's cheek with her own. Her eyes at least had not
changed. They were as bright, as blue, and very nearly as
dazzling as the sea.

"*Darling*!" she said. "What a frightful house! But how nice
to see you! You're not going to live in it, are you? You really
couldn't? I'm sure it's got black beetles, and a basement, and
the sort of old-fashioned range that simply eats up coal! You
must tell me everything! But I'd better put the Tick away first—
it belongs to George Robertson, and he's rather mean about
his things! He was quite frightfully peeved when I ran into a
lamp-post and smashed the windscreen of the car he had before
this one—and it was more or less dropping to pieces anyhow
and well overdue for the scrap heap!"

The three years since they had last met were gone. Pippa
was just the same. The current young man's name had been
Jocko then, it now appeared to be George. That was all.
Whatever it was, he would be considered as a provider of cars,
flowers and other unconsidered trifles, and more or less treated
like dirt whilst kind, stodgy Bill Maybury looked on with a
tolerant smile. Carmona had a moment's faint wonder as to
what James would do or say if she were to start borrowing
cars and being continually here, there and everywhere with one
infatuated young man after another. All at once she shivered
and felt cold. Too silly—because the sun was really hot today.

The garage was a converted stable balancing the large
Victorian conservatory on the other side of the house, denuded
now of its palms, its climbing heliotrope, its plumbago, its
begonias and pelargoniums. When the Tick had been put away
with the narrowest escape of a grazed mudguard, Carmona led
the way up a flight of steps into the tesselated hall.

Pippa's comment was frank.

"Darling, how fierce! Too, too like the kind of hotel one's
grandmother might have stayed at!"

Carmona laughed.

"Well, we really are rather like a family hotel at the moment.
We've got the Trevors here. You remember Maisie and Tom?"

"Of course—he was your guardian. Rather a lamb."

"And Adela Castleton——"

Pippa made a face.

"Darling—not *the* Lady Castleton! Because I don't know if I can bear it! I've a sort of idea I met her once, and she looked at me as if I must have got there by mistake! That kind of nose, if you know what I mean!"

Carmona knew quite well. It was the kind which lent itself to disapproving of the young. She passed hurriedly to Esther Field.

Pippa burst out laughing.

"Aunt Esther! Is she here too? Still dropping stitches and calling everyone 'My dear'? Well, I must say you are doing the relations proud!"

"She's the only real one. The rest are just because of being guardians and things, but Esther was my father's sister."

"And Alan Field's stepmother. Carmona—where *is* Alan?"

"I don't know."

They had passed out of the hall into what Octavius Hardwick had called the morning-room, an apartment which looked north and never got the sun, its natural gloom being further intensified by a carved overmantel of some black oriental wood and curtains of indigo plush.

Carmona shut the door. It wasn't the slightest use hoping that Pippa would drop the subject.

"You don't *know*? But, *darling*!" Pippa's eyes were alive with interest. "Surely Aunt Esther——"

"She hasn't the slightest idea."

"You mean he just broke it all off and disappeared?"

"Something like that."

She wouldn't turn away. It didn't really make things any worse to speak of them. Sometimes it made them better, and—it was only Pippa.

"But Carmona! Darling, you've simply got to tell me all about it! When I had your wire to say it was all off I wanted to rush to you! But Bill put his foot down—you know, he does sometimes. He said I couldn't do any good, and he was sure you'd rather not, and it wasn't reasonable to expect him to put up about a hundred pounds for me to fly home just to hold your hand. I could see his point, you know, and when he is like that I do find it's better to do what he says. Darling, you *did* understand, didn't you?"

"Of course."

"You must tell me all about it now! What did you quarrel over?"

"We didn't."

Pippa's voice rose a third of an octave.

"Didn't quarrel? But, *darling*!"

Better get on with it.

"He just didn't turn up."

"On your wedding day!"

"Yes."

"Darling, how perfectly frightful! You don't mean to say you were there waiting at the church!"

"Yes."

It was hurting horribly. Much more than she had thought it would. It was hurting like hell. The grey church, cold and dark, with that odd smell which empty places have. Empty— at least thank God for that! Only Tom, and Maisie, and kind Esther there to look on whilst she waited for Alan who didn't come. A parson and a verger too, but they didn't count. Grey old men quite alien from what was happening to her, their own days of quick anguish and hot tears all past and gone. She looked vaguely at Pippa, but she did not see her. She saw the empty church.

"Darling, how *frightful*! But what on earth made him do a thing like that? If he wanted to break it off, why didn't he do it properly? I just can't imagine Alan—*Alan* getting cold feet at the last minute and not being able to come up to the scratch! Carmona, he must have *written*! Something must have happened to the letter—or to him!"

Carmona moved her head. It was the slightest of movements. It said, "No."

Pippa Maybury repeated what she had said before.

"Something *must* have happened to him!"

This time it was Carmona's lips that moved.

"No—he wrote afterwards. The letter came next day. He said he couldn't go through with it—he wasn't cut out for marriage, and he was going to join a friend on a horse-breeding ranch in South America."

"And that was all?" Pippa stared. "Well, darling, I really

do think you were well rid of him! He was a charmer and all that, and marvellous to go about with, but when it comes to husbands"—she shrugged and laughed—"well, you know, there's something to be said for having them solid. After all, they've got to run the show, and pay the bills, and do all the unpleasant sort of things like income tax, and washers on taps, and spiders in the bath, and I don't really see Alan making much of a show of it. Speaking quite frankly, you know."

Carmona didn't see it either. She never had. She had always known that if there was anything unpleasant to be done, she would have to do it herself. The thing that had been broken in her was the conviction that Alan needed her. It was a conviction that went right back into her childhood. He was selfish, he could be cruel, he had a fatal knowledge of his own charm and of other people's weaknesses, but—he needed her. And then when she found out that he didn't, that he could push her aside and put the width of the world between them, something broke. She said,

"No——"

Pippa gave her a light pinch.

"Wake up, darling! You said that as if you were about a hundred miles away,. and the one thing one ought never to let oneself do is to go dreaming back into the past. Fatal! And it isn't as if you had got left on the shelf, or anything like that. Why, it was no time at all before you married James. To tell you the truth, I didn't think you'd have had the spirit."

"Thank you, Pippa."

"Well, you know, you were always one of the quiet ones and you might have taken up good works, or gone into a mouldering melancholy—like the girl in Shakespeare who sat. on a monument and smiled at grief, which I always thought a particularly stupid thing to do, because young men aren't really interested in monuments and they wouldn't bother to climb one. And now tell me all about you and James! He isn't nearly as good-looking as Alan of course."

"Not nearly."

Pippa nodded vivaciously.

"Husbands don't need to be. And I always thought Alan overdid it. After all, looks are more in the woman's line, don't you think? Anyhow I'm dying to see him again."

"He's away," said Carmona.

"Away!"

"He'll be coming any day now. He has been doing a job under U.N.O.—something to do with tracing people who have disappeared. He speaks a lot of languages, so they find him useful."

"Doesn't it take him away a lot? It sounds as if it might."

"It does rather." After a pause she said, "Sometimes I go with him. I went over to the States with him in the spring."

Pippa stared.

"It sounds a bit detached. I hope he turns up in time for me to see him. And where is everyone else? You say you've got the house packed with relations. Where are they?"

"Down on the beach. I hope you won't find it dull here. There's nobody young."

Pippa looked through her eyelashes.

"Too, too reposeful. Not all the time, you know, but every now and then—relations, I mean—the nice quiet elderly sort who have never had anything happen to them."

"Do you suppose anyone is really like that?"

Pippa burst out laughing.

"Marvellous if they all had buried secrets! But, no, I'd really rather be soothed. Where are they?"

"Down on the beach—and we should just have time for a swim before tea."

CHAPTER II

THE tide came up slowly. There was a shimmer of heat over the sea and no breeze. Esther Field sat on a cushion in the shade of the beach hut and knitted diligently. Since this year she was giving shawls as Christmas presents to the three or four old pensioners whom she had inherited from Penderel Field's mother, and since this particular shawl was almost complete and of a lively shade of crimson, she both looked, and was, extremely hot. Billows of red wool flowed from her in every direction.

"Extra big," she was explaining to Lady Castleton who was sharing the patch of shade. "For old Mrs. Mount. She gets larger every year and is really quite proud of it, so of course it wouldn't be the least bit of good my giving her anything skimpy."

They had been at school together thirty years ago, when Adela Castleton was Adela Thane with a brother in the Army· whose occasional visits provided the other girls with a thrill. They had neither of them changed very much. Esther had always been large, and kind, and dowdy, and Adela had been beautiful. She had kept her looks wonderfully. The celebrated profile, the celebrated complexion, the celebrated figure were all still intact. If they had become a little fixed, a little—how shall one say, stereotyped—the effect was sufficiently imposing. She made Esther Field look like a rag-bag, and Maisie Trevor of that out-dated smartness which is so much worse than just being dowdy. Her own dark blue linen was exactly right, and so was the simple shady hat which had probably cost more than Esther had ever paid for one in her life. She glanced at the billowing shawl and said,

"Really, Esther—I don't know how you can! Do put that ghastly thing away and give us all a chance to get cool! You don't have to think about Christmas now!"

"I've dropped a stitch, dear. You see, that is why I have to get on—I'm always dropping stitches. I can't think why they won't stay on the needle. Other people seem to manage it, but I've never been able to. That is where I miss Carmona so much. She always used to pick them up for me. It's lovely being here with her now." She raised her voice a little. "Darling, if you wouldn't mind—I'm afraid there's another one gone."

Carmona came over and knelt beside her. Pippa lifted her head from her folded arms to say lazily,

"Darling Esther, why not do a drop-stitch pattern and have done with it?"

"Well, dear, I don't suppose I should ever manage to drop the right stitch. It doesn't do for it to be just any one, you know. You have to follow a pattern, and I do find patterns so difficult. This is one I learned when I was at school, and I don't seem to be able to manage any other."

Carmona put the shawl down again in her lap and went back to where the sun was glinting on the silver gilt of Pippa's hair. Not a breath stirred. She thought Colonel Trevor must be having a very hot walk. She wondered why one sat in the sun and baked, and thought Maisie really had the best of it when she said it would be much cooler up at the house and she would go and look for an amusing book.

Carmona waited till she had gone, to say,

"She won't find one."

Pippa yawned.

"Uncle Octavius didn't rise to light literature?"

Carmona shook her head.

"Scott, Dickens, Thackeray, in sets—handsome bindings and very small print. And all the works of Mrs. Henry Wood—East Lynne, you know. And frightful memoirs, like the ones Esther solemnly brings down here every day and never reads. Uncle Ocatavius had never read them himself—nobody has ever read them, because the pages have never been cut. But she thinks they will improve her mind if she can get it off her knitting long enough to give them a chance, so she brings out her pet paper-knife that Penderel gave her and waits for the moment to be improved."

In the shade of the beach hut Adela Castleton said suddenly,

"That girl's happy, isn't she—the marriage is turning out all right?"

Under the droopy hat which had seen better days Mrs. Field's placid face took on a startled expression. Her hair was never tidy for very long. She pushed back a strand of it now and said quickly,

"Oh, *yes*. My dear, what makes you ask?"

"She doesn't look like she used to," said Adela Castleton. "Alan wasn't any good for her, but she used to have that kind of lit-up look with him. It wouldn't have lasted of course—it never does. Do you ever hear from him, Esther?"

"No."

"You've no idea where he is?"

"He said he was going to South America."

"You never knew why the engagement was broken off?"

"No."

"And she married this James man practically the next minute?"

"It was three months, Adela."

"Well, what do you call that? I call it the next minute. And a good thing too. Tom was delighted. James has always been a pet of his. I've hardly seen him myself since he was a boy and used to spend his holidays with Mildred Wotherspoon. Is it true that he fell in love with Carmona at first sight? I can't think why anyone should, but the most extraordinary things do happen."

Esther Field ruffled up like a hen with one chick.

"Really, Adela!"

"What have I said? I'm very fond of Carmona, but nobody is going to pretend that she is the kind of beauty who would turn a man's head at the first glance. She has the sort of looks that grow on you, and they generally give a girl the better chance of happiness. Beauty doesn't always do that." Her voice dropped a little. "Do you remember how lovely Irene was?"

The vexed look left Esther Field's face. Warmth and kindness flowed from her.

"Oh, my dear, yes! I don't think there was ever anyone as pretty as she was that last summer."

Adela bit her lip. What a fool she had been to speak of Irene. She couldn't imagine what had made her do it. A little quick jealousy over Carmona, a small cold wish to prick Esther Field, and here were her eyes smarting and the old wound aching as if it had never healed. Irene had been more than ten years dead—everything healed, everything passed. What had possessed her to speak of those old forgotten things?

Esther Field was remembering too. Irene Thane, the young sister whom Adela had loved like her own child—lovely, bright, and tragically dead at twenty. They said it had been an accident—but was it? A warm summer day and a still sea, and Irene swimming out into the blue and never coming back. . . .

They said it must have been cramp. The best swimmer in the world may have cramp——

The word came to her lips.

"Had she ever had cramp before?"

Adela's face hardened.

"Everyone gets it some time."

"Oh, I don't think so, dear. I've never had it myself. It wouldn't be safe to swim out very far if one did. And Irene was such a good swimmer—so graceful in the water too. You know, my dear, I am so glad you spoke of her. It does always seem so sad when no one ever talks of them—like shutting them away and trying to forget. It's difficult of course when one has had a shock. I felt like that when Penderel died, but I knew I couldn't do it, because if I did I should feel as if I had lost him altogether—never speaking of him, you know. And it would have been awkward too—his name being so unusual, and strangers being so very apt to remark on it. I used to have it on my visiting cards—only one doesn't visit so much as one used to—at least not formally. But I have always called myself Mrs. Penderel Field, and then they say, 'Not *the* Penderel Field?' and we often have quite a nice little talk about him. It is such a pleasure to find that he is remembered. Do you know, his portrait of Lord Dainton has just been bought for the Tate Gallery, and really the Daintons didn't care very much about it at the time it was painted. Now, if it had been that lovely thing he did of Irene—I always did like that— but Lord Dainton was such a very plain old man, you wouldn't have thought he would have wanted to be painted at all. And *The Times* says it is Penderel's masterpiece! Of course he *was* Lord Chancellor."

"I always thought it a very fine portrait," said Adela Castleton firmly.

Esther Field sighed.

"I've never been any good at art, dear. Penderel used to tell me not to try. He said there was only one thing worse than the out and out Philistine, and that was the Philistine who pretended he wasn't. And when I said I couldn't think why he ever wanted to marry me, he said it was because I had the only two virtues indispensable in a wife, a sweet temper and a light hand with pastry. He had such a sense of humour, and he did love my lemon meringue tart. Do you know, that new clever young man Murgatroyd is going to write a life of him. He came to see me, and when I told him about the lemon meringue he said that was the sort of personal touch he wanted. He has just written what everyone says is a very brilliant book about Mr. Parnell. The papers all say things like his 'being a live wire' and 'having quite a new approach'— if anyone knows what that means."

"It generally means something unpleasant," said Adela Castleton.

Esther Field dropped a stitch without noticing it.

"Oh, my dear, I do hope not! And as I said to him, 'Well, I'm afraid I can't help you very much, because it was my stepson who went through his father's papers for me.' I was really too ill to do it myself, and so much of the early stuff had to do with Alan's mother, so I didn't feel——" She dropped another stitch.

"My dear Esther, you mustn't dream of just handing those papers over to anyone! You will certainly have to go through them yourself."

"I know, dear. But I can't. You see, I'm not sure what Alan did about them. I was ill, and he managed everything."

"You must know what he did with the papers."

Esther looked vague.

"He managed everything—and it's nearly ten years ago— Carmona and I had that cottage—there was so little room. Of course they must be somewhere. I promised Mr. Murgatroyd I would have a good look, and he said he would put an advertisement in the South American papers—for Alan, you know."

Adela Castleton pressed her lips together. She was of the opinion that it would probably be better for Esther and everyone else if Alan Field were to remain on the other side of the world. There had been so many stories about him. Men didn't like him—didn't trust him—never had. There was a time when he used to run after Irene. So many young men did that, and he was only a boy—twenty-one—twenty-two. Old enough to be quite terribly attractive—and a trouble-maker. That last year Irene had seen a lot of the Fields. . . . Irene swimming out to sea and drowning there. . . . A sudden attack of cramp? . . . She had never had cramp in her life. . . .

"Oh dear!" said Esther Field. "I've dropped two more stitches! No, three! Carmona darling——"

When the stitches had been retrieved Carmona stood up. She was still holding the shawl. The man who had come down the cliff path looked at the little group and saw her like that, in her white dress with the folds of crimson wool falling down it to her feet. He stood for a moment to take in the scene. Quite a decorative effect. She had, if anything, improved in looks. Pretty would always be the wrong word for her, and no one would ever call her beautiful, but there was something about her that pleased the eye—a charm, a grace. Since Hardwick was away, they might have quite a sentimental meeting.

His eyes travelled to Esther Field. She really hadn't changed a bit. He supposed she never would, the soft-hearted, muddle-headed old thing. He felt quite fond of her as he remembered how easy it had always been to get round her.

Neither of the Trevors was in evidence. Esther's maid had told him they would be there—"Such a nice party, Mr. Alan. Mrs. Field was ever so pleased about it. Colonel and Mrs. Trevor, and Lady Castleton—quite a reunion as you might say, not to speak of meeting old friends we used to see when we went down to Cliffton regular every summer. The only pity is Major Hardwick not being there."

Somehow, he felt, they would be able to do very nicely without James Hardwick. And without the Trevors too. Maisie was all right—she might even be useful—but old Tom had always given him a pain in the neck. Adela Castleton—no, on second thoughts, Adela might be worked into the game. It would be tricky of course, but he could do it—oh, yes he could do it. And to play a tricky game well was half the fun.

He came across the shingle to the beach hut, and Carmona saw him. It was just as if someone had struck her a sharp blow. The shawl slipped from her hands and fell. She didn't know whether she was hurt or not. There was just that sense of shock and of everything being wrenched a little out of focus. His voice and the touch of his hand on her shoulder——

"Carmona!"

He was smiling and looking down into her eyes just as he used to do. And then he was on his knees by Esther Field, an arm about her, kissing her.

"Well, old dear, how are you? But I needn't ask—you look

marvellous. I'm even a little hurt. The wanderer returns, and nobody has been pining for him!"

"Oh, my dear boy! Oh, Alan, my dear, dear boy!"

He endured an embrace which entangled him in crimson wool. Half a needleful of stitches slipped and were lost. He disengaged himself, laughing, and turned to Adela.

"Lady Castleton—how nice to walk right into a family party! Emily told me when I turned up at Esther's flat, so I thought I would come down right away. Pity about Hardwick not being here. I was looking forward to meeting him."

Carmona had not moved. She did not move now, but she spoke.

"I hope he will be here tomorrow."

Alan Field said, "Delightful!"

The numbness went out of her. The shock of the blow was passing and she could feel again. What she felt was not what she had expected to feel. Whenever she had thought of seeing Alan again there had been an intolerable sense of shrinking, but now that he was here it was gone. He stood looking at her with the smile which used to twist her heart, and all she felt was the prick of anger.

As he stepped into the sunlight, she saw that he looked more than the three years older. Whatever he had been doing in South America, it had not done him any good. There was the old charm, the old grace of movement and manner, the old ease, but it seemed to her as if something had gone out of all these things. Or was it that something had gone out of her? That little glow of anger persisted. It was outrageous of him to blow in like this. . . . He had come to see Esther. There was nothing outrageous about that. . . . It wasn't Esther's house. . . . It belonged to James Hardwick whom she had married after Alan had let her down. . . . And James wasn't here. . . . If he had been, would even Alan have had the nerve to walk in like this?

He had the nerve now to laugh in her face and say, "Well, Carmona, how about it? I hope you are going to ask me to stay, because, quite frankly, I'm broke to the wide."

Pippa sat up and stretched.

"Who isn't?" she said. "Hullo, Alan, where have you blown in from? I haven't seen you for ages."

"Darling, you couldn't very well—I was in South America."

"Why didn't you stay there?"

"Partly because I was broke, my sweet, and partly becaus someone was advertising for me. I thought there might be money in it, so I came home only to find it was a bloke who wants to go through my father's papers. Seems there's a boom in Penderel Fields, and he wants to cash in on it and write a life."

Pippa stared.

"Well, I shouldn't think Carmona could put you up. Frankly, I think you've got a nerve to ask her. And anyhow the house is pretty well crammed."

Esther Field had scrambled to her feet.

"No, no, you can't stay here—of course not! The house is really very full indeed. It wouldn't do at all. Carmona mustn't think of it. Come up to the house with me and we will have a talk. You remember the Annings? They used to take p.g's, and you stayed there once or twice when we had the house too full."

He laughed.

"Oh, yes, I remember the Annings."

"Well, Mrs. Anning is quite an invalid, but Darsie carries on. It's really quite a boarding-house now. I met her yesterday and I happened to mention you. And I don't think she is full up, so perhaps—But come up to the house, my dear, and we will talk it over. I have to take that cliff path slowly."

Carmona had not said anything at all. Her expression was grave and still. Alan Field turned to her now, his eyes dancing.

"Well, Carmona? Time seems to be getting on, and I lunched on a sandwich. Talks with Esther are rather apt to be lengthy. Am I invited to dinner, or is the house too full for that?"

She smiled, and said in her natural voice,

"Oh, I think we can manage dinner, Alan."

CHAPTER III

ESTHER FIELD sat by the window and fanned herself. They were in the morning-room, which was the coolest room in the house. She had left her knitting in the hall, but the climb up the cliff path had heated her. She was worried too, because after the first shock of surprise she could see very well that Alan had put them all in a very difficult position by coming here. He really had no business to walk in on them like this. The more she thought about it, the less she liked it and the surer she was that it really wouldn't do. James wouldn't like it—not after the way Alan had treated Carmona. He couldn't be expected to, though she wasn't sure how much he really knew. Husbands and wives didn't always tell each other everything. Even Pen——

Her thought jerked back to Alan. What he ought to have done was to stay at the flat and ring her up from there. Emily would have looked after him.

Alan laughed and said,

"Well, old dear? Where have you got to—'He really oughtn't to have given us a shock like this'? Yes, I guessed as much. I can generally see through you. Well, I always was a bit funny, you know. When I think of a thing, I like to do it right away."

In spite of continued fanning Esther's high flush persisted. She said quite simply,

"You oughtn't to have come here."

He made an airy gesture.

"Because Carmona and I were once engaged and very sensibly didn't get married? Really, darling—we're not Victorians!"

She said again, "You ought not to have come. Why did you come back from South America?"

He smiled.

"I told you—to go through my father's papers for that man Murgatroyd. Though I don't expect you to believe that it's all filial piety, because of course it isn't. I can't really afford that sort of thing—at least not free gratis and for nothing. But if there's going to be a boom, I've at least as much right to be in on it as anyone else."

The brown eyes which were Esther Field's best feature gazed at him doubtfully.

"But, Alan, Mr. Murgatroyd wouldn't be buying the letters. People don't do that when they are writing a biography."

"Quite right—they don't. But there might be money in it all the same."

"I don't see how."

"You will, all in good time. You see, I've got to have money. One can't, unfortunately, get on without it. And as it is, I've got a chance of a really good thing. If it comes off, I'll be made for life and no more trouble to anyone. But I've got to have a sprat to catch my whale with."

Esther went on looking at him.

"What has all this got to do with your father's papers?"

"Everything or nothing, according to how things turn out. It mightn't be necessary to bring them into it. It all rather depends——"

"On what?"

He produced one of his most charming smiles.

"On you. Just what are you prepared to do about it, darling?"

"*I?*"

"Yes, you. It's quite simple, you know. I didn't get much out of my father's estate, did I?"

"You got all there was, Alan."

"I know, I know—there were only a few hundreds, and you let me have them. The money was yours—you needn't rub it in."

"You had already had your own mother's money. Has it all gone?"

"Every sou, darling. What could you expect?"

She had known what the answer would be. To Alan money was something to spend. Whatever she gave him today would be gone tomorrow. He could charm her heart, which Pen used to tell her was as soft as butter, but she came of a long line of shrewd business men to whom money meant something to save, and he couldn't altogether charm her head. She said,

"I'm afraid I gave up expecting you to be sensible a long time ago."

He nodded.

"I've been a fool, darling—you needn't tell me that. But this thing is a cert. Listen and I'll tell you about it. It's this horse-breeding business. I've been working with a chap called Cardozo. We get on like a house on fire. He's got a small ranch and he's been doing very well. Now he's got a chance to take over a much larger place—going concern, good stock, good water supply—everything just right. He's prepared to put up two thirds of the capital, and he'll take me in as a partner if I can find the rest. It's the chance of a lifetime."

"And how much would you have to find?"

"Oh, three or four thousand. Cardozo hopes he may get the owner down a bit, but even if he has to pay the full price it will be dirt cheap."

Esther Field had stopped fanning herself. She didn't feel hot any more. She had never liked saying no to Alan, but she was in no doubt that that was what she must do. In so far as she could help him out of income she would do so. But capital was a different matter. It had come from her own family, and it must go to Carmona and Carmona's children. She said in her kind voice,

"Oh, my dear, I don't see what can be done about that— I don't really."

"Don't you? Well, I do. This is my chance, and I'm not going to miss it." His voice, which had hardened, melted suddenly. "You know, old dear, you'd never regret it. The thing is an absolute dead cert, and I'd pay you back—say five hundred a year after the first two years. Interest too if you like. Come now, I can't say fairer than that. What about it?"

Esther Field looked away. If she had been another kind of woman she might have been angry. As it was, she only felt ashamed. Did he really think that she or anyone else could believe that he would pay the money back? He was Pen's son, and she had loved them both very much. He had ease, charm, grace, and the caressing ways which mean so much to a woman, but she had known for years that he was not to be trusted. And the money wasn't hers. She regarded herself as holding it in trust for Carmona and her children. She hoped very much that Carmona would have children.

Watching her, he was aware that he had failed. These large, soft women were only easy up to a point. There was a hard core of resistance, and when you came up against it you were done. All right, if she wanted it that way she could have it. He took out a packet of cigarettes, lit one, and pushed the packet back into his pocket.

"As you see, my case is gone. Candidly, I had to pawn it to get my train fare."

"Alan——"

"It's true."

It might be, or it might not. She said,

"I can let you have enough to be going on with until you can find something to do."

"My dear Esther, I *have* found something to do. I mean to do it. But I've got to have some capital. If you won't help me, I must get it elsewhere. There's the life of my father! With the material I can give this chap Murgatroyd it will have a very good chance of being a best seller. Without that material—well, I suppose the libraries will take a certain number of copies and Murgatroyd will have something to put in his pocket. But you know how it is—biographies are dull." He blew out a little cloud of smoke. "They are damned dull because all the interesting parts are left out. But if they weren't left out—if the public could buy the true story of who pulled the strings which made the great man work, and just why he did this, that, and the other—especially the other—don't you think the book would boom?"

Esther turned a bewildered look upon him.

"I don't know what you mean."

"Don't worry—I'm going to explain. In words of one syllable if necessary. To put it quite clearly, darling, my father kept a number of letters which he might more discreetly have destroyed. They constitute what I think the Press would call 'a revealing correspondence'. I feel they would make any book a best seller, and I don't see why Murgatroyd should be

the one to cash in on that. But I'm willing to go fifty-fifty
with him, and if you ask me, that's a pretty generous offer.
There'll be an advance, and there'll be royalties. If he agrees
to my terms he can go through the papers and take what he
likes. If he doesn't agree, I'll publish the letters myself and
scoop the lot."

Esther Field sat in a stunned silence. The smoke of his
cigarette hung in the air. After the sun-drenched brightness
on the other side of the house the room seemed dark. Alan
stood in front of the black mantelpiece with the ebony carving
above it. He looked confident and assured. His fair hair shone.
If there were lines about the eyes and lips which had not
been there three years ago, this shaded light was kind to
them. She looked at him, and looked away.

"You can't!"

"Oh, yes, I can. You gave me a power of attorney, you
know, after my father died—when you were ill."

"I can revoke it."

His bluff had been called. He had not reckoned on her
knowing that. He made a light gesture with his cigarette and
said in a laughing voice,

"Well, darling, the one thing which would make the whole
affair go with a bigger and better bang would be a legal struggle
between us as to the ownership of the papers. You see, even
if you got the originals, I should have had copies made, and
anyhow I'd have read them, and I have a pretty good memory.
You wouldn't be able to prevent the facts from—how do they
put it—transpiring. So you see, it's no go unless you are
prepared to hand over the money yourself."

Esther's mind had not followed him. It had remained fixed
upon Pen's letters. What could there be in them that she did
not know? They had been happy together. He had had his
moods, his struggles, his torments of the imagination. Artists
were like that, up one day and down the next. They needed
someone to rest them, someone who would just go on being the
same. Security—yes, that was the word—they needed someone
who could give them the sense of security. That was what she
had been able to do for Pen. Nobody could take it away from
her. She remembered how he used to look at her with that

queer twisted smile of his and say, "You're a comfortable woman, Esther."

Her eyes had returned to Alan. Sometimes he looked so like Pen that it hurt. She said, labouring to find words,

"But, Alan—you couldn't—do a thing like that. Not your father's private letters. I don't know what they are—or when they were written. I suppose he may have written a great many letters he wouldn't have wished to see published. He was always very attractive—to women—and they wrote to him. He didn't make any secret of it, only of course he didn't tell me their names—only that it was a lot of silly stuff, and he wondered why there had to be so many fools in the world. He used to laugh and tear the letters up and put the pieces in the fire. I shouldn't have thought he would have kept—any of them."

"Well, he kept the ones I am talking about. And I can tell you something, he didn't laugh at them. He kept them, and he answered them."

"How do you know?"

"Because the answers are there. The whole correspondence is there—his letters and hers. I suppose she didn't dare to keep them herself, and she couldn't bear to destroy them.'"

Esther Field said, "She?" And then quickly, "No, don't tell me! I don't want to know! Don't tell me anything!"

He laughed as if he were amused.

"My dear, you won't be able to help knowing—when the letters are published. If they *are* published! They needn't be of course. I don't exactly want to hurt your feelings. I'd much rather let sleeping dogs lie and get the money some other way." He turned to look at the clock on the mantelshelf, a monumental affair in black marble, with a blue face and squat gold hands. "Half past six! How time runs away in these family reunions! What time do you dine?"

Esther said mechanically,

"It's cold supper at eight."

"All right. Then I think I'd better drop in on Darsie and see if she can put me up. If not, it'll have to be the Anchor—that is, unless Carmona can be induced to change her mind."

Esther's flush had faded. She looked as if her thoughts were far away, but at the sound of Carmona's name she roused a little.

"No, no, you can't stay here—it wouldn't do at all——"

"What—with three chaperones!"

Her voice shook as she said,

"It wouldn't do. You ought not to have suggested it. Go and see whether Darsie can take you in. I have about fifteen pounds in the house—I could let you have that to go on with. And then something can be arranged."

He smiled benignly.

"Of course it can. And you're not to worry—it will work out all right. Things always do if you take them the right way. Well, I'll be seeing you!" He blew her a kiss and went out of the room.

She heard the hall door shut, and saw him go past the window with a suit-case in his hand. The gloom of the room closed round her.

CHAPTER IV

ALL the houses along the cliff bore a strong resemblance to one another. Some were larger, some had more turrets and fewer balconies, others more balconies and fewer turrets. The Annings' house had more turrets. When Colonel Anning left the East and retired it had seemed to him a very handsome and commodious residence. Through the years during which prices rose and the value of money fell he began to suspect that he had overhoused himself. Even before his death it had become very difficult to find a staff or to pay the bills. It was when his death still further reduced her income that Mrs. Anning began to supplement it by taking in paying guests. Now, apparently, Darsie was running the place quite frankly as a boarding-house.

Alan Field made a wry face at the thought of it. Boarding-houses were mostly stocked with old ladies. Darsie wouldn't like that at all. She had been pretty hot stuff in the old days—

an exciting creature with a flashing temper and sudden flares of passion. He wondered what she was like now.

She opened the door herself. Well, he would have known her. Or would he? He really wasn't sure. She couldn't be thirty yet, but she had a dried-up look. Of course those dark girls didn't wear so well. Where she had been slim she was thin, where she had been pale she was sallow. Her eyes seemed to have shrunk, and there were lines between them.

He said, "Well, Darsie?" and she stared at him for what seemed quite a long time before she spoke.

"Alan——"

She said it in rather an odd sort of way, almost as if she wasn't sure about him—under her breath too. She might have been talking to herself. And then she said,

"What do you want?"

He stepped past her into the hall.

"Aren't you going to say how do you do to an old friend? You mayn't have noticed it, but I've been away for three years—in South America, to be precise. And now that I'm back again nobody seems to be killing the fatted calf. I find it a bit damping."

Her face was closed against him—all the blinds down and the shutters fastened. She said,

"How extraordinary! Or is it? Would you expect, let us say Carmona, to be killing fatted calves? You left her waiting for you at the church, didn't you? At least that was the story I heard."

He smiled.

"Rather a public place to discuss our friends, don't you think?"

She should have sent him away—she knew that. Only there were too many bitter memories—too many bitter words which had said themselves over and over in the endless night watches but never to him. Now he was here, and they brimmed up in her.

There was a little room on the left where Mrs. Anning had been used to do the flowers. Darsie used it as an office now. She flung open the door.

"You can come in here if you like, but I don't think we have anything to discuss."

Alan came in smiling.

"Well, what I really wanted to talk about was the question of whether you could give me a bed for the night. Esther seemed to think you might be able to manage it, because Carmona appears to be full up."

It was like having cold water thrown in her face. It steadied her. You can't run a boarding-house without finding out that it doesn't pay to lose your temper. But—take Alan in? Something in her blazed again.

"So Carmona hasn't room for you. How surprising!" Her voice had an edge to it.

He gave the slight shrug of the shoulders which she remembered.

"That seems to be the general idea. I'm the big bad wolf, and James mightn't like it—not even with Esther and the Trevors to do propriety. Cold supper is permitted, so I shan't have to trouble your housekeeping, but after that the line is drawn. Rather silly, I think." He laughed. "After all this time you would think we could bury the past! Something in not very good taste about digging it up again!"

Two burning spots of colour had come into her cheeks. They gave her back the old lost glow.

"And that goes for me too, I suppose?"

"It goes for everyone. One has one's good times—we had some very good ones if I remembered rightly. But you can't bring them back again. You know that, and so do I. We are sensible people, and sensible people know when they have had enough. What on earth is the good of pretending? If a thing is done, it's done. Where's the sense of starting a feud about it? There may be more good times ahead, or there may not, *quien sabe?* They either come along or they don't. You can't just turn them on to order."

She knew very well what he was at. He wanted to smooth her down, to have everything comfortable and easy between them. Unpleasantness of any sort was a challenge. The fact that Carmona wouldn't have him to stay would make him determined to get his foot in at Cliff Edge. Her own flaring antagonism was a challenge. It wasn't in him to refuse it. He would spare no pains to charm it out of her. She had a sharp

stab of self-contempt as it came to her that she would give
almost anything to be charmed—to believe in him again. Bad
enough if she could, but how much worse to let herself go
sliding down into the pit with open eyes. She said,

"You do like everything comfortable and easy, don't you,
Alan?"

"Don't we all?"

"We don't all get what we want. How easy do you think
my life has been?"

He said in his warmest voice,

"I was so terribly sorry to hear about your mother."

"Thank you—she is pretty well. Just vague, you know.
Her illness was brought on by worry. About me. I suppose
you have forgotten what I told you the last time we saw each
other."

"My dear——"

She said in a low, steady voice,

"I told you I was going to have a child."

He threw up a hand.

"My poor darling, what could I do about it? I was broke—
absolutely. My turning up in the affair could only have made
it worse. As it was, you must have been very clever about it—
there doesn't seem to have been a breath of scandal. How did
you manage?"

He might have been any interested friend. She thought,
"He is not human. He doesn't love, or hate, or get in a rage.
He just likes to drift along with everything going his way. He
doesn't mind what he does to keep it like that, and he doesn't
give a damn about anyone else."

She said without any expression at all,

"I don't know that I was clever, but I managed. A married
friend took me in. They had no child, and they adopted
mine. They have gone to Australia, so I shall never see him
again."

He said, "So that's all right!"

His tone was one of heartfelt relief. What could have been
luckier—the convenient friend, the adoption, and, to crown
it all, the Antipodes. A narrow shave, but they had come
out of it. And why in the world should Darsie be looking at

him the way she was? Whatever else had changed, her temper
hadn't.

As she looked at him with blazing eyes and said, "I could
kill you for that!" the door opened and someone came a step
into the room—a pleasant looking woman in her late thirties.
She came in just that one step, stood for a moment uneasy and
embarrassed, and backed out again. The door closed upon her.

Alan Field burst out laughing.

"That's torn it!" he said. "What a little spitfire you are,
Darsie!"

Mrs. Burkett almost ran up the stairs, knocked at the door
of the bedroom next to her own, and hardly waited for a reply
before bursting in. Even at the time, and in the midst of her
perturbation, she was conscious with gratitude of the marked
improvement in her own health. At the beginning of her fortnight's visit the ascent of the stairs had left her breathless
and certainly in no state to hasten along a passage and enter
her aunt's room in this precipitate manner.

Miss Maud Silver looked up from her knitting in surprise.
She had been enjoying the cool breeze from the sea. Such an
airy room, and the view quite delightful. The sun on the blue
expanse of the bay, and now this cool breeze springing up.
The holiday had indeed been a successful one, and dear Ethel
quite restored to her usual excellent health. A pity that she
had to go back tomorrow, but this was the first time in her
married life that she had ever been persuaded to leave home
without her husband or at least one of the children. It was
something of an achievement to have detached her for so long.
It was these placid thoughts that were interrupted by Ethel
Burkett's entrance. She certainly did look well. Quite brown
too, but then the weather had been so fine. She looked well
now, but as certainly flushed and agitated.

"My dear, what is the matter?"

"Oh, Auntie—the most extraordinary thing, and so embarrassing!"

Miss Silver was concerned.

"Had you not better sit down and tell me about it? What
has happened?"

Mrs. Burkett sank into a chair.

"Oh, I expect it's nothing really. But so unexpected—from Miss Anning. She always seemed so controlled. And then coming in on them like that. I suppose I ought to have knocked—but of course I had no idea she had anyone with her. I thought I would just drop in and have a little chat. She has been so kind and made us so comfortable, and as I was taking the early train tomorrow, I just thought——"

Miss Silver interrupted her in a mild but firm manner.

"A very nice thought on your part, my dear. But you are not telling me what has happened to embarrass you. You went to find Miss Anning, and when you found her she was not alone?"

"I'm telling it very badly," said Ethel Burkett, "and you have such a logical mind. Well, I went to the office just to see if she was there—and of course I had no idea she had anyone with her, but when I opened the door, there she was standing back against the writing-table and saying the most extraordinary thing to one of the handsomest young men I have ever seen in my life. He really was, Auntie."

"My dear, you sound quite melodramatic."

Ethel Burkett nodded.

"But Auntie, that is just what it was—like a scene in a film. And that is what made it so embarrassing, because you don't expect to walk into a scene from a film when you are staying in a quiet private hotel—now do you?"

Miss Silver's cough indicated dissent. She had known melodrama crop up in some very unexpected places. She said dryly,

"Perhaps if you were to tell me what made the scene an embarrassing one——"

"Oh, but it was. You see, he was by the mantelpiece, and she was over by the writing-table like I told you. He seemed quite easy and comfortable—he looked like that sort of person. But Miss Anning—well, I would hardly have known her. She was as white as a sheet, and her eyes were blazing, and just as I came a step into the room, she said, 'I could kill you for that!' And, oh dear, she really did sound as if she meant it. Of course I came away at once and shut the door, but I don't know how she could have helped seeing me. And it does make it so very awkward, doesn't it?"

Miss Silver had resumed her knitting—one of those small coatees considered suitable for the new baby, in this case an expected addition to the family of Ethel's brother Jim. After ten childless years his wife Dorothy had presented him with a boy, followed two years later by a little girl. Now there was to be another baby. Their cup of happiness was full, and Miss Silver proposed to mark the occasion with one of her finest, lightest coatees in a delicate shade of blush rose. She smiled across the fleecy wool and said,

"When people are angry they often say foolish things that they do not mean. Miss Anning has a hot temper."

"I should never have thought so."

"She has it very well under control, but it is there. We had better not speculate as to what may have roused it now. Very good-looking young men are often responsible for a great deal of unhappiness. I believe Miss Anning used to be a very attractive girl."

"Was she?" Ethel Burkett's tone was one of surprise.

"Oh, yes, my dear. That nice Mrs. Field who is staying at Cliff Edge was telling me about her. You remember Miss Anning introduced us, and down on the beach I have been able to help her once or twice when she was in difficulties with her knitting. She does not find it at all easy to keep her stitches on the needles, and I have been trying to teach her the continental method of holding them. It makes a dropped stitch almost impossible, but I am afraid she is not at all an apt pupil."

Ethel Burkett was not interested in Esther Field as a knitter. She said,

"And she told you about Miss Anning?"

"Oh, yes. The Fields used to take a house down here every year. Her husband was quite a famous artist, but he has been dead for some years. They knew the Annings quite well, and she said how much Darsie Anning had changed from the pretty, lively girl she used to be. You know, my dear, I have frequently had occasion to remark that it is just these gay, spirited girls who are apt to become repressed and over strict in middle life. It seems strange, but I have seen it happen."

"Perhaps they go too far, and find out that it doesn't do," said Ethel Burkett.

CHAPTER V

LATER on that evening Miss Silver paid her accustomed visit to Mrs. Anning. She was, as usual, engaged upon the piece of embroidery which had been begun before her illness, and which never seemed to come any nearer to completion. A spray of wild roses in one corner had been very nearly finished, but the bow of blue ribbon with which it was tied was no more than an outline. It was upon this bow that Mrs. Anning worked continually, drawing a needle full of pale blue silk through the fine canvas. There was no knot on the end of the silk, so that it just went in and came out again, but it kept her happy for hours at a time. She would occasionally give a kind of half attention to the wireless, but there was always a risk of there being something in the programme which disturbed her. Miss Silver could see at a glance that something had disturbed her tonight. The hand that plied the embroidery-needle was shaking, and the usually fair placid face was puckered into lines of distress. She looked at Miss Silver and said in a troubled voice,

"Darsie doesn't come. She doesn't tell me anything. She sent the foreign girl up with my supper. Nobody tells me anything, but I know he is here."

"Someone whom you wanted to see?" enquired Miss Silver. She took a chair and leaned forward to look at the embroidered roses. "What a pretty pattern, and how well you have carried it out."

Mrs. Anning made a stitch and pulled the blue silk through.

"I heard his voice," she said. "We don't talk of him because of what happened. Darsie used to be so pretty and bright—but we don't talk about it now."

Miss Silver had begun to knit. She said very kindly,

"It is always better not to recall unhappy things. There are happy memories too, are there not, and pleasant things that happen from day to day?"

Mrs. Anning gazed at her in a piteous manner.

"I was so fond of him. We all were. And Darsie was so pretty——"

At about this same time or a little later Alan Field stepped out of the french window which led from the drawing-room at Cliff Edge and, turning, spoke over his shoulder.

"It's a great deal cooler out here. Lovely breeze. You are missing all the best of it in there. Why not come out?"

The meal had been a dreary affair. Esther looked as if she had been crying. She probably had, but there really wasn't any need to let everyone know about it. Quite unnecessary for the modern woman to show more of her original face than she wanted to. But of course Esther had no social tact. Then, as if those pink eyelids and her silent air of reproach were not enough, there was old Trevor's hard stare and Lady Castleton's quite extraordinary capacity for imparting a chill to the atmosphere. He had never liked her, in spite of her looks. After all, a woman needs something besides beauty, and she had always been too inclined to throw her weight about. He preferred a more feminine type. And if she thought she could take this glacial line with him, she would just have to sit down and think again. There might be a good deal less of her high-and-mightiness by the time he was through with her. Carmona too. What business had she to sit there at her own table in what almost amounted to complete silence? More attractive than she used to be, and perfectly composed, but scarcely saying a word. If it hadn't been for himself and Pippa, with old Maisie Trevor's constant trivial flow in the background, they might have passed for a company of ghosts. The prospect of just sitting round in that cluttered drawing-room was too much for him. Make a move to the terrace and there was always a possibility of breaking the party up.

Since no one answered his invitation, he repeated it.

As far as Colonel Trevor was concerned, you took your exercise in the open air, and when you had taken it you came into the house and sat down in a civilized manner. He observed stiffly that he had not yet read *The Times*, and left it at that.

Esther Field said,

"I think not, Alan."

Carmona said nothing at all.

To everyone's surprise, Adela Castleton rose to her feet.

"It is rather hot in here," she said. As she moved towards the window, Esther Field spoke in a shaky voice.

"Adela, do you think—should you not have a wrap? Is it really wise?

She had leaned sideways to catch at the folds of a floating skirt. Adela smiled down at her with an air of assurance.

"Oh, yes, Esther."

Esther Field let go of the filmy stuff.

Lady Castleton came out upon what was by day a singularly hideous terrace adorned with a number of massive urns. In the evening light the effect was softened, the harsher outlines blurred. The old figureheads in the garden below loomed up with a certain air of mystery. The sea beyond the cliff had begun to darken. In an hour or two the breeze would carry a chill. Now it was a breath of enchantment.

Adela Castleton said.

"You are quite right—the air is delightful. Shall we go down towards the sea?"

There were steps that led to the garden. She moved towards them, catching up her floating black. Alan followed her, puzzled. It was quite obvious that she wished to speak to him. A great many women had had the same wish in the past, and had made some such opportunity.

A light breeze after a hot day, dusk and the scent of flowers or the tang of the sea—there was nothing he didn't know about it. But Adela Castleton—that did puzzle him.

When they were about half way down the garden, its cement paths still giving out the heat, she stopped and said in an authoritative manner,

"You have been upsetting Esther. Is that what you came back for?"

He was lighting a cigarette, its red tip glowed. He put away the packet before he answered her. Then he said,

"You are a good friend. Of course anyone could see she had been crying—but you know, she cries very easily. We had been talking about my father."

"Yes, I know that. I also know what you said to her."

He blew out a little cloud of smoke.

"Oh—she told you?"

"Yes, she told me. I went into her room before dinner and found her crying bitterly."

"About this Life of my father? I naturally don't want her to be distressed about it, but if there is to be a Life at all, it must be a faithful one. My father had a good many sides to his character. The side Esther knew wasn't the only one. He was very fond of her—who wouldn't be—but she was not the only woman in his life."

"I suppose not. Do you really mean to make that public?" He sketched a deprecatory gesture.

"I don't know what Esther told you, but this is how it is. There is a boom in Penderel Fields. Unfortunately, we possess very few of them—as far as I know, only some sketches and his portrait of Esther. And I don't see her consenting to part with that."

"Why should she?"

"I'm not saying that she should. She values it very much, and I wouldn't dream of asking her to make such a sacrifice." She said crisply,

"You surprise me."

"Do I? Well, to continue. It is now proposed that there should be a Life of my father. I only had a few hundreds out of his estate, and I think it is fair that I should have a share of any profits on the book—especially as the papers without which it cannot be written are in my possession. Some of them are very interesting. There is, for instance, a batch of letters which would make any biography a best seller. Esther did not know of their existence, and she is upset at the idea of their being published. I suppose some such difficulty is bound to arise over any Life. If the personal element is left out, the thing is as dry as dust, and nobody will read it. If you show the man as he was, somebody's feelings are bound to be hurt."

"And you propose to sacrifice Esther's?"

"I don't want to in the least. I am, in fact, prepared to sacrifice my own advantage. I could publish this correspondence myself. There are about a hundred and fifty letters. I could, I daresay, produce quite a readable life. But the letters would do the trick on their own—they are of a highly

personal and romantic nature. I say I could do this, but for
Esther's sake I don't want to—do try and believe that. I am
very fond of her and I don't want to hurt her. But I'm in a
difficult position. If I can produce a certain sum of money
I can secure a partnership in an excellent going concern run by
the chap I've been working with for the last three years.
Other things being equal, he would like to give me the chance,
but he must have the money. It's a question of purchasing a
larger ranch, and if I can't raise the amount, he'll have to
take in someone who can. If Esther will enable me to avail
myself of this chance, I shall be only too glad not to distress
her by publishing those letters."

Adela Castleton said, "Blackmail!"

He drew on his cigarette.

"I don't think there is any point in using words like that.
Wiser not to, you know. Especially for you."

"And why for me?"

The breeze from the sea had a sudden chill as she spoke.

"Can't you guess?"

"No. How should I?"

He said in his agreeable voice,

"The correspondence I mentioned consists of letters which
passed between my father and a young girl who had become
infatuated with him. She begins it. He replies in the manner
of an older man writing to an over enthusiastic girl—he is
pleased and flattered, but there is a certain restraint. He
has known her since she was a child, he sees her often. The
tone of the letters changes, gets warmer. Presently they are
writing every day. Before long they are lovers."

The cold seemed to have got into Adela Castleton—she was
stiff with it. Her lips would hardly move. She forced them
into difficult speech.

"You can't—publish—letters like that——"

"I don't know about can't, but I would much rather not.
You don't ask me who the girl was."

"I am not—interested."

"You don't think so? Perhaps not. But I am going to tell
you. The letters are signed, 'Irene'."

She turned and went from him without a word.

CHAPTER VI

HE made no haste to follow her. He had given her plenty
to think about. Let it sink in and it would do the trick all
right. He thought she would go to almost any possible length
rather than allow her sister's letters to be published. There
were plenty of people who would remember Irene's beauty, and
her sudden tragic death. These people were Adela's friends—
and enemies. She was of the type that makes enemies. The
story of an attack of cramp while swimming out too far would be
blown sky high. That final letter would finish it—"We can't
go on like this. I am taking the only way out. I can't go on
living without you." That must have been written on the
very day she was drowned. A newspaper cutting was folded
inside the envelope, and a photograph of the Penderel Field
portrait. A lovely creature, as beautiful as Adela and much more
feminine. No wonder his father had fallen for so much grace
and charm. He speculated as to how long the affair would have
lasted if she had not brought it to an end in the way she did.
It must have been a horrible shock to Penderel Field. Extraordinary that with all that tragedy and passion going on around
them neither Esther nor Adela had been aware of it. Or had
they achieved a deliberate blindness? Irene lived with her
sister, Esther with Penderel Field. They all met constantly.
Was it possible that there had been no suspicions? He wondered.

He was half way through a second cigarette, when he heard
Pippa call his name. She came down the terrace steps. The
dusk drained the colour from her pale green dress, but a
tracery of sequins glittered. An attractive creature. That hair of
hers reminded him of thistledown. Bleached of course, but not
so very much. He remembered her at twelve years old with
long fair plaits.

As she came up to him, he glanced appraisingly at the
double row of pearls she wore. Difficult to tell, of course,
but he thought they were real. He seemed to remember something being said about them at the time of her marriage. They
came from Bill Maybury's side of the family, and she had worn

them on her wedding day. Well, pearls or no pearls, he was pleased to see her. The prospect of returning to the drawing-room was not an alluring one.

She came up to him with a laughing, "Let's go out along the cliff—let's go quite a long way! I really can *not* endure any more gloom. I'm sure I don't know what has happened to everyone. Colonel Trevor just sits and glares at *The Times*. Aunt Esther has obviously been crying her eyes out. Carmona doesn't utter. Lady Castleton has gone to bed with a headache. And I don't feel I can bear any more of Mrs. Trevor's early Edwardian scandal. I feel I should like something a little more up to date."

"And you think I could oblige?"

She had a light, pretty laugh.

"I'm quite sure you could. I'm in the mood for something really thrilling.

They went down towards the gate in the wall.

"Well, you know, I'm a bit of a back number. I've been away three years."

"So you have! What have you been doing?"

"Oh, quite a lot of things. Three years is a long time. Things that were a nine days' wonder so soon get out of date. Nobody cares any longer, except perhaps the actual people concerned."

He held the gate for her to pass out on to the cliff path. The tide was full. The breeze blew stronger here, ruffling the thistledown hair. As they turned to the right, it was behind them. He threw away the end of his cigarette and said lightly,

"I suppose it might still interest Bill to know about that little jaunt of yours to Trenton in—let me see—wasn't it June three years ago?"

It was as if a door opened between them and shut again—sharply. She had caught her breath—he would have sworn to that—but her laugh followed in a flash, and her light, tripping words:

"What on earth are you talking about?"

He said.

"You, darling—and Trenton—and Cyril Maynard."

She laughed again.

"And Bill—you haven't forgotten Bill?"

"Oh, no. But you had, hadn't you? I thought he might be interested."

"My dear Alan, I haven't the *slightest* idea what you are talking about."

"Oh, just scandal, and how old it has to be before it stops being of interest to anyone. I was going to develop the theory that it would go on being interesting for just as long as there was anyone left who cared. Now, it always seemed to me that poor old Bill cared quite a lot—about you."

"How kind of you to say so! He *is* my husband, you know."

"And that, my dear girl, is the point. Being your husband and fond of you, he might take rather a dim view of the fact that you and Cyril were week-ending at Trenton three years ago."

She had been walking so quickly that he had fallen a pace behind. She stopped now, whirling round with a stamp of the foot.

"If that is your idea of a joke!"

He shook his head.

"Oh, no—it's my idea of a fact. You see, I was there. I saw you arrive. And I watched him go into your room at somewhere round about midnight, and when I had the curiosity to look at the hotel register I found you were down as Mr. and Mrs. Cyril Smith. I was at school with Cyril, and there's no mistaking that fist of his. Also there was no Mrs. Maybury on the register, and no Cyril Maynard. It just struck me that old Bill might take an interest."

He looked to see what she was doing with her hands. There was light enough to discover that they were clenched in the pale green stuff of her dress. He was smiling as she said,

"Are you going to tell him this fairy story? Do you suppose he would take your word against mine?"

"No, of course not. I should merely suggest his taking a look at the register. Cyril's writing is really quite distinctive— once seen never forgotten, and I imagine that Bill will have had plenty of opportunities of seeing it."

There was a short tight silence before she said,

"And you think he would go down to Trenton and look at the register?"

"Yes, I think so. He wouldn't believe me—or at least he would tell himself that he didn't believe me—and he would go down to Trenton for the express purpose of calling my bluff. Only, as you know, it wouldn't be bluff."

There was another and a longer silence. Then she said, "What do you want?"

He laughed.

"Sensible girl! The whole thing can be settled without hurting anyone's feelings. Bill is the best fellow in the world, and I have always thought you a very charming girl. Why should I want to upset your marriage? I loathe unpleasantness of any kind. But one must live."

"Blackmail?"

He sighed.

"Darling, do let us avoid melodrama. So out of date. Why not settle the thing to our mutual advantage in a civilized manner?"

She said with a sudden quick heat,

"I can't think why someone hasn't murdered you, Alan!"

"My dear Pippa, you surprise me. Look out, there's someone coming!" His voice dropped.

The someone turned out to be two people with arms entwined—Miss Myrtle Page who worked in a beauty parlour and was quite a good advertisement for its wares, and a boy friend, one Norman Evans, clerk in a local solicitor's office. When they had turned the next corner Myrtle said,

"Ooh! Did you hear that?"

To which Norman responded that he wasn't deaf, thank you, and what about another kiss.

Away behind them Alan shook his head and said in a reproving voice,

"That's what comes of letting your temper fly. They heard what you said all right."

"So what?"

He laughed.

"So if you've got any idea about pushing me over the cliff you'd better think again, because they heard you say why

hadn't anyone murdered me, and they heard me call you
Pippa. In the long run it will be cheaper to come to terms
with me than to let yourself in for a hanging."

She began to walk back in the direction of the house.
There was more breeze going this way and she was glad of
it.

They walked slowly and in silence. For his part, he had
said as much as he meant to. Women only worked themselves
into an obstinate state if you argued with them. He had said
enough, and what he had said would say itself over and over
again through the hours of a wakeful night.

Just before they came to the garden gate she spoke without
turning her head.

"What do you want?"

CHAPTER VII

CARMONA reached her room with a feeling of unutterable
relief. The evening was over, and whatever happened or
didn't happen, no one could make them live it through again.
It had begun with an impression of approaching storm—dark
clouds coming up from a long way off and brooding overhead.
They had come, they had hovered, and they had passed.
There had been no explosion.

She was astonished at the trend of her own thoughts. What
cause could there be for this sense of dread and strain? If
she lived, and if Alan lived, it was more or less certain that
they would meet. This might not be pleasant, but it was
inevitable. To decline or avoid such a meeting would be to
give it too much importance. The only reasonable and self-
respecting way was to revert to the old family relationship and
behave as if nothing had happened to rupture it. That there
should be a certain feeling of strain was natural enough. What
surprised her a good deal was that this feeling was not in the
main a personal one. As far as she herself was concerned, she
could go back. She had schooled herself to endure, and then
to leave the past behind. She had married James Hardwick.

She had to look elsewhere than in her own feelings for the sense of dread.

That Esther had been seriously upset was plain. She had been crying. She cried easily when anything upset her. But the unhappiness which had hung about her like a cloud tonight seemed too deep to spring from any except a really serious cause. Quite obvious that it was Alan who had upset her. Looking back across a three years gap, it was not difficult to guess that he had been demanding money. There had never been any end to his asking, but at long last there had been an end to Esther's giving. Her no had been said with kindness, but with finality and without undue emotional disturbance. There must be something more than money to account for her state tonight.

And Adela—what on earth had come over Adela Castleton? A brief absence in the garden with Alan, and she had returned with the look of an automaton—sitting down at the small table from which she had risen, laying out her patience cards with a kind of stiff precision, her face colourless, her eyes fixed and empty, and in the end sweeping the pack together and getting to her feet to announce that she had a headache and thought she would go to bed.

It was with her departure that there was some slight lessening of the strain. Pippa came in, blew a kiss to the assembled company, said she was all in and had better vanish before she fell asleep in everybody's face. Then, after a brief interval, Alan to make his excuses.

"It's quite lovely out on the cliff. You ought to have come, Carmona. Well, Darsie tells me her front door shuts at some extraordinarily early hour, and I forgot to get her to give me a key, so I had better be off. She made a tremendous favour of taking me in at all, and I can't afford to put a foot wrong. She seems to be full up with old ladies who go to bed at ten. They don't think men are quite nice, and I gather she is rather stretching a point in allowing one inside the gates. I'll come up in the morning if I may." There had been the old careless smile in his eyes as he looked at Carmona.

She went on undressing, putting her dress on a hanger, sliding it on to a brass rail in the immense gloomy wardrobe which took up nearly a whole side of the room. She thought suddenly what a dreary room it was, with its faded carpet, its dun wall-paper, its curtains turned from green to grey by the salty air. It had been Octavius Hardwick's room, and it came to her that he had probably died there.

She had reached this cheerful point and was slipping her nightgown over her head, when there was a soft knocking on the door. It was followed immediately by the entrance of Pippa in pale yellow pyjamas. She shut the door behind her and said in an energetic whisper.

"If Alan gets himself murdered he'll only have himself to thank for it! I thought you had better know!"

She then sat down on the edge of the vast Victorian bed and burst into tears.

"Pippa!"

She tossed back her hair.

"Can't people be put in prison for blackmail?"

"Yes, they can."

"And what is the good of that? They know damn well you would rather die than go into court and say what it was all about!"

Carmona had come over to stand beside her.

"What *is* it all about, Pippa? Do you want to tell me?"

The blue eyes were full of angry tears.

"I've got to tell someone, or I shall blow up! Spontaneous combustion! People used to believe in it like anything! You just go up in smoke—poof! And all that's left of you is a horrid smell of burning and some amusing tales about your having been carried off by the devil!"

"Pippa!"

There was another vigorous toss of the head.

"And you needn't think I'm joking, because I'm not! It's that swine Alan, and——"

Carmona broke in.

"He's blackmailing you——"

She found that she wasn't surprised—that nothing Alan did could surprise her. She had a deep sense of shame.

Pippa said,

"If Bill knew, he would kill him! But if Bill knew, then it

would kill me, so what is the good of that? There just isn't a thing I can do about it, and Alan knows it!"

Carmona sat down on the bed beside her.

"Do you want to tell me?"

"I've always told you things, haven't I?"

"Sometimes people tell you things, and then they wish they hadn't."

Pippa shook her head.

"I shan't do that. You make me feel safe." She looked piteously at Carmona. "You know, that's why I married Bill— I always did feel safe with him. People like that aren't awfully exciting, so you go off and have a bit of fun with somebody else, but somewhere inside you deep down you know perfectly well that you can't do without them."

"Yes, I know. The bother is you might go too far and not be able to get back. Is that what Alan is holding over you?"

Pippa nodded.

"I went off for a week-end with Cyril Maynard. Bill said people were talking. We had a row and I thought I'd give them something to talk about. I didn't care what I did. You don't, you know, when you're angry—you only want to score the other person off. Bill had to be away that week-end— some stupid manoeuvres or something—and I went off with Cyril. I hadn't ever done anything like that before—I swear I hadn't—but I just didn't care. We went to Trenton, and we had dinner on the way and danced afterwards, so we didn't get down there till late. I don't know why Alan was there, but he was. We didn't see him, but he saw us arrive, and he went and looked in the hotel register and saw that we were down as Mr. and Mrs. Cyril Smith. And afterwards he saw Cyril go into my room."

"Oh, Pippa!"

There was a violent shake of the head.

"No—no—it isn't what you think! The minute he came in I knew I couldn't do it. I'd been getting cold feet all the evening, and the way Cyril looked at me was the *end*. I felt as if I should kill him if he touched me, and I told him to get out. First he pretended to think I was joking, and then he got really frightfully angry, and in the end it turned into the

most ghastly sort of melodrama. Because I got hold of the
bell-pull—it was one of those old-fashioned places where
they have a thing like a long woolly rope hanging down
from the ceiling—and I said I would pull it and scream the
place down if he didn't go away at once. So he went, and I
bolted the door. And I got up frightfully early and had a
taxi to the station."

Carmona felt a good deal of relief.

"Why don't you just tell Bill and have done with it? He
would believe you, wouldn't he?"

"Oh, yes, he'd believe me. It's not that. It's just—Carmona,
I *couldn't* tell him! I really couldn't! It would hurt him—
dreadfully, and he would never, never, never think quite the
same way about me again. He doesn't dance, but he knows
I adore it, and he likes me to have fun, and go about, and
do the things I want to. And he thinks he can trust me. If
he thought he couldn't——"

Carmona was silent for a moment. Then she said,

"You had better tell him, you know."

"I'd rather *die*! And that isn't just a way of talking—I
mean it. I'm not a good person—I never have been, and I
probably never shall be. But Bill actually thinks I am. Idiotic,
isn't it? But I don't think I could go on if he stopped. You
know what a toy balloon looks like when you prick it—well,
that would be me." She dragged the back of her hand across
her eyes like a child. "I shall just have to do what Alan wants."

"What does he want?"

Pippa said, "My pearls." She put up her hand to where
the double row dripped down over the filmy yellow of her
pyjama top. "He knows I haven't any money except my
allowance from Bill, but I've got these, and they are worth
quite a lot. He'll be kind enough to take them and call quits.
He says he can get them copied for me so that no one will
ever know, damn him!"

Carmona said out of depths of bitter certainty,

"Money always did run through Alan's fingers. He would
only spend what he got and come back for more."

Pippa stared at her.

"There wouldn't be any more."

"That wouldn't stop him. He would go on holding it over you—pushing you to get what he wanted—from Bill—from anyone. They say a blackmailer never leaves go. You would find yourself being pushed until you were ready to do almost anything to get the money. For God's sake, make up your mind to tell Bill!"

Pippa sprang to her feet.

"I'd rather kill myself!" she said. "Or him!"

CHAPTER VIII

EARLIER that day Chief Detective Inspector Lamb looked up from his desk as the door opened. It was Detective Inspector Frank Abbott who presented himself, that very fair hair of his immaculately smooth, his tall, slim figure immaculately clad.

"You wanted to see me, sir?"

Lamb fixed him with a stare which had long since ceased to terrify.

"Shouldn't have sent for you if I didn't."

His own appearance was solid rather than elegant. He filled his massive chair, and looked as reliable as the oak of which it was made. His strong black hair was going a little thin on the top but retained its tendency to curl over the temples. His voice carried a pleasant country accent. He might, in fact, have served as an example of the old type of police officer at his best. He said now,

"Sit down. I want to talk to you."

"Well, sir?"

Lamb drummed on his knee.

"It's about that fellow Cardozo."

"Cardozo?"

"No, you don't know about him—you were out on the Notting Hill case. Well, this chap came in with a yarn about his brother having disappeared. Philip Cardozo, only he writes it with an F and has some kind of a dago way of saying it."

"Felipe."

"You've got it—Fayleepy. Funny sort of way to say Philip.

I don't know how anyone gets their tongue round that sort of lingo. This one spells his name J.O.S.E. and calls it Hosy. Doesn't seem much sense in it to my way of thinking, but there you are. This Hosy came in about a week ago and says his brother is missing. Says he was coming over from South America, and it might have been on the *Marine Star* from Rio, or it might have been some other boat, or he might have taken a plane to Lisbon and come on from there. The point is, he hasn't turned up here, and Hosy thinks something has happened to him. Very excitable little chap. You know how these foreigners are—waving his hands about and putting in a lot of words I couldn't make head or tail of."

Frank Abbott felt some regret at having missed the interview. It might have brightened the official round, and would certainly have proved a good deal more entertaining than the affair of the grocer's teeth in the Notting Hill murder case.

Lamb drummed on his desk.

"To start with, there wasn't any evidence to show that Felipy ever set foot in this country. Hosy says he had a very particular reason for coming over, and if he didn't come one way he'd have come another. Says he thinks he'd have come by plane. Well, if he did, it wasn't under his own name. And I don't mind saying I thought the whole thing was a lot of fuss about nothing. If this chap had slipped in under an alias he'd want to keep quiet. In fact Hosy might have wanted to see Felipy, but Felipy mightn't have been so keen on seeing Hosy. People don't always want to meet their relations."

"They do not—and with reason."

Lamb frowned.

"Well, that was a week ago. I told him how many people disappear every year, and that about threequarters of them turn up again."

Frank cocked an eyebrow.

"I can't make out why you were seeing him at all, sir."

Lamb jerked open a drawer, looked for something that hadn't ever been there, and shut it again with some force.

"Oh, he came along with an introduction. You know the sort of thing—— Sir Somebody Something in the South American business line who wants to oblige Signor Somebody

Else who doesn't mind putting in a word for Hosy who is some kind of an agent of his. As I say, I told him his brother would probably turn up, and no call to think anything had happened to him. He waved his hands a lot and talked nineteen to the dozen about his brother being murdered, and went away."

"Is that all, sir?"

"No, it isn't. I shouldn't be talking to you about it if it was. He's been here again. This time he says he's found his brother."

Frank began to say something and stopped.

"Picked up out of the river."

"Dead?"

"Quite a time. We'd passed on Felipy's description, and he was sent for to identify the body. He says it's his brother all right, and he swears he's been murdered. The post mortem shows a blow on the back of the head. Well, it might have been accidental, or it mightn't. You can go down and look into it."

CHAPTER IX

GOING in through the Annings' front door at ten o'clock that night, Alan Field encountered Darsie coming out of her office. He smiled and said,

"Punctual to the moment, you see."

The smile met with no response. She said, "Thank you. Goodnight," and turned back into the little room. She went across to the bookcase and appeared to be selecting a novel.

Alan's smile deepened as he followed her, closing the door behind him.

"Don't I get a few kind words?"

She turned round, her face quite blank.

"I haven't got anything to say to you, and you know it. You are only here because——"

He broke in with a laugh.

"Because I pointed out that it would make a good deal of talk if you turned me away. The house isn't full, and it would certainly give Esther and all the rest of them up at Cliff Edge something to think about if you refused a nice eligible boarder like me!"

"That is why you are here. It is the only reason. I have nothing to say to you. Goodnight."

She walked past him, turned the key in the front door lock, shot the bolt, and went on up the wide, easy stair without looking back. It gave him a good deal of amusement to reflect that he had made her take him in, and that she was hating every minute of it. How stupid women were. All this time gone by, and she couldn't even pretend she didn't care!

He slept soundly, and woke with pleasant anticipations. Esther would pay up, and so would Adela when it came to the pinch—he had no real doubt about it. And there was Pippa— he was going to enjoy dealing with Pippa. She didn't like him much, and she had never been at pains to hide it. She was going to pay for that.

By ten o'clock he was asking the late Octavius Hardwick's elderly butler for Mrs. Field and being informed that she was in the morning-room. It was the place to which she had taken him yesterday, and gloomier than ever. The mist which would presently melt into heat had not yet cleared. It hung before the windows.

Esther looked up from a small writing-table of the same black wood as the hideous overmantel. She did not refuse his affectionate kiss, but she did not respond to it. Her eyelids were pink and swollen.

He took her hand and put it to his lips.

"My dear, you've been crying."

"Yes——"

"I haven't been very happy myself. You looked wretched last night, and I felt it was all my fault. But there isn't any need—there really isn't. Everything can be arranged. Suppose we talk it over a little."

He pulled up a chair and sat down, whilst she watched him between hope and doubt.

"You won't publish those letters?"

"Darling, do you suppose I want to? It's just that I've got to have the money. If there is any other way of getting it, I'll be only too thankful. You don't suppose I want to upset you, do you? We can have a comfortable talk and settle the whole thing provided you are willing."

He saw the tears come up in her eyes and went on in a hurry.

"Now, my dear, I don't want you to say anything—I just want you to listen. It was all very sketchy yesterday, and I think perhaps you got a wrong impression of what I was asking you to do. To begin with, there isn't any question of your parting with capital—I know you've got strict views about that—because I'm really only asking for a loan. I'm afraid I wasn't quite frank with you last night. The whole thing is very confidential, and if the least word of it got out, we should be sunk. So I employed a little camouflage. But thinking it over in the night—I couldn't sleep, you know, so there was plenty of time—I realized that I had no right to keep you in the dark."

Esther's soft brown eyes remained fixed upon his face. He certainly had her attention. What he would have liked to know was whether he had her belief. He wasn't so sure. He made haste to go on.

"That story I told you about Cardozo wanting to buy a horse ranch——"

"It's not true?"

He laughed.

"Only partly. He does want to buy a ranch, and he will probably want me to come in with him, but—well, he hasn't got the money. Or at least—look here, I'm going to tell you the whole thing, only it's a top number one secret. You mustn't breathe a word to a soul—you'll see why in a minute. Here it comes. Somewhere back in the last century a relation of Cardozo's, a great uncle or something, came by a considerable treasure—and it's no good asking me how, because Felipe is rather inclined to draw a veil over that part of it. There was quite a lot of stuff buried up and down the coast and islands of the Spanish Main in the sixteenth and seventeenth centuries, and a good deal of it has never been found. My guess is that old Cardozo tumbled on a cache. He had his own reasons for keeping quiet about it. He got the stuff away anyhow, and he got it to Rio. And a week later he was picked up with a knife between his shoulders in a back street. And that was that. His affairs were in a bad way. His house was sold to pay his debts, and there wasn't very much left. His next of kin was a young nephew. When he came of age, the family lawyer handed him a sealed envelope which had been deposited with the firm only a day or two before his uncle's death. It told young Cardozo about the treasure and where it was hidden."

Esther Field was remembering all the stories she had ever heard about buried treasure, from the romantic kind over which she had pored in youth, to the more sordid variety which cropped up every now and then in the police court or the newspapers, hand to hand, so to speak, with the gold brick and the confidence trick. Her feelings must have shown in her face.

Alan laughed.

"You think it sounds phoney, and so it does. But it isn't. I've worked with Felipe for three years, and he's as straight as a die. Let me go on telling you about it. Old Cardozo got away with the stuff and got it to Rio, and when he got it there he buried it again—somewhere in his house or garden. It was an old family place, and if he hadn't been bumped off when he was, he could have cleared all his debts and revived the ancient glories. Well, he told his nephew where the stuff was, but the house had been sold—there was no way of getting at it. It has changed hands twice since then at a top price, but the Cardozos have never had enough to buy it in. Just think what a situation! An immense fortune waiting, and just having to wait because they couldn't get a few thousand pounds together! But now the house is coming into the market again. Felipe has done everything he can—sold his ranch and scraped up every penny—but we are still about five thousand short——"

He paused there until she said,

"Even if you believe this story, how do you know that the treasure is still there, or that it is so valuable?"

He laughed.

"Darling, you're just not thinking. If anyone who owned that house had suddenly burst into wealth, the Cardozos

would have known about it. They have naturally always kept
an eye upon the place, and so far from anyone getting rich,
each time the house has been sold it has been because the owner
found it too expensive to keep up. It's a regular mansion."

She went on looking at him.

"You know, Alan, it does all sound——"

"Fishy? Well, of course it does. There have been no end
of phoney yarns about buried treasure, but don't you see,
there wouldn't have been those yarns if there hadn't been
something to tell them about. Treasure really was buried,
and some of it was found. Of course if a fellow blows in out
of nowhere and says he's got a map showing where Blackbeard
buried his pieces of eight, you tell him to go and show it to
the marines. But this is different. It's the real thing—no
funny business. You know me, and I know the Cardozos. I
can trust Felipe as if he was my own brother. You've only
to put up the money, and you'll get it back inside a year with
anything you like to name in the way of interest."

She said quickly,

"I'm not a money lender, Alan."

He was aware of having made a false step.

"No—no—of course—I shouldn't have said that. You
are all that is kind and generous, and don't I know it? Now
just think over what I've told you. I give you my word it's
all on the level, and no possible risk. You'll get your money
back, and you shall burn those letters yourself."

As he spoke, the door opened and Carmona came in.

CHAPTER X

HE could not be unaware of Esther's relief. She said in a hurry,

"We were going down to the beach, weren't we? If the sun is coming through, I had better go and put on my hat."

As the door closed behind her, Alan broke into a laugh.

"The eye of faith!" he observed.

Carmona said,

"Not entirely. This is the dark side of the house. It really is clearing on the other side. Alan, you are worrying Esther. Why?"

He said lightly.

"Do you know, you haven't changed in the least. You are still beautiful—and devastatingly frank."

She did not smile.

"Alan, I'm serious."

"You always were."

"I want to know what is going on."

"I'm afraid I can't tell you."

"Esther will."

"I wonder."

"I suppose it's the old story—you want money."

"How right you are! I always did, didn't I? Only this time it's really a final demand."

"Wasn't that what Hitler used to say?"

She would have to pay for that. He said smoothly,

"A bit old-fashioned, darling, aren't you? If you go back to before the war you might just as well go back to before the Flood. Too dating!" He laughed suddenly. "This is the first time I've really seen you since our own particular crash, and we're talking about Hitler! Who'd have believed it!"

She looked steadily back across the three years gap. What she couldn't believe was that she had ever come within an hour or two of marrying this stranger. He looked like Alan, he spoke like Alan. There was a horrible duality of the familiar and the strange. It must always have been present, but she had kept her eyes to the surface charm. Familiarity had bred not contempt but tolerance. There had been the long-cherished illusion that he loved her, and that she could help him. He had had a bad childhood until he came under Esther's care. He was not too steady, not too truthful. Money ran through his fingers. But he had the loving ways which could only spring from a loving heart. She saw the illusion now for what it was. There was no love in him, and no kindness. There never had been. There was only one person who mattered, and that was Alan Field. She had a passionate wonder as to why it had suited him to come so near to marrying her. Why up to that very last day had it been to his interest—and then all at once not to his interest? She said,

"It's all a long time ago."

He burst out laughing.

"Hitler—or us? In either case, how true!"

"Alan, why did you do it? I've always wanted to know."

"Oh, didn't he tell you?"

"What do you mean?"

"He didn't? But how very amusing!"

"I don't know what you are talking about."

"But you shall, darling—you shall. It's much too good a joke to be wasted. I had no idea he wouldn't have told you—made the most of such a romantic situation. Or perhaps he was afraid you wouldn't think it so romantic. Now I wonder whether you will."

Her heart had begun to beat rather hard. He was going to hurt her, and he was going to enjoy it. She didn't quite know why, but she knew that she was going to be hurt. There was cruelty under the laughter in his eyes. She said,

"I don't—want—to know."

"But you are going to, my sweet. Husbands and wives should know everything about each other, don't you think? Of course he wasn't your husband then, but it didn't take him very long to console you, did it? I really need not have had any qualms about taking the money."

"What money?"

"Oh, that is the joke. The great James Hardwick in his

original role of Sultan! He sees you, you take his fancy, and he offers me five thousand pounds to clear out!"

The room shook about her. She said,

"It's not true——"

His voice was hard with contempt.

"Of course it's true! I was broke. The best I could do was to get myself married to you. Well, it wasn't too good a best. You couldn't touch your capital, and the interest didn't amount to such a lot. Five thousand down wasn't to be sneezed at. I didn't sneeze. Hardwick put down the cash, and I cleared out."

Her "No——" came faintly from stiff lips. She had to get out of the room—somehow, anyhow.

She never really knew how she did it. The stairs were misty, the landing unsteady to her feet. Voices came from the open door of her room—Mrs. Beeston and the daily help making up the great cumbersome bed in which Octavius Hardwick had slept in solitary state—in which she and James would have to sleep tonight. There was to be no privacy—either now—or then. She found that she did not want it now. What would she do if she was alone? Sit down and think—that James had bought her. A shudder went over her heart. For as long as she could she would keep that thought at bay.

She went into the room, opened a drawer, and took out the shady hat which she had worn yesterday. The mist was lifting. It was going to be hot.

Mrs. Beeston was a big woman with a plain sensible face. She said, "A little more of that sheet, Mrs. Rogers," and turned it down over the yellowing blankets. Then, to Carmona,

"Mr. James will be coming today?"

Carmona said, "Yes."

"If he will be here for dinner, ma'am, we couldn't do better than a nice salmon mayonnaise. Always very partial to it, Mr. James is."

"Yes, it would be nice."

"Going to be hot again, and I thought if you could see your way to it, ma'am, it would be a good thing if you could call in at Mr. Bolding's, for the sooner I have that fish cooked and in the fridge the better pleased I'll be."

"Oh, yes, Mrs. Beeston, I'll do that."

"And a nice cucumber and anything you can see for the salad. I've got some of my own bottled strawberries for an iced sweet, and I've saved the top of the milk for cream."

"That will be lovely."

She went into the dressing-room and shut the door. Her hat swung from her hand. As she stood at the mirror putting it on she could see the dark reflection of the room behind her—marble-topped washstand, mahogany chest of drawers, and the single bed against the wall. She would have given anything she possessed to tell Mrs. Beeston to make up that bed for James tonight, but she just couldn't do it. Mrs. Beeston mightn't talk—she was the old dependable sort—but Mrs. Rogers had a small persistent trickle of gossip full of 'I said to her', and 'She said to me', and 'Only fancy anyone doing a thing like that'. It wasn't any good, she couldn't face it. If it really came to the point, it would be easier to face James and have it out with him. There would at least be the lash of anger to drive her.

She did not feel it yet. She thought how strange it was that she should feel nothing but this sick dismay. It would be easier to be angry, but you cannot be angry at will.

She came out of the house, and saw that the sun had broken through and the mist was rolling up across the sea. She walked down to the shops and bought the things Mrs. Beeston wanted. Mr. Bolding had a fine cut of salmon for her and hoped that they would all enjoy it. He remembered her from the time when she was twelve years old and they used to come down for the holidays.

She took her basket back to the house and went down to the beach to join Esther Field.

It was a long, hot day. Alan had gone away and did not come back again. Having planted a thorn, he believed in leaving it to fester. The more you let a woman alone, the more frightened she became. Meanwhile he was going to bathe. He swam out to the point, lazed about there until the tide came up, and then swam back again. After which he made an excellent lunch and slept away the hot hours of the afternoon.

Miss Silver saw her niece Ethel off by an early train, and

later strolled down on to the beach. Passing the hut which belonged to Cliff Edge, she stopped to speak to Mrs. Field and enquire how she was getting on with her knitting.

"Very badly indeed, I'm afraid."

Miss Silver became aware that there was something wrong. Those swollen eyelids, that tremor in the voice. She sat down beside Esther Field, discovered a number of dropped stitches in the red woolly shawl, and began to pick them up. Presently her kind voice and the cheerful ordinariness of her conversation had their effect. Alan couldn't really mean to publish his father's private letters—you didn't do things like that. And you didn't hand over large sums of money to a wild extravagant young man who had dissipated far too much already. He wasn't a boy any longer, and it was time he turned to some sensible employment and settled down. Perhaps a small share in the ranch he had mentioned—he had always been very fond of horses. . . .

She began to take an interest in the new way of holding her needles. It would certainly help her not to drop stitches, but she was afraid she would never be able to remember about looping the wool over her left forefinger instead of her right. She said so, and was assured that it would all come with practice.

Mrs. Field shook her head doubtfully.

"I'm afraid I'm really rather a stupid person," she said. "I can do the kind of things I learned when I was young, but I don't seem to be any good at new ones. Do you think that might make one not really able to understand someone else's point of view?"

Miss Silver said in a meditative voice,

"I suppose it might."

Esther had an impulse towards confidence. She said,

"There is my stepson—I don't know if you have met him. He is staying with Darsie Anning."

"A tall young man with fair hair—very good-looking?"

Esther Field nodded.

"He is—isn't he? He is like my husband, you know, and he has the same kind of charm. But he doesn't settle down to anything."

She told Miss Silver a good deal about Alan Field, finishing up with,

"He wants me to advance quite a large sum of money for something which I'm afraid I don't think at all sensible. But of course he thinks it very unkind of me to refuse."

Miss Silver looked shocked.

"My dear Mrs. Field!"

The tears rushed into Esther's eyes.

"I know, I know—I oughtn't to do it—I mustn't do it. But if I don't——"

Carmona was coming towards them across the sands. Esther felt an odd relief. She didn't know what she might have said if she had been able to go on talking to Miss Silver. It was so easy to talk to her. But she might have said too much. She hoped that she had not done so already.

The next moment she was thinking that Carmona looked pale. There were shadows under her eyes. Her voice had a lifeless sound as she greeted Miss Silver and asked,

"Where is Pippa? Have you seen her?"

"I think she has gone out."

"Out?"

"She called something down over the cliff. I think she said she was taking that horrid little red car. I only hope it's safe."

Carmona sat down in the patch of shade.

"Oh, I expect so."

Embarked on the topic, Esther found it easy to go on.

"You know, she does fly about too much. I thought she really didn't look very well this morning. Of course, with all the stuff girls put on their faces, you can't tell, can you?"

Miss Silver said, "No, indeed," but opined that the general effect was often pleasing.

They continued to talk about make-up, a subject upon which one would not have supposed them to be particularly informed, but which appeared to interest them in no small degree.

By the time they had finished their chat Esther was feeling a great deal better. The world about her had again become the world she knew—one in which pretty girls made up their faces, young people fell in love and got married, and no one really wanted to do wrong or to act unkindly. When sorrow visited this world it was endured with courage and with the consolations of a simple faith. Friends were kind, and in due time cheerfulness returned. She became more and more persuaded that Alan could not possible have meant what he said.

To Carmona their talk was like something on a radio programme which you hear, but to which you do not listen. It went by, but never once broke in upon the closed circle of her mind. She lay on the beach and let the small hot pebbles run through her fingers.

Miss Silver took her way home in rather a thoughful mood. That very good-looking Mr. Field appeared to have had a disturbing effect not only on the Annings' household, but also on Cliff Edge. Very good-looking young men were rather apt to produce this effect upon a distinctively feminine household. There was obviously some link with a young and perhaps gayer Darsie. Mrs. Anning's words could really bear no other construction. And now here was this nice Mrs. Field who had certainly been upset to the point of prolonged weeping, to say nothing of Carmona Hardwick whose thoughts appeared to be quite painfully turned in upon themselves. She showed no traces of tears, but if Miss Silver was not very much mistaken, she was at this moment suffering from some kind of shock. There was, further, the rather strange conduct of Mrs. Maybury, an exceedingly pretty young woman of whom she had caught only a glimpse upon the previous evening. She had then appeared to be very far removed from the type which prefers solitude to company. To come down for so short a visit and then go off by herself in this way might have nothing at all to do with Alan Field, but it was obviously causing Mrs. Field some anxiety.

As she walked along the hot cliff path with her knitting-bag on her arm she reflected that human nature was of all studies the most absorbing. The knitting-bag was a new one presented by her niece Ethel upon the occasion of her birthday. The remnant of chintz from which it had been made was most tasteful, the pattern embracing a great number of flowers all blooming together in a profusion seldom conceded by nature, and the lining an agreeable shade of green. A much appreciated feature was the addition of a row of useful pockets to hold everything from pattern-books to spare needles and balls of wool. Her thoughts followed Ethel Burkett on her journey with affection, picturing with pleasure her prospective reunion with the family from whom she was never willingly parted.

It being by now close on one o'clock, Darsie Anning would be engaged in superintending the dishing-up of lunch. Even with a good refrigerator, food must be a problem in such weather as this, and with a foreign staff you really could not be too particular. Miss Silver was therefore surprised as she crossed the upper landing to see Miss Anning come a little way out of her mother's bedroom and then turn back again.

"Now, Mother, I really must go and see about your lunch. Marie will bring it up to you."

Mrs. Anning's voice sounded fretfully through the half open door.

"I don't like these foreign girls, Darsie. I keep on telling you, but you don't do anything about it. My mother had a French maid when I was a girl. She read our letters. I should like you to send Marie away. I don't like her to be left with me. I don't know why you don't stay with me yourself. I don't want you to go away and leave me."

Miss Anning came out half way upon the landing and saw Miss Silver. At the sound of a fretful sob she drew her brows together and said, "Oh dear!"

Miss Silver coughed.

"Could I perhaps be of any use? I could sit with your mother until her lunch comes up. I know what a busy time this is."

Darsie Anning gave a short brisk nod.

"That is very kind of you. Mother, here is Miss Silver come to pay you a visit."

Mrs. Anning was in a state of unusual agitation. She had a high flush and a wandering eye. Miss Silver was asked with insistence to see that the door was really shut.

"It has a way of springing open, and these girls stand at the crack and listen. Foreigners are all spies—you can't trust them. But you can't trust anyone, can you?"

Miss Silver said,

"I should be very sad if I believed that."

"I have been sad for a long time," said Mrs. Anning. "My husband died, and Alan went away, and then we had no money, you know. He said he couldn't marry her because he had no money either. Young people can't live on nothing, can they? But Darsie has never been the same. People always said how pretty she was, and she used to be so gay. She took away all her photographs, but I hid one in the cover of my needle-book. Would you like to see it?"

The photograph was a snapshot, tucked in between two of the little pinked-out flannel leaves which had been meant to hold needles. It showed a dark girl with a lively laughing face, and a handsome fair young man. Mrs. Anning snatched it away again almost before Miss Silver had time to look at it. Her fingers shook as she put it back into hiding.

"He oughtn't to have gone away!" she said in a sudden loud voice. "You can't do things like that and not be punished! You ought to be punished when you do wrong! It says so in the Bible—'An eye for an eye, and a tooth for a tooth'! Perhaps that is why he has come back, so that he may be punished. I thought about that when I heard his voice. I told Darsie it was his voice, and she said no. She oughtn't to tell lies about it, ought she? As if I wouldn't know Alan's voice—*Alan Field*!"

She was running on in this way, when the door opened. The French girl Marie came in with the tray—a cutlet in aspic, salad, a drink of iced lemonade, all very nicely served. Marie's eyes took darting glances here and there in the room. She set down the tray upon a small table which stood ready for it and went out again, leaving the door unlatched. Mrs. Anning said loudly and angrily,

"She wants to hear what I am saying about Alan Field! Well, let her hear it! Why should I care? Anyone may hear it, because it is true! He ought to be punished! I told you she listened at doors!"

CHAPTER XI

JAMES HARDWICK drove up from the station, and thought that for once in a way the tail end of an English summer was doing itself proud. The weather looked like lasting too. Tomorrow he and Carmona would swim out to the Point and take their time about coming back.

Carmona! In less than ten minutes he would be seeing her again. When he was away from her, this was what he looked forward to—this moment of anticipation when he could savour to the full the thought that he was coming home. Every meeting held the romance and the promise of the first time, when they had not really met at all but he had looked across the crowded theatre and loved her.

They turned in at the hot cement drive. He paid off his taxi and walked up the steps between the empty urns and into the hall, which seemed dark and cool after the outside glare. As he set down his suit-case, the grandfather clock at the foot of the stairs was striking seven. It was very large and very ugly, and it struck with a whirring note which had alarmed him very much when he was a little boy. He waited for it to stop, and caught the sound of voices through the open drawing-room door. Esther Field said,

"Oh, no, Alan."

James stood where he was. Unbelievable that Alan Field should be here in this house. Esther must have been speaking about him, not to him. He went on down the hall and into the room.

There were seven people there having drinks, but the one he saw first was Carmona, in a white dress, with her hat thrown down upon the arm of a chair beside her. Her dark hair was a little ruffled, and she was pale. She had a lemon drink in her hand with lumps of ice in it frosting the glass. He saw her first, but in the next instant he saw Alan Field at her elbow. The others in the room were the Trevors, Adela Castleton, Esther Field, and Pippa Maybury.

Carmona came to meet him. She was much too pale. He

put his hand on her shoulder and just touched her cheek with his lips—any husband greeting any wife in the presence of a party of old friends. But inwardly he was the lover who wished them all at Jericho so that he might catch her up in his arms and hold her close. It was the lover who was aware that there was no response. He might have been touching one of those wax models which you see in a shop window. She didn't look at him. As soon as he had touched her cheek she drew away. Whilst he was speaking to the Trevors, to Adela, and Esther, whilst Pippa Maybury was telling him he must be dying for a drink and mixing him one, she had gone back to her old position and stood there aloof and withdrawn.

He came with his drink in his hand to stand beside her and speak to Alan.

"You here, Field? How very unexpected!"

"Oh, I don't know. One is bound to come back some time. I had business with Esther, but it shouldn't take very long. I'm at the Annings'. You will remember Darsie in the old days. Shockingly gone off, poor thing, and no wonder. What a life—trying to scrape halfpennies out of cranky old women! I'd rather shoot myself!"

He put down his glass and turned to Carmona.

"Well, I'm afraid I must be pushing off—they dine at half-past-seven. In this weather! Esther, old dear, I'll see you in the morning. Oh, just a moment, Pippa——"

They went out of the long window together. Presently Pippa came back. There was a flush of colour in her cheeks. She was fingering her pearls. The party melted away to change.

James arrived from the bathroom to find Carmona pinning an old-fashioned pearl brooch on to the front of her thin yellow frock. She turned from the glass and put out a hand to hold him off.

"No—I want to talk to you. But not now—there's no time."

"Carmona, what is the matter? What is that fellow Field doing here?"

"He came to see Esther. You heard what he said—he has business with her."

"I suppose he wants money."

"I suppose he does."

Right up to this moment she had gone on feeling numb or, rather, not feeling anything except a kind of cold emptiness. Now there began to be pain—hot stabs of it. Her heart shook and was afraid. She said quickly,

"Esther is upset. I can't talk about it now—I don't want to. We must get through the evening first."

There was a heavy gilt clock on the mantelpiece. He glanced at it and said,

"I'd like to know what all this is about, It isn't only Esther who is upset. You can tell me while I dress. We've got thirty-five minutes."

"No—James, I can't."

He looked at her keenly.

"Darling, what is all this? You'd better get it off your chest, you know. Has Field been annoying you?"

"Not—like that."

He gave a short half-angry laugh.

"Not like what? Come along, out with it!"

His voice rasped, because in the very moment of speaking it came to him what Alan Field might have done. If he had told Carmona the thing which he, James, had always hoped she would never know, it would account for that shocked look. Difficult to believe the fellow would give himself away to that extent. Difficult, but not impossible where Field was concerned. It could be his idea of paying off an old score.

Carmona went back a step. They had never talked about Alan. Why were they talking about him now? She could not remember that James had ever used such a tone to her before. Something in her shrank, and then sprang into anger. He saw her eyes widen and go bright.

"Carmona—what has he said to you?"

"Don't you know?"

"I think you had better tell me."

She went back again until the foot-board of the bed brought her up short. She stood against it with a trapped feeling and said, "No."

James Hardwick came over to her and dropped his hands lightly on her shoulders.

"Tell me what he said."

It had been a mistake to touch her. The gentlest creature will fight if hands are laid on it. Something very old came up in Carmona. Her anger flared. She looked at James as if she hated him and said,

"He told me you paid him to go away and let you marry me!"

And on the last word she twisted loose and ran for the door. The handle left a bruise across her palm, but she didn't feel it until afterwards. She was any wild thing wrenching free from the trap, sense and reason gone. If he had touched her, tried to hold her back, she might have screamed.

The door fell to behind her. She had a moment's horrified realization that she really might have screamed if he had tried to hold her back. But he had not. He had made no move to follow. She stood there with the door between them, and was glad that she was angry.

James Hardwick remained where he was. He was barefoot, with a thin dressing-gown over his under-pants. He could hardly pursue Carmona through a house littered with guests. Now that he knew what was wrong he could wait. There had always been the possibility that she might come to know. He would much rather it had not happened, because Field would certainly have put it in the most offensive light, and she was bound to be hurt. It was really a good thing that she should have had that spurt of anger. It would hurt her less that way. He hated her to be hurt.

He went on with his dressing.

CHAPTER XII

A LONG evening for everyone. Afterwards, when everything that had been said or done was being sifted over, Beeston was to be asked a number of questions. How had this one looked, and what had the other said? Did anyone seem disturbed, nervous, depressed, or in any way upset? He opined that it was very difficult to say, sir, and the day had been a hot one. It did cross his mind that Lady Castleton might have been out in the sun a bit too long, seeing she had gone to bed with a headache. She and Mrs. Field, now, they were neither of them as young as they were and perhaps better to have stayed in in the heat of the day, but as to the others, no, he wouldn't go so far as to say they were out of their usual. Mrs. James had quite a colour, and Mrs. Maybury the same and talking very lively. Naturally, they would all be pleased about Mr. James coming home, and coming from abroad, he would have all manner of interesting things to talk about. The work he does, he comes in contact with all kinds of foreigners, and for those that take an interest in such, well, sir, it makes interesting talk. The impression was conveyed that James Hardwick was a good host and that whatever he might have had on his mind, he did not allow it to interfere with the entertainment of his guests.

Carmona got through the evening very well. There were times when she was frightened, but they did not last. Quite suddenly and without any warning she would have the feeling you get when you look over an unexpected drop to something far below—there is a moment of panic fear, and then you stop looking, and it is gone again. For the rest of the time anger burned in her hard and clear. She thought of the things she would say to James when they were alone together. Meanwhile she could play the graceful hostess to his gracious host.

If she had been less taken up with her own affairs she might have felt some concern about Pippa, who had certainly allowed her glass to be filled too often. As her colour rose and her tongue ran faster, Esther began to look uncomfortable. Adela Castleton, intent upon her patience cards, raised an eyebrow, whereupon Pippa burst out laughing and said,

"Now I've shocked everyone!"

James poured her out a cup of coffee.

"Too many drinks," he said easily, "It's too hot for them this weather. Take a nice long pull at Mrs. Beeston's iced coffee and come out on the terrace with me. It should be getting cool there now."

She gave a curious little shudder.

"No—no—I don't want to do that. I hate your uncle's garden—don't you? And it looks worse at night. In the day it's just plain ugly, but in the dusk all those figureheads and things, they *lurk!*"

Carmona found herself watching them. He had done that very well. But then James did do things well. He had just that touch of distinction which made everything he did seem right. Through her sense of shock and anger she knew that he was carrying the whole situation as very few men could have done, and carrying it with at any rate the appearance of perfect ease. Now he was starting Maisie Trevor off on one of her favourite lines of chatter, and had drawn Colonel Trevor into saying something pleasant about Bill Maybury whom everybody liked. It was for her to respond to Maisie and to import Esther into the conversation. Esther—and if possible Adela Castleton.

But Adela afforded no possibilities of any kind. Her beautiful pale face remained bent over the patience cards which she fingered with delicate precision, the solitaire diamond which almost hid her wedding-ring flashing under the light, the blood-red ruby on the other hand making one bright spot of colour against the white of her skin and the black of her dress.

"And I really am the only one who knew all the ins and outs of the affair," said Maisie Trevor. 'Of course I 'was quite a girl at the time, but you know what an interest one takes in that sort of thing, especially when everyone drops their voices and tells you to run away and do the flowers or something like that. He was such a distinguished man, and *married*, and she was only a year older than I was, so naturally I took the very deepest interest. And she told me the whole thing the night before they ran away."

Echoes of an old musty scandal dead and gone for a generation—heartbreak and pain, shame and sin and suffering, buried now beneath the indifferent years. Carmona tried to look as if she was listening. It was all so far away and long ago.

Adela Castleton swept her cards together as she had done the night before. The heat, the lights, the voices, Maisie Trevor's voice and her interminable stories! She stood up.

"Will you forgive me if I go to bed? I was stupid to be out in the glare for so long. It has brought my headache on again."

Carmona was all solicitude.

"Can I get you anything?"

Adela looked vague.

"I don't think so. I have some very good tablets. I'm just not sure—where I put them. Perhaps if you—will come up with me——"

Her face was stripped of life and colour. Difficult to recognize the assured Lady Castleton. As they went out of the door, Carmona slipped an arm about her, and had the impression that it was welcome.

The tablets were in a drawer of the old-fashioned mirror. Yellow curtains, a shiny yellow eiderdown, and Adela sitting on the side of the bed and saying,

"Somewhere on the dressing-table, I think. Yes, that's the bottle. I don't take them once in a blue moon, but when I do it means at least eight hours of good deep sleep—and I feel I need it tonight. Perhaps you would give me a glass of water from the washstand."

She tipped two of the tablets into her hand, lifted it to her lips, drank the water Carmona brought, and thanked her.

"Would you be very kind and just look in on your way to bed? Once I'm off nothing wakes me, but it would be nice to know that you would just look in. I haven't had a head like this since—oh, I can't remember!"

Carmona saw her into bed and went down to the others.

The longest evening ends. This had not been so long as counted in time, but there are other factors. Endurance is one of them. Just how much strain can anyone endure? The Victorian drawing-room with its garlanded carpet, its gold and white overmantel, its china cabinets, and its brocaded chairs, held more than one who might have been asking that question.

Perhaps no one was sorry when the evening drew to an end. Good-nights were said, and the women went up the stairs, their murmur of conversation dying away as they receded. Doors closed, Carmona, left to the last, crossed over to Adela Castleton's room and turned the handle gently. Two windows open to the cooler north, and a breeze coming in—the vague outline of the bed. At first no sound, but as she took a step forward and then stood to listen, the regular rise and fall of Adela's breathing. She waited until she could be quite sure of it, and then went out and closed the door again.

Downstairs James poured drinks, and presently went to latch

the windows. He stood for a moment at the long glass door of the terrace. There was a cool air coming in from the sea. The water was dark and the sky luminous. The old figureheads stood up black and strange. He said,

"It seems a shame to shut out the air, but Beeston would certainly expect us all to be murdered in our beds if we didn't."

"Your uncle had him a long time?"

"Oh, ages. I used to be sent down by myself, you know. There was a deadly feud between my aunt Mildred Wotherspoon and the Hardwicks. I don't know what it was about, and it had been going on for so long that I don't suppose they even knew themselves by then, but they wouldn't meet. I used to be sent down with a label sewed inside my pocket from the time I was about seven, and the Beestons looked after me. Uncle Octavius used to pat me on the head and tip me—half-a-crown to start with, rising to a fiver at twentyone, where it stopped dead. He used to mutter, 'Poor Henry's boy', and go away, to our mutual relief. It was Beeston who provided the statutory bucket and spade and showed me the best places for prawns. And Mrs. Beeston let me have a glass bowl with sea anemones in it, and bring in seaweed, and shrimps and winkles and any old thing."

Colonel Trevor finished his drink and set down the glass.

"You're not thinking of staying on here, are you?"

James turned from the window.

"Oh, no, it can't be done. This kind of house just isn't possible any more."

They parted on the wide upstair landing with its tall ebony clock ticking in a staid old-fashioned way and the patterned carpet giving out a faint musty smell. James knocked on the door of what he still could not help remembering as Uncle Octavius' bedroom and went in.

Carmona was sitting on the edge of the bed. She had got through the evening, and she had been glad that it was over and glad to be alone, but as one moment after another went by, her courage ebbed. She still wore the pale yellow dress and the pearl brooch. Her hands were clasped in her lap. They were clasped so tightly that James' wedding-ring was cutting into her finger. But she did not feel it. With the sound of his step and the opening of the door she had begun to feel too many other things, and to feel them too intensely. There could be no more putting off. They had come to the place where they must speak the truth to each other and take what came of it. And she was afraid. Not of James, but of what she might be going to find out about him. She thought that he would tell her the truth—she did think that. But she didn't know what that truth was going to be. He had bought her from Alan Field. He had paid five thousand pounds for her. She could still raise the hot flare of anger when she pressed this home, but it failed again and left her shaking with an inward cold, because if James wasn't James at all, but someone she had never known, then where was she to turn, and what was she to do? Just for a moment it came to her that there wasn't anyone she could turn to—except James himself. And if there wasn't any James, then there wasn't anyone at all.

He shut the door and came over to her.

"Well, my dear, I suppose we have got to talk this out."

She said, "Yes." That is to say, her lips made the right movement, but there wasn't any sound.

He sat on the bed beside her.

"Do you mind so much?"

Her lips said, "Yes," again, but there was still no sound. She sat there, not looking at him, not really looking at anything.

His heart wept for her. Well then, they must get on with it. How did one begin? Now that he had to talk to her about it, all the words which would have to be used were coarse and crude. He said,

"You don't want me to touch you, do you?"

A long shudder went over her. He said quickly,

"All right, I won't. But it would be easier if you would let me put my arm round you."

The shudder came again.

He said, "Very well, I'll tell you."

It was quite extraordinarily hard to begin. His mind went back to seeing her that first time in her white dress with her birthday pearls at her throat, and Alan Field smiling beside her, leaning over to whisper in her ear. As the scene sprang into memory, all light and colour, he began to bring it back to her in words. Once he had started, the words came. He told her about sitting there in the box with the Trevors and seeing her like that. He said,

"I fell in love with you then, and I planned to meet you between the acts. The Trevors would have introduced me—they were talking about you a lot—but Maisie turned faint and we had to take her home. I was due in Cairo next day and no getting out of it. It was fifteen months before I could get away, but I heard about you in a letter from Maisie, and from Mary Maxwell who had been staying in the same house. I ran across her and her husband in Alexandria and she used to talk about you, so I knew that you weren't married or engaged. As soon as I got home I went down to see the Trevors, and they told me you were marrying Alan Field in a week's time. Maisie was all for it, but Tom said he would break your heart and that he would give his right hand to prevent it. I would have given more than that, but there didn't seem to be anything I could do."

Carmona lifted her head.

"What business was it of yours?" she said. Her voice was small and cold.

"I loved you. You were unhappy."

"How did you know—I was unhappy?"

"I saw you on my way down to the Trevors. You were in a window-seat of the London train as my train came into the junction. I don't think you saw me, but you were looking straight at me and I could see how unhappy you were. Both trains were only just moving."

Yes, she had been most desperately unhappy then. She was going to marry Alan not because she needed him, but because he needed her, and with every day that passed she knew most certainly that it wasn't enough. Too late to draw back, too late to strike him such a blow, too late to do anything but go through with it as best as she could.

James waited to see whether she would speak. The pale profile bent a little, but the lips did not move. He went on.

"I didn't think there was anything I could do. If I had thought he would make you happy I would have made up my mind to it. But I knew he wouldn't. Tom Trevor was right—he was going to break your heart. You see, I happened to know quite a lot about Field. He wasn't fit to be in the same room with you, let alone marry you. I went through hell. And then—something happened."

She gave a little startled gasp and turned to face him, lips parted, eyes suddenly bright. That was what she had always wanted to know—what had happened, and why, and how.

If James was surprised he did not show it. He went on speaking in the same quiet voice.

"I had an old-standing engagement to dine with a man called Edwards and meet his wife. When I got there it was quite a party, and we all went on to rather a hot-stuff night club. It wasn't much in my line and I wasn't in the mood for it, but I couldn't very well fall out. When we'd been there about half an hour Field turned up with a fairly noisy party. They had all been drinking, and they kept on. After Field had slipped and brought his partner down he stopped trying to dance and took to talking instead."

This was the hardest thing he had ever done in his life. If there was any way out of telling her he would have taken it. There wasn't any way. It would hurt her damnably, and he had got to do it.

She lifted her eyes to his face and said, "Go on."

"He talked—about how he had never had any luck. You can't get anywhere without money, and he had never had any. It didn't give you a chance. And now the best he could do was to tie himself up for a beggarly few hundred a year. I'm not going to tell you everything he said, but it was all along those lines. I went over and sat down at his table. The girl who was with him was practically out. I said, 'You're getting married in a day or two, aren't you?' And he said yes, worse luck, but you'd got to live hadn't you, and he was down on his uppers. I said, 'If someone were to offer you a good round sum down and a fresh start in, say, South America, what would you say about it?' He wanted to know what I meant by a good round sum, and I told him. It seemed to sober him up. He stared at me and said, 'You're joking!'. I said, 'Look here, you're drunk. I can't do business with you like this. If you'll come home with me and put your head in a bucket of water, we can talk'."

Carmona said nothing. She kept her eyes on his face and said nothing.

James went on.

"Well, that was how it was. He knew what he was doing all right. I fed him black coffee, and he wasn't drunk when he made the bargain. England was getting a bit too hot for him, and he had quite a fancy for South America. And he was quite frank about the money—said yours wasn't going to be very much good to him because it was all tied up on you and your children, whereas if he had some capital to play with, there were no end of things he could do. I saw him again next day and we fixed up the details. He was to have his passage and some spending money, and the main sum down when he reached Rio. And he wasn't to see you. He was to write and tell you the truth—that he wasn't within a hundred miles of being good enough for you, and that you would be better off without him."

"He didn't write."

James put out his hand towards her, but she drew away from it.

"I went—to the church—to marry him. He didn't come."

"I know. I didn't mean it to be like that."

It was almost as if she were appealing to him not to have let it happen, and as if he were putting out a hand to steady her—not in any physical touch, which would have sent her shrinking away into her own loneliness, but with some quiet assurance of safety. That was the curious thing about what was happening between them—under the shock, the hurt, the anger which had ravaged her, there was the instinct which looked to him for security and knew that he could give it. It was this instinct which had drawn her into marrying him. Everyone had been pleased, but everyone had been very much surprised. She knew that they were wondering how she could. So soon, and after such a hurt. They didn't know, and she could never tell them, that when she was with James the pain and humiliation dimmed and faded out. If she could be with him all the time, it wouldn't come back. So when he asked her, she married him.

After they had been silent a little while he said,

"We haven't ever talked about Field. Does it still hurt such a lot?"

She looked at him piteously.

"I thought—he needed me. I knew—it wasn't going to be easy, but I thought—I could do it. Then I began to wonder—whether I could. I had to make myself—go on. When I went to the church—and he didn't come—it was—I don't know how to say it——"

"You had been trying so hard, and then what you were trying to do wasn't wanted. Was that it?"

She moved her head in assent.

"He didn't want—any of the things—I thought—I could give him. Now I know that all he ever wanted was the money—and it wasn't enough——" Her voice went away until the last word could only be guessed at.

He leaned forward and took her hands. This time she did not draw them away. The fingers clung to his, but when he tried to loosen them so that he might put his arms about her they clung and wouldn't let go.

"Carmona—darling!"

But she shook her head.

"No—*please*—*James*——"

He let it be as she wanted.

The tears were running down her face. Presently she took away her hands to find a handkerchief and dry them.

CHAPTER XIII

JAMES put out the dressing-room light and drew back the curtains. He looked out upon the same scene which he had watched from the drawing-room—dark waters, luminous sky, and the odd shapes of the things with which Uncle Octavius had cluttered up his garden. What was new was something that stirred amongst the clutter, a tall shape amongst the other shapes which had lifted once to the sea and would never move again. Someone was going down the path which led to the cliff.

He stood there, frowning a little. Difficult to imagine that anyone from inside the house would be choosing this time to take a walk. It would certainly not occur to either of the Trevors or to Esther Field. He thought about Pippa Maybury. It was the sort of thing she might do it if came into her head, but not alone—quite definitely not alone. He remembered Alan Field's "Can I have a word with you, Pippa?" and that she had gone out on to the terrace with him and come back looking—well, how had she looked? Excited—frightened? The impression was so momentary that he couldn't be sure of it. He couldn't be sure about anything. The moving figure could be someone who had no manner of business to be there. He thought he would just go down and make certain that everything was quite all right. If, for instance, someone had gone out of the house, one of the doors or windows would be ajar or at least unlatched. If, on the other hand, someone was lurking in the garden—he recalled Pippa's use of the word with dislike——

He thought he would just go down and see what was happening. The bare possibility that Alan Field might be hanging about——

He opened the door into the bedroom and saw that Carmona was asleep. The overhead light had been turned out, but the room was full of a soft glow from the lamp on his side of the bed. She lay turned away from it, her hair dark against the pillow. He closed the door again, slipped on shoes, and caught up a torch and a light raincoat. As he came out on to the landing, the clock struck the quarter after midnight.

He found what he was looking for at the first trial. If anyone was getting out of the house in the middle of the night, it was a hundred to one they would use the glass door in the drawing-room. And there it was, the door he had locked as he talked to old Tom Trevor about the Beestons an inch or two ajar. He had locked it all right an hour ago—he was sure about that. Someone had come down and opened it. He switched off the torch, pushed the door wide, and went out on the terrace.

Standing now and listening, there was nothing either to hear or see except what he might have heard and seen on any summer night of all the nights he had slept or waked at Cliff Edge. But that someone had been there he was in no doubt, and the open door bore witness. With the torch in his hand but not switched on, he walked down the path to the gate which opened upon the cliff.

Carmona woke. It was later. She had fallen into depths of sleep almost as soon as her head touched the pillow. It was as if she had made a long journey and come to the end of it with nothing left but utter weariness and the need to sleep. When she dried her tears, it was as if she had wiped away with them all the pain which had brought them to her eyes—the pain, the anger, the deep humiliation. She no longer felt anything at all. All she wanted was to be left alone, and to lie down and go to sleep. Now she woke to the sound of running footsteps. She opened her eyes upon the glow in the room. The windows on either side of the dressing-table were dark beyond it. The footsteps ran and stumbled. There was the sound of a sobbing breath. She had the confused instinct to see without being seen. To do that she must switch off the light. She pushed back the sheet and the thin blanket and got out of bed.

As soon as the lamp was out, the windows sprang into view, no longer dark. She made her way towards the nearest and leaned out. Someone ran across the terrace and was gone. She could hear the small sound which the glass door beneath her made as it fell to. Her mind was still not quite awake. The thought of James came into it. Not his step—no. A much lighter step than that of any man. But—the thought came again and more insistently—where was James? She had the feeling of time gone by. How much, she didn't know, but more than it would take for him to undress and come to bed.

She drew back from the window, went to the dressing-room, and put on the light. The clothes he had worn were tumbled on a chair, his dressing-gown beside them. The raincoat which had hung behind the door was gone. The torch was gone from the dressing-table. It had lain up against the mirror behind the brushes which she had given him for a wedding present. It was gone.

She went back into her bedroom, crossed to the door, and opened it, all a good deal as if it was part of a dream. A low-powered bulb burned at the head of the stairs. The footsteps she had heard in the garden were in the hall, but they were not running now. She heard them come from the drawing-room with a slow, lagging fall, and at the foot of the stairs they stopped, as if there were no strength to go farther.

Carmona waited. The breeze between window and door made her shiver a little in her thin nightdress. The footsteps began again. They climbed the stairs, dragging on every step. She heard them come, and in the end she saw.

Pippa pulled on the newel at the head of the stair as if that last step was indeed the last that she could take. It was her right hand that pulled on the newel. Her left hung down by her side. Her face was ghastly pale, and all across the front of her dress from the knees down there was a frightful red stain.

CHAPTER XIV

PIPPA leaned on the newel. Her breath came in shallow gasps. Then all at once she made a sideways thrust like a swimmer pushing off and took her stumbling way across the landing to the door of her room. It was closed. Her hand came up groping and failed twice to find the knob. The third time it gave under the fumbling touch and she went forward into the dark and was lost.

Carmona had stood there frozen, her heart thudding against her side. Now, with a quick shiver, she came back to thought and action. Oddly enough, the first thing that came to her was that she had done well to let Pippa go by, because if she had touched her she might have screamed and waked the house. Even then Carmona had a horrid certainty that no one must wake and no one must know. Adela Castleton wouldn't wake. Her room was the nearest, but she had taken her sleeping-draught, and she wouldn't wake.

She crossed the landing, opened the door, and went in. Darkness met her. As she shut the door again and felt for the switch, there was a quick shuddering intake of breath not more than a yard or two away. Her fingers found the catch, light flooded the room, and she saw Pippa standing there, her eyes wide with fear, her hand stretched out as if to ward a blow.

Under the high-powered bulb overhead, so much brighter than the mere glimmer on the landing, everything was quite frightfully distinct—the vivid stain on the white dress, the smudged stain on the hands.

Carmona said in a voice which surprised her because it sounded so like her own,

"Don't look like that. It's only me." And then, "What has happened?"

Pippa said, "He's dead——" Her hands came slowly down.

Carmona reached behind her and locked the door. It wasn't until she had done this that the thought of James came to her again, and dreadfully, because she didn't know where he was, and Pippa hadn't said who was dead. She said it now.

"Alan—Alan is dead——"

There was such a sense of relief that Carmona almost cried out. Just one word, a name, and the blood had turned back to her heart. She came across the little space between them and said quick and low,

"Get out of that dress! And hurry! You can tell me afterwards."

Between them they got it off, bundling it up upon itself. The stain had soaked right through. Stockings were stripped and thrust into the bundle. It was like undressing a child. Pippa's hands pushed feebly at the white chiffon of the dress, fumbled at the clips of the suspender-belt. Her hands—the stain on them was dry. It wouldn't come off on anything else now, but it must be got rid of. The dress must be got rid of.

Why?

Carmona said, "You had better tell me. You said Alan was dead. Did you—kill him?"

Pippa gasped and shook her head.

"No—no!"

"You had better tell me."

"I went—to meet him——"

"Why?"

"He was going to town—in the morning. He said—he would see Bill—so I went——"

"Where?"

"The beach hut."

"But it was locked—we always lock it."

"Key on the hall table. He put it—in his pocket." A shiver went over her. "As simple as that."

Carmona said, "Go on! Here, you'd better have something round you."

A filmy black wrap hung over the foot of the bed. It had gold and silver stars on it. Over the inky folds Pippa's small pointed face was chalky white, her scarlet lipstick standing out like the patches on the face of a clown. The mouth opened and said,

"I went. The door was open. There wasn't any light. I stumbled over—something—and came down. I didn't see the stain—on my dress—I just knew it was wet—and my hands—" She had begun to shake all over.

"You said Alan was dead? You did say that."

"Yes—he was dead——"

"How do you know?"

"I had a torch. I put it on—to see." Her tongue was suddenly loosed. She began to sob, and between the sobs there was a jumble of words. "He was there—just inside the door. He was dead—someone had stabbed him. I didn't do it—I swear I didn't! How could I—I hadn't anything to stab him with! My dress was all wet—and my hands! Oh, Carmona!"

"Are you sure he was dead?"

"You wouldn't ask—if you'd seen him——" Her voice stopped. She shuddered dreadfully.

Carmona said, "We ought to call the police."

Pippa stared at her.

"They'd say I did it. No—no—we can't! Carmona, we can't! I'd have to say I went there to meet him in the middle of the night. I'd hate to tell Bill, and he'd want to know why— the police would want to know why. Do you want me to tell them Alan was blackmailing me and I was giving him my pearls so that he shouldn't tell Bill? How long do you think they would believe I hadn't done it if I told them that? I'd rather kill myself! Carmona, don't you *see*?"

Carmona saw. During the last few horrible minutes she had been becoming more and more conscious not only of Pippa's position, but of other things as well. Where was James?

It must be very late. Uncle Octavius had had a craze for clocks. There was one in every room, and they all kept very good time. The one on the mantelpiece in Pippa's room was of green and gold china. A bulging cupid held up the clock face on either side. Between them the hands stood at twenty to one. She had been here with Pippa for how long? Five minutes—ten?

She asked quickly, "When were you to meet Alan?" And Pippa said, "Twenty past twelve."

The time echoed in Carmona's mind. At twenty past twelve she had been deeply and dreamlessly asleep. James had gone to his dressing-room. He hadn't come to bed. Where was he then? Where was he now? If they were to call the police, it must be done without delay. She couldn't bring herself to say that it must be done.

It was half an hour before she returned to her room. They had crept downstairs and burned Pippa's stained dress and stockings in what remained of the kitchen fire. Pippa had scrubbed and washed at the scullery sink. The Beestons slept at the top of the house. Down in the old-fashioned half-basement it was safe enough to stir up dying embers and let water run.

They went up at last, sure that no stain was left. When she had seen Pippa into bed, Carmona went back to her own room. It was in darkness, as she had left it, but it was no longer empty. She had no sooner opened the door than she knew that James had come back. The sound of his deep, quiet breathing reached her. She went softly round to her own side of the bed and got in. Not until she lay down did she know how tired she was. Too tired to think or to remember. Too tired to be anyone, or to do anything except go down, and down, and down into the sleep that closed about her.

CHAPTER XV

IT was Colonel Anthony from Ralston who gave the alarm.
For seven months in the year irrespective of weather he went
down at what his wife called a horrible hour to take his morning
dip. Ralston being next to Cliff Edge and served by the same
path to the beach, his way across the shingle led him quite
close to the Hardwicks' hut. He at once perceived that there
was something wrong. The door, which should have been shut,
stood wide, and from it protruded a man's foot and ankle.
There was a stiffness, there was something about the angle of
that jutting foot, which halted Colonel Anthony. He took a
couple of steps to the right, and saw a dead man lying just
inside the hut. He lay on his face. There was a wound in
his back, and there was no doubt about his being dead. There
had been a lot of blood, but it was dry now. There was no sign
of a weapon.

Colonel Anthony gave a sharp exclamation, turned on his
heel, and made his way back up the cliff path at a very creditable
pace. At a quarter past seven James Hardwick was being
informed that Inspector Colt would like a word with him—
"if you please, sir". James said, "All right, Beeston," pulled
on a pair of slacks and an open-neck shirt, and went down.

Inspector Colt was waiting for him in the gloomy study to
which it had been Uncle Octavius' wont to retire when he felt
disposed for a nap. It contained a number of monumental chairs
covered in rubbed black leather and a very large sofa, but the
Inspector had remained upon his feet—a tall man with sandy
hair and a face like a horse. He extended a sizable hand with
a key on the palm and said,

"Good-morning, sir. May I ask if this is the key of your
beach hut?"

James looked at it.

"Well, it might be. But I don't know how you came by it.
We always lock up when we come in, and it ought to be on the
hall table. I'll just have a look."

"You won't find it there," said Inspector Colt. "When

the police were rung up to say there was a dead body in the hut——"

James had turned towards the door. He turned back.

"A dead what?"

"A dead body," said Inspector Colt. Neither his face nor his voice had changed. He continued without any perceptible break. "Proceeding to the spot, we discovered the door of the beach hut standing open, and the body of a man lying just inside. The key was on the floor beside him. I should like to know whether you can throw any light upon its being there."

James said sharply, "Who was the man?"

"Colonel Anthony identifies him as Mr. Alan Field."

"Field? Good God—we've got his stepmother staying in the house! He was here only last night!"

"So Colonel Anthony informed us."

James reflected that since the neighbours always knew everything, it was as well not to be outdone in the way of offering information to the police. He said in a suitable tone of distress,

"This will be a most terrible shock to Mrs. Field. She is very fond of him."

"You are connected?"

"Mrs. Field is my wife's aunt. Field has been abroad for the last three years—I believe in South America. He turned up quite unexpectedly the evening before last. I myself was away. I only returned last night—at seven o'clock, to be precise. We have a number of guests in the house. They were having drinks in the drawing-room. Field was there, but went away soon afterwards. It looks as if he must have had the key of the hut. He may even have been the one who locked it—I don't know."

There was more on these lines. Inspector Colt took down the names of the guests—Colonel and Mrs. Trevor, Lady Castleton, Mrs. Field, Mrs. Maybury.

"Did they all know Mr. Field?"

"I should think so."

"You are not sure, Major Hardwick?"

James smiled faintly.

"Well, no. You see, I didn't. As I told you, I only got here last night, and up till then I had only met Field once or twice."

Colt said in his expressionless voice,

"But Mrs. Hardwick was once engaged to him."

"Oh, yes—they were more or less brought up together. But it didn't come to anything. It was before I met her."

"Was there any disagreement, any quarrel, when he was here last night?"

"Oh, no—nothing like that——. Just a social gathering. It broke up almost at once."

"May I ask why?"

"It was after seven. Everyone had been out in the sun, and I was just off a journey—we all wanted to wash and change. Field was staying at Miss Anning's—they dine at half-past seven. It was like that."

"There was no quarrel?"

"Of course not."

He went upstairs.

Carmona was brushing her hair. He shut the door behind him, went over to her, and took the brush out of her hand.

"Listen, darling! Inspector Colt is downstairs from the local police. Alan Field is dead. I'm not asking you whether you knew that already—I'm not asking anything at all. I'm telling you what you will now be expected to know. Colonel Anthony found our beach hut open. Alan was just inside on the floor. The key was lying beside him. He had been stabbed in the back—no, as you were—we don't know anything about that! *He had been stabbed.* Now this is what I've said." He told her briefly. And then, "They know you were engaged to him *before I met you.* They'll want to see everyone in the house. Colt is very hot on finding out whether there was any quarrel. I said no, of course not. Now you'll have to go and tell Esther. I'm sorry, but it's your job. Then there are the others. Use your judgement. Tell them not to say too much. Stick to answering questions, and if it's any way possible, stick to the truth. Lies have a way of doubling back and tripping you up. And now hurry! I'll go down and tell him you're not dressed, but you'll be as quick as you can."

CHAPTER XVI

At half-past-eight that evening Inspector Abbott stood at
the door of the Annings' house and asked for Miss Silver.
It was the French girl Marie who opened the door to him. In
spite of the heat which had only just begun to drop out of the
day she looked trim. Her eyelashes flicked up provocatively
and then fell again to lie demurely upon the smooth skin of
her cheek. Frank reflected that she probably knew most of the
answers to most of the questions, and considered that it might
be worth his while to find out what she knew about Alan
Field. But he must see Miss Silver first.

He was invited into what had been the drawing-room of the
house. Two elderly ladies were playing double patience at a
table by the window. A third was reading a thriller in the
sofa corner. Miss Maud Silver, in an olive-green dress
adorned by her favourite brooch in the shape of a rose carved
from bog-oak with an Irish pearl at its heart, sat knitting at
the farther end of the room. There was a fluff of pale pink
wool in her lap, and she was engaged in conversation with a
massive woman who was expressing very definite views about
the government.

The eyes of all these ladies turned towards the unexpected
guest. It may be said that they approved him. Miss Silver did
more. Gathering up her knitting, she rose and went to meet him.

"My dear Frank—how extremely pleasant! I had really no
idea that I was to expect you today."

This, and an affectionate greeting, took them as far as the
hall, where he dropped his voice to say,

"Will you come out with me—or is there anywhere we can
talk?"

Miss Silver considered.

"Just a moment. I will ask Miss Anning," she said, and
crossed to the office door.

Frank saw it open, heard the murmur of voices, and was
aware of Darsie Anning coming out. He had an instant
and strong impression of—well, what was it? It hit him as if a

stone had been flung. He ought to know what it was, but he didn't. You wouldn't, after all, know just what kind of a stone had hit you.

He was being introduced—"Inspector Abbott." And Miss Silver was saying, "Miss Anning is kind enough to let us use her office."

Darsie Anning's dark eyes rested for a moment on his face. No one would ever have guessed how gay and bright they used to be. She said in reply to a murmur of thanks, "I was just on my way to sit with my mother. The room is quite at your service," and went away from them up the stairs, a rather stiffly upright figure in her dark brown linen dress.

Frank thought, "What a house! A French maid from a farce—chorus of old ladies—and Miss Anning who should have had a part in quite a different play. He was frowning as they went into the office and shut the door.

As soon as they were seated he said,

"Something is the matter there. What is it?"

Miss Silver arranged her wool.

"With Miss Anning? She has a difficult, harassing life. Her mother is an invalid—"

He said, "No, it's not that. Why don't you want to tell me?"

She gave him a small grave smile.

"Perhaps because I do not want you to make too much of it. I am sorry for Miss Anning, but if I do not tell you someone else will. I believe there was once, if not an engagement, an understanding between her and Mr. Field. His tragic death would naturally be a shock, especially as he had been staying in the house."

Frank nodded.

"I see. You know, I come into this from rather an odd angle. I'll tell you about that presently. When the Chief told me the murdered man was staying at this address, it really did seem too good to be true, because I had had your picture-postcard only a day or two before. Perhaps I had better not tell you what he said when I came back with the information that you were staying here too."

Miss Silver assumed an expression of reproof. She held Chief Inspector Lamb in high esteem, and preferred to forget the occasions on which she had been obliged to consider his manner to be lacking in some of the finer shades.

Frank made haste to purge his offence.

"Well, you know, he does feel that you crop up. Somewhere under all that solid worth there is a lurking vein of superstition, and he has the feeling that you might for all he knows crop up on a broomstick."

Miss Silver was not placated.

"You sometimes talk great nonsense, Frank," she said.

It was a remark she had often had occasion to make before, and as a rule it was accompanied by an indulgent smile. This being notably absent, he perceived that he had better make a diversion.

"I do, don't I? And we're in the middle of a serious business. I apologize. Let me tell you about José Cardozo—or, as the Chief endearingly calls him, 'Hosy'."

Miss Silver was knitting after the continental fashion, her hands low, her eyes fixed intelligently upon Frank Abbott.

"And who is José Cardozo?"

Frank gave a short laugh.

"Well, for the past three weeks he might have been described as a thorn in the Chief's flesh—wished on him with a letter of introduction and wanting to know what has happened to his brother."

"There is a brother?"

"There was. Or maybe there still is. That is one of the snags. Name of Felipe. José says Felipe was coming over here from South America. He might have come by sea, or he might have come by air. He might have come under his own name, or he might not. He was on very important business of a private and family nature, and he carried a valuable document. Here we run into another of the snags. There is no evidence to show that Felipe ever set foot in this country. The nearest you can get to it is that José says he met a man about a fortnight ago who says he saw Felipe in London a week before that in the company of a fair, good-looking Englishman. He didn't speak to them, and he has now returned to South America, so it doesn't get one very much farther."

Miss Silver's needles clicked.

"A fair, good-looking Englishman?"

"According to José's friend as reported by José. But let me come a little more up to date. The first I heard of any of it was day before yesterday morning when the Chief sent for me, Got a good piece off his chest about letters of introduction in general and 'Hosy' and his letter of introduction in particular. It seems Cardozo had been in again, and this time he said he had found his brother."

"He had found him?"

"He had identified a body picked up out of the river—dead about three weeks. The post mortem showed a blow on the back of the head. Might have been the reason why he fell into the river—might have been acquired accidentally after falling in. Actual cause of death drowning. José swore it was his brother, and that he had been murdered. The Chief told me to go down and look into it. Well, I went, and I saw José. He was in a very excited state and quite sure that his brother had been bumped off for the sake of what he carried. He said it was a very important family document, and that there was a great deal of money involved. Pressed to suggest what use a family document would be to the stray dockside murderer, he became very grand opera and let off as good a piece of recitative as I have heard, all on the lines of 'A stray murderer? When have I said so! Is it a stranger who follows Felipe to rob him, or is it the serpent he has nourished in his bosom?' Naturally, it is the serpent—the one that he has taken into his confidence, and who has now repaid him by robbery and murder. Finishing up with a torrent of fancy invective. When I enquired who he supposed the serpent to be, he threw up his hands and said it wasn't a case of supposing, and he had always distrusted him. Felipe had a simple, open nature. He loved the serpent like a brother, and where he loved he trusted. But José had detected the serpent's perfidy. He had warned Felipe, and they had quarrelled. All this in Rio, where José had been a little while before on business. Now it was quite clear to him that his brother had been murdered by the perfidious ingrate, and so forth, and so on. When I could get a word in edgeways I asked for the serpent's name, and—I suppose you can guess it."

Miss Silver looked across her pink wool and said,

"Alan Field."

"Was that really a guess, or do you know something?"

Miss Silver said sedately,

"I am acquainted with Mr. Field's stepmother. She is the widow of Penderel Field the artist, and she is a very nice woman. She mentioned to me that her stepson had been associated on a horse ranch with a Mr. Cardozo."

"I see. Of course you are right as usual. Alan Field was the name which José produced. Well, so far so good. Only of course there was no evidence to speak of. There were no papers—certainly no valuable family document. José identified the body, suggested Field as the murderer, and said his friend's description of a fair, goodlooking Englishman would apply."

Miss Silver inclined her head.

"Alan Field was very fair. He was also outstandingly handsome."

Frank nodded.

"Yes. Now, all that belongs to yesterday. Let us come to today. There are two remarkable developments. First of all, the murder of Alan Field. The Yard got early information about that, because he came down from London and they wanted anything we could give them about where he was staying and what his contacts had been. I went off to see Cardozo, and found he had been round to the local police bright and early this morning and had told them there was something he ought to have mentioned. His brother Felipe Cardozo had had a bad accident when he was a boy and had broken his right leg in two places. He said it had passed out of his mind, but came back in the watches of the night, and he thought he ought to let them know, because if bones had been broken, would not the post mortem make that clear? Perhaps he had been a little hasty in identifying the body."

"And had he?"

"That's the question. I saw the chap who did the post mortem, and he says if Felipe Cardozo broke his leg as described by José, then he isn't the corpse, and that's all there is about it. From which I deduce that either José really had been too hasty in the first place, or that having identified the body as his brother's, he had now some strong reason for wishing he had held his tongue. And the reason which presented itself in rather a forcible manner was the murder of Alan Field."

Miss Silver continued to knit in a thoughtful manner. She said, "I see." And then, "Pray continue."

He did so.

"To sum up. On Tuesday morning José identifies a body as that of his brother Felipe and more or less accuses Alan Field of having murdered him for the sake of 'a family document.' On Wednesday night Alan Field is stabbed in a beach hut at Cliffton-on-Sea. On Thursday morning José goes to the police and says he had forgotten to mention that his brother had a broken leg, and perhaps he had been a bit too hasty in identifying the corpse. Difficult to resist the suspicion that José had had the bright thought that it would be healthier for him if he could disabuse the police of the idea that he had any motive for the stabbing. If the corpse wasn't his brother, why kill Alan Field? Felipe might still be alive, and an affectionate brother would go on searching for him."

"It is a possible explanation. But I think you have something more to tell me."

"Well, I have. Just once in a way, you know, one does have a piece of luck. Do you happen to remember Ernest Pearson?"

Miss Silver thought for a moment.

"A slight stoop—thinning hair—brown eyes—and rather hollow checks—"

"A very good portrait. Do you remember where we ran across him?"

"Oh, yes. He was the butler at the Grange in the Porlock case, which the newspapers would insist on alluding to as the Spotlight Murder. He turned out to be a detective employed by a private agency."

Frank nodded.

"Yes, Blake's. Quite reputable people. Pearson used to be in the Force, but was invalided out. He retains an immense respect for it. Well, as I was coming away from the local station I bumped into him. Not the long arm of coincidence this time, because he had heard I was on the case and was waiting for me."

"You interest me extremely."

"And I am going to interest you a good deal more. Pearson asked if he might have a word with me, and we walked along together. He said he wasn't easy in his mind. Chief Inspector Lamb would speak to his character when he was in the Force, and there wasn't anything anybody could say against him since he retired from it and entered the employment of a private firm—Blake's being a high-class agency and not one that would lend itself to any funny business. He was very earnest about it all. There was one's duty to one's client, and there was one's duty to the law. Blake's gave good service, but if it was a case of the duty to the client coming up against the duty to the law, Pearson was of the opinion that the law had it every time, and that you couldn't be a party to anything of, so to speak, a criminal nature, especially not when it might lead to your being involved in a murder case. And that was where I began to prick up my ears."

Miss Silver's needles clicked.

"I am not surprised, my dear Frank. What had he to tell you?"

Frank leaned back in his chair and regarded her with pleasure. Part of the bond between them lay in the fact that to talk to her was to be conscious of a quick and sympathetic intelligence which not only followed every point, but so stimulated and clarified his own thought as to render it capable of something just beyond its previous best. He said in his rather lazy, cultured voice,

"Quite a surprising tale. Mr. José Cardozo had employed him through his agency to trace and to shadow a Mr. Alan Field recently arrived from South America after three years' absence. Now Blake's happened to know something about Alan Field. Before he left the country they had been employed by an irate husband on two separate occasions to shadow him with a view to divorce proceedings. No precise evidence was obtained, and the matter was dropped. But Blake's learned quite a lot about Alan Field—amongst other less reputable things the fact that he had a well-to-do stepmother, and that she had a London flat where he was a constant visitor. Pearson had been employed on the case and he remembered the address. He went there on Wednesday morning, and learned that Alan

Field had been there the day before and had gone on to look up his stepmother at Cliffton-on-Sea. Pearson is very good at extracting information from people who wouldn't dream of handing it out to the ordinary pressman or detective. He describes Mrs. Field's housekeeper as 'a very respectable person,' which is just what he is himself. *He reported to José Cardozo.* So you see, José knew Alan Field's whereabouts and Mrs. Field's address at Cliffton by the early afternoon of Wednesday. He knew them in time to run down there by train or car and stab Alan Field in the beach hut belonging to the house where his stepmother was staying."

CHAPTER XVII

MISS SILVER continued to knit. She had a thoughtful expression and she did not appear to be in any hurry to speak. Frank Abbott watched her. That she could have stayed for twenty-four hours in the same house as Alan Field or been the repository of his stepmother's confidences regarding him without receiving some very definite impressions, he was unable to believe. To what extent she was prepared to impart them was another matter.

After a lapse of time which made him wonder whether he was to be told anything at all she said,

"I have felt uncertain in my own mind as to just what I had better do. I have no professional connection with this case, and no direct evidence to offer to the police. There are, on the other hand, certain things in the background which you will be bound to hear about, and I have been considering whether you had not better hear about them from me."

"And you have decided?"

She did not answer his question directly.

"I have always been of the opinion that the truth is best for all concerned. The worst thing that can happen to a guilty person is to evade justice and so be able to persist in crime. This evasion may cast a terrible shadow of suspicion upon the innocent. What complicates a case like this is the fact that it is not only the criminal who may have reasons for shunning the light."

Frank's irreverent mind recalled a couple of lines by Owen Seaman written, to the best of his recollection, on the subject of the blackbeetle:

"He loves the dark because his deeds are evil,
He loathes the blessed light."

He did not, however, venture to quote them.

Miss Silver continued.

"There are passages in many people's lives which they would find it painful to disclose. There are things which they would give almost everything they possess to conceal. But to become involved in a murder case is to find a searchlight directed upon their private lives. They are very much afraid of what it may reveal, and this fear may produce the appearance of guilt."

He nodded.

"Yes, we have seen that happen."

"I will ask you to bear it in mind. But first, in what capacity are you here?"

He laughed.

"I got sidetracked over Pearson! As soon as I reported my conversation with him to the Chief he rang up Maynard Wood who is the Chief Constable down here, and they fixed it up between them that I should come along and have a finger in the pie. And now what have you got to tell me?"

Miss Silver pulled on her ball of pale pink wool.

"How much do you know already?"

"I have seen the statements which Colt took from the people at Cliff Edge. I hope to see the people themselves tomorrow. Do you know them all?"

"I have met them. Miss Anning introduced me. As I told you, she knew the Fields very well some years ago. I have been helping Mrs. Field with her knitting—she has really been very badly taught—and whilst sitting with her on the beach I have met other members of the house-party."

"It is not her house, I gather."

"Oh, no, it belongs to her niece's husband, Major Hardwick. He has been abroad and only returned yesterday evening. That is to say, not more than a few hours before the murder."

"And how well did the Hardwicks know Alan Field?"

"Mrs. Hardwick was brought up with him. She was left an orphan at the age of twelve. Mrs. Field and another of the guests, Colonel Trevor, were her guardians. They are, by all accounts, very much attached to her. Three years ago she was engaged to Alan Field and about to marry him, but he left the country and has not been back again till now."

Frank's fair eyebrows rose.

"Any reason given?"

"No—he just went away. The Fields have friends down here, and there was quite a lot of talk about it. The affair went as far as the bride going to the church and waiting there for a bridegroom who never came."

He laughed.

"After all these years you can still amaze me! You have been here—how long—a fortnight, and you know everyone's family history!"

Miss Silver smiled.

"That, my dear Frank, is an exaggeration. The Annings are old friends of Mrs. Field's. I have been staying in their house, and since the first day or two it has been my practice to spend a little time with Mrs. Anning after dinner. An invalid's life is sadly restricted."

He nodded.

"So Mrs. Hardwick was jilted at the altar—is that it? And nobody knows why. When did she marry Hardwick?"

"About three months later."

"And she didn't see Field again until he walked in on Tuesday. Any evidence as to how she reacted to the prodigal's return?"

"Mrs. Field mentioned that they were all very much surprised. She had not heard from her stepson for three years."

"Room for quite a lot of emotions. But I'm told he dined there that night, having booked a room here in the house of another old flame." He made a French quotation which would have incensed his respected Chief. It was the opinion of Chief Inspector Lamb that if a thing couldn't be said in English it had much better not be said at all. "Sounds like a case of *'On retourne toujours a ses premiers amours.'* Tell me about Mrs. Hardwick. What is she like?"

"A charming girl—sensitive and rather quiet. About twenty-four or twenty-five."

"Happily married?"

"There is no reason to think otherwise. I have not met Major Hardwick."

"And the rest of the house-party—have you met them?"

"I have met Colonel and Mrs. Trevor, and Lady Castleton. They are old friends of Mrs. Field's and have known Carmona Hardwick since she was a child. Colonel Trevor is a keen gardener. His wife is a silly woman with a taste for bygone scandal. Lady Castleton was a famous beauty and is still very handsome. She is rather an imposing person, and does a good deal of public speaking in the Conservative interest and on various philanthropic subjects. Then since Wednesday there has been a Mrs. Maybury at Cliff Edge, a very pretty lively young woman who was, I believe, at school with Carmona Hardwick."

He nodded.

"One of my various cousins is married to a man in Bill Maybury's regiment. Everyone likes him and thinks she leads him a dance, but Jenny says there's no real harm in her. What I don't know, and should like to know is, had she any previous acquaintance with Alan Field?"

"I believe they all belong to the same set, and would therefore know each other, but how well I cannot say."

"He didn't by any chance jilt her as well as Mrs. Hardwick and Miss Anning?"

"I never heard any suggestion that he did."

Frank repeated the last of the three names he had mentioned.

"Miss Anning—have you any idea as to the circumstances in which her affair with Field was broken off? Of course three years is a long time to keep up a grudge, but women don't take kindly to being jilted, do they? There's the old hackneyed 'Hell hath no fury like a woman scorned'—usual incorrect quotation, but let it pass. Mrs. Hardwick has married, but Miss Anning has not, and she looks very much as if she might have been through hell. What were her reactions to Field's return?"

Miss Silver made no reply. After a short pause she turned the conversation back to José Cardozo, enquiring whether there was any evidence of his having been seen in Cliffton-on-Sea on the night of the murder.

"Well, nothing decisive. A man who seemed to be a foreigner came into the bar at the Jolly Fisherman at about half-past-nine. There was a girl with him whom they took to be a foreigner too. They had a few drinks and went away before closing time. Colt has turned up someone who came out of the Fisherman at about the same time and says he saw them get into a car and drive away. I don't know why Cardozo should have brought a girl with him or had a girl with him, and it was probably someone quite different, but you never can tell. Colt doesn't seem to have been able to pick up anything that gets us nearer than that. He says that as far as he can make out Cardozo neither rang up nor came to this house, so just how he was going to make his contact with Field one doesn't know."

Miss Silver gazed at him in a meditative manner.

"On so fine an evening Mr. Field would be unlikely to stay indoors. It is possible that Mr. Cardozo may have counted on this."

"And on such a fine evening a car parked anywhere near enough to this house to be within watching distance would certainly have been both noticeable and noticed."

Miss Silver remained silent for a time. Then she said mildly,

"But the murder, Frank, and therefore we may presume, the interview which led up to it, must have taken place after darkness had fallen."

Just what did one make of that? He didn't know, but he was to return to it afterwards. Meanwhile his mind went back to Miss Anning's maid. If anyone had been watching the house or had attempted to communicate with Alan Field, she was the most likely person to know something about it. Colt had drawn a blank there. A worthy chap, but not perhaps the lightest of hands with a girl. He thought he would see her himself. He said so with a quick change of voice and manner.

"That girl—the one who let me in—I'd like to have a talk with her. But first just tell me—how does she strike you?"

Miss Silver made a curious oblique answer. She said,

"Mrs. Anning does not consider that she is trustworthy."

CHAPTER XVIII

MARIE BONNET came into the room in a demure manner. She had no objection to an interview with this policeman who had so distinguished an air. She knew instinctively that her approach must be a subtle one—she must present an appearance of refinement, of delicacy. She achieved a very creditable imitation, and insensibly he began to feel less uneasy at having let Miss Silver go. For that was the astonishing thing, Miss Silver had refused point-blank to stay, and she had gathered up her knitting and departed before the girl came into the room, remarking with a considerable degree of firmness that she had no professional connection with the case and would rather not be present. Such a thing having never in his experience happened before, he was unable to feel easy about it.

He looked up as Marie came. Not pretty, with something about her that took the eye—very smooth, pale skin, good ankles, and quite expensive stockings. He had too many female cousins not to know just as much about nylons as they did. Marie's nylons were of good quality, and if he wasn't mistaken, just out of the packet. It would have surprised him very much to learn that she had bought them herself.

He asked her to sit down, and she did so, crossing her legs in a manner that brought the nylons rather more into view and then pulling her skirt down to cover them. It was a black skirt, very neat, and the shoes were trim. He had her name, and he addressed her as Mademoiselle Bonnet, at which mark of courtesy she gave him one quick upward glance and then looked down again.

"Mlle. Bonnet, you know, of course, that Mr. Field who was staying here has been murdered."

"Yes, indeed—*le pauvre m'sieu!*"

"I gave you my name when I came in—Inspector Abbott. I am a police officer from London. Since Mr. Field was staying in this house, you will, I am sure, understand that I should like to ask you a few questions."

"But yes, m'sieu." Her voice was soft. She was all compliance.

"Mr. Field was here how long?"

"On Tuesday evening he arrives here at half-past-six—seven—I do not know. He sees Miss Anning. They talk—he is perhaps an old friend."

"Who told you that?"

She made a slight gesture with her hands. They were well kept, the nails bright with polish.

"It is known. Besides——" She flashed him a look that promised, tantalized, and withdrew.

"He didn't dine here that evening?"

"No, he went out again. He is to dine at Cliff Edge where he has friends. Later when dinner is over Miss Anning tells me that a room is to be prepared for him. Next day he is here for breakfast, for lunch, and for dinner. Then someone assassinates him—*le pauvre, m'sieu!*"

"Yes. I'd like to come back to Wednesday evening. Had you ever seen Mr. Field before?"

"Me, m'sieu? But no!"

"Heard of him?"

She shook her head.

"But no, m'sieu!"

"Then how did you know, right away on that very first evening, that he was an old friend of Miss Anning's?"

She looked up startled, wary. Then she smiled.

"It is very simple, m'sieu. As I said, it is known. And besides—I came past the door when they were talking. It was evident that they were not talking as strangers."

She found herself confused under his glance. Blue eyes should be smiling eyes, but his were as cold and pale as the shadows on ice. He said in a voice as chilly as his look,

"You listened."

"But no, m'sieu! I would not do such a thing!"

His smile was not a reassuring one.

"You happened to hear. These old houses are quite solidly built. Suppose you tell me just how you happened to hear."

"M'sieu doubts my word?"

"M'sieu doesn't think you could have heard anything to speak of through that rather solid door."

"I did not say that it was shut!"

"Oh, it was open?"

"Evidently, since I could hear what Miss Anning said."

"And what did Miss Anning say?"

Her breast heaved.

"Why should I tell you? If you do not believe my word, why should you believe what I say?"

"I don't promise that I will. I should like to hear how the door came to be open when Miss Anning was talking to her old friend, and I should like to know what you heard—or whether you did in fact hear anything at all."

The very smooth white skin became slightly tinged with red. The lashes lifted to disclose a flash of anger. She said in a voice that was no longer as quiet and demure as it had been.

"Does one lie because one does not tell everything at once?"

His light glance dwelt on her.

"I don't know—does one?"

When a girl is angry she will sometimes tell the truth. She was certainly angry. He wondered if she was going to tell it now.

"Then I will tell you! And it will be the truth that I shall tell! If you do not believe me, it will be because you are stupid, and that will not be my fault! On the Tuesday night when I was coming into the hall, there was Mrs. Burkett going into this room where Miss Anning and Mr. Field were talking. She had the door open and she was going in, but she stopped. She stopped because Miss Anning was speaking, not loud, but as one speaks when one would be glad if one had a knife in one's hand. And would you like to know what she said? It frightened Mrs. Burkett, and it frightened me. Until that moment I did not know that Miss Anning and Mr. Field were more than strangers. But one does not speak so to a stranger, m'sieu—I tell you that! One speaks like that only to a lover, or perhaps to a husband! I do not suppose that Mr. Field was the *husband* of Miss Anning!" she emphasized the word quite strongly. "Oh, no, I do not suppose that—not for an instant!"

"Mlle. Bonnet, what did you hear Miss Anning say?"

"She said, m'sieu—and it was not only I who heard her, but Mrs. Burkett who is the niece of your friend Miss Silver —she said, speaking to Mr. Field, 'I could kill you for that!'"

Frank Abbott has been considered to bear a very strong resemblance to the portrait of his grandmother, the late Lady Evelyn Abbott, whose cold and formidable temper had made her disliked and feared by a large family circle. Cousins would hasten to say that the likeness was more in feature than in fact, and that in spite of it he really had quite a number of human feelings, but when, as at this moment, his features sharpened and the blue of his eyes went pale and cold he could produce a very similar effect. He thought Marie Bonnet was telling the truth, and he thought he knew now why Miss Silver had so carefully dissociated herself from this affair. He recalled the picture-postcard to which he had already alluded. Dated four days ago from Cliffton-on-Sea, it had read in part: "Ethel and I are greatly enjoying the sea breezes. She leaves on Wednesday, but I shall be here for another week." Ethel was Mrs. Burkett. Her husband was a bank manager in the Midlands, and she was Miss Silver's favourite niece. Since this was Thursday evening and she was to leave on the Wednesday, she would already have returned to her husband, her three boys, and to little Josephine.

He turned a chilly stare upon Marie Bonnet and said,

"One of those remarks to which it is difficult to find the correct answer. May I ask what Mr. Field said in reply?"

"But he said nothing, m'sieu. It is all so quick. Mrs Burkett opens the door, I hear Miss Anning say, 'I could kill you for that!' and then Mrs. Burkett makes an apology and comes out in a hurry. She shuts the door, and me"—with a slight shrug of the shoulders—"I do not wait, I am gone."

Frank Abbott considered. Mrs. Burkett would certainly have repeated what she had heard to Miss Silver. He could check up on this girl's story. But just why had she told it to him? There were a number of reasons—the simplest a desire to get herself into the lime-light. Others—a grudge against Miss Anning? A desire to draw a red herring across the path? At the moment no discernible motive for this.

He asked sharply, "Why do you dislike Miss Anning?"

She opened her eyes widely. They were not anything particular either in shape or colour, but she could do tricks with them. This one registered innocent surprise.

"But, m'sieu——"

"I know—you don't dislike her, you never thought of such a thing, and all that. But you don't really like her very much, do you? Suppose you tell me why. Is she strict—harsh—particular about little things like perquisites? You needn't be afraid of telling me. She doesn't look as if she would be too easy, and I won't pass it on."

He smiled, and after a moment she smiled too. Her lashes fell.

"But, m'sieu, I do not dislike Miss Anning. She is my employer."

"How long have you been here?"

She shrugged again.

"In England—ten years. In this house four months. The money is good. When I have saved enough I shall go home to France."

"And you do not dislike Miss Anning."

"No, m'sieu."

Spite is a thing that is difficult to conceal. It had been apparent from the first word she spoke. It came to him that he had asked Miss Silver what she thought of Marie Bonnet, and that she had given him rather a curious answer. She had said, "Mrs. Anning does not consider that she is trustworthy." *Mrs.* Anning. So it was the invalid mother who was disliked. He said smoothly.

"How fortunate that is! It isn't pleasant to be—disliked. Is it possible, then, that Miss Anning had made you feel that she dislikes you?"

Marie threw up a hand.

"She would have no reason! I know my work, and I do it! She is fortunate that I have stayed so long! It is not everyone who would remain, and so I have told her! She says, 'My mother is old—she has had an illness. She does not mean to insult you.' And I say she is not so old, and she is not so ill that it is permitted to her to say these things! 'That French girl!' Am I ashamed that I am French? And, 'She listens at doors!' Is it that I wish to listen to what a mad old woman says? And, 'Why do you keep these foreigners? I don't like them!' Do I like her? I should like to ask her that!"

"So it is Mrs. Anning who dislikes you and whom you dislike so much."

Marie smiled. The anger had gone out of her.

"Why should I dislike a mad old woman?"

CHAPTER XIX

EMERGING from Miss Anning's office, Frank Abbot made his way towards the drawing-room. Manners demanded that he should say good-bye to Miss Silver, but it is not to be denied that he had an ulterior motive. He wanted to check up on Marie Bonnet's story and to know what Mrs. Burkett had heard when she walked in on Miss Anning and her old friend Alan Field.

There was an even more formidable concentration of elderly ladies, the party having been reinforced by a couple of visitors. From the sudden hush which greeted his entrance he deduced that they knew that he was a police officer, and that they had been discussing the murder of Alan Field.

To his suggestion that Miss Silver might care to take a stroll along the cliff path she replied that it would indeed be pleasant, and most kindly shepherded him into the hall, where he waited whilst she went upstairs to put on her hat and gloves. Returning with a pair which had been the gift of her niece Dorothy—white net with a fancy stitching, so cool, so easy to wash—and a hat of black straw with a ruching of lilac ribbon, she accompanied him into the evening air, which she described as most refreshing.

They made their way to a seat overlooking the bay, where she commented upon the pleasing effect of a sky reflected in a sea just ruffled by the breeze, and produced an apposite quotation from her favourite poet Lord Tennyson :

"The trenched waters run from sky to sky."

Frank cocked an eyebrow.

"I've never heard that one before."

She said sedately,

"It occurs in one of the early poems."

He smiled.

"What a pity we can't just sit here and swop quotations. The time, the place, the revered preceptress—what could be more favourable? Yet we must recur to the sordid annals of crime. It is a pity, but when duty calls——"

Miss Silver gazed at the shoaling colours in the bay. She might have known no more about crime than an occasional headline in the morning paper.

After waiting for her to speak, and discerning that it was not her intention to do so, Frank Abbott proceeded to a frontal attack.

"It's no use, my dear ma'am. You see, I've got to know whether Marie Bonnet was speaking the truth. She wouldn't unless it suited her book—I am pretty well sure about that. But she had a grudge against the Annings, and she would be pleased to do them a bad turn. At the same time there is a motive, if not for invention, at least for a little embroidery. If there's any truth in what she says, your niece Ethel walked in on an interview between Miss Anning and Alan Field. Marie happened to be passing at the time, and she says both she and Mrs. Burkett heard Miss Anning say, 'I could kill you for that!' Now if anything of this sort happened, I am quite sure that Mrs. Burkett must have told you about it. Did she?"

When Miss Silver continued to say nothing, he allowed his voice to sharpen.

"It is the question of the credibility of a witness, you know."

She turned to face him with a faint protesting movement.

"You need not tell me that. I merely wished to give the matter my full consideration before I replied. Marie Bonnet's statement is substantially correct."

He nodded.

"I thought so. Is she also correct when she says that Miss Anning was speaking 'not loud, but as one speaks when one would be glad if one had a knife in one's hand'?"

Miss Silver's tone held a slight shade of reproof.

"I am really quite unable to say. You must remember that I was not there."

"But your niece was. I feel sure, when she repeated Miss Anning's words, that she also gave you some indication of how they were spoken. She would not perhaps use quite so dramatic a metaphor, but I suppose once more I may take it that Marie was substantially correct?"

"You may take it that Miss Anning had lost her temper. Just what provocation she had, none of us are in a position to know. As I said to my niece Ethel at the time, though she has it very well in control, Miss Anning's natural temper is a hot one. If she and Mr. Field had known each other when they were boy and girl—and this was, I believe, the case—and if some attachment or engagement had existed between them, such a phrase as was overheard could mean no more than an angry impulse and the revival of an earlier, cruder way of speech. It could mean very little."

He said in his most serious tone,

"Very little—or a good deal more. When a woman says that she would like to kill a man, and within thirty-six hours that man is discovered to have been murdered, one can't quite discard the remark as negligible."

"No—I see that."

He looked at her with a curious expression.

"Do you know, I wish you would tell me why you are so much concerned about Miss Anning."

She said sedately, "I am living in her house."

He laughed.

"I'll give you a nice homely quotation straight from the soil—'Soft words butter no parsnips.' I have known you to live in a house for whose owner you did not appear to feel any such protective passion."

"My dear Frank—such exaggerated language! I really cannot let it pass."

There was more than a hint of sarcasm in the smile with which he met this rebuke.

"You defend her as if she were a favourite niece."

She said with gravity,

"I hope that even in such a case as that I should not allow myself to be swayed by personal bias."

"Then will you tell me just why you take Miss Anning's part? If Marie had not told me what she and Mrs. Burkett had overheard, you would not have spoken of it—now would you?"

"Not perhaps at this stage, Frank."

"And I should like to know why."

After a minute she said,

"I am not obliged to answer that question, but I will do so because I do not wish you to mistake the motive for my silence. I have none, except a natural feeling of compassion for a woman who has been hardly done by, and who now finds herself in a position which must be painful to her. I think it probable that she suffered considerably when her engagement to Mr. Field was broken off. His return would revive these painful impressions, and it was impossible that his murder should not accentuate them to an almost unbearable degree. I did not wish to contribute anything to her distress."

He said,

"You do not take into account the possibility that it was she who stabbed him?"

Miss Silver made no direct reply. Instead she asked a question of her own.

"Is it true that though Mr. Field was stabbed, no weapon has been found?"

"Perfectly true. If the murderer had his wits about him he probably threw it into the sea."

"If he did so, it may quite easily be washed up again. A strong current sets into the bay."

He gave a short laugh.

"I notice we both say *he!* But I must point out that you haven't answered what I asked you."

"Which was?"

"Whether you have not taken into account the possibility that it was Miss Anning who did the stabbing."

"Is there any evidence to support such a theory?"

"There is quite a strong motive."

"I imagine that might be the case with quite a number of people. There is, for instance, Mr. Cardozo."

"Oh, yes. I'm not really suggesting that Miss Anning has the stronger claim. I just wondered why you are being so careful not to suggest that she had a claim at all."

Miss Silver watched the gradual dimming of the light upon the sea. After a little while she said,

"I met Mr. Field very briefly. He had great good looks and a great deal of personal charm. I received the impression that he was entirely taken up with himself and his own affairs. The charm was being rather deliberately used. When I began to hear him discussed, this impression was confirmed. He was considered to have behaved very badly both to Miss Anning and to Mrs. Hardwick. From what Mrs. Field said about him it was plain that he was making extravagant demands upon her for money, and that not for the first time. She was, in fact, so deeply troubled that it came into my mind to wonder whether he might not be bringing some kind of pressure to bear."

Frank whistled.

"What do you mean by pressure?"

She made no reply.

"Do you mean blackmail?"

"I think he was the type who might have had recourse to it, in which case there may be quite a number of people who had a motive for wishing him out of the way."

CHAPTER XX

FRANK ABBOTT went up to Cliff Edge in the morning, where he talked with Mrs. Field, Major and Mrs. Hardwick, the Trevors, Lady Castleton, Mrs. Maybury, and the domestic staff, which consisted of the butler Beeston and his wife, and Mrs. Rogers who came in by the day.

Running through these names later on with Inspector Colt, he had some comments to make.

"I suppose it's natural to be agitated by a murder in your own beach hut, especially when the murderer is to some extent a connection of the family."

Inspector Colt opined that it would be liable to shake you up a bit. "Mrs. Field now—she is said to have been very fond of him. Spoilt him by all accounts."

"Oh, I'm not thinking of her. She's normal enough. Nice woman—fond of a troublesome stepson, shocked at his death, but with just that hint of relief which people don't always realize themselves."

"I'm told she was very well thought of when they used to be down here a lot some years ago."

"The Trevors, on the other hand, are not afflicted at all— at least Colonel Trevor isn't. He makes no bones about it. Shocking thing of course, but the fellow was a waster and no great loss to anyone. Mrs. Trevor kept telling me how handsome dear Alan was, and how all the girls fell in love with him—but it was just blah! She has no real feelings on the subject. People who have are Mrs. Field, Major and Mrs. Hardwick—their house of course, and she had been engaged to him—and, less understandably, Lady Castleton and Mrs. Maybury. They are the two who intrigue me, you know, because I can't see why. Like everybody else they hadn't seen him for three years, and as far as comes to light, they knew him in the sort of way you know a mass of people who live more or less in the same set, but with whom you are not really intimate. Take Lady Castleton. Rather a hard type. Looks— she was quite a famous beauty—money, position—she has always had everything. And quite a place of her own in the philanthropic world—makes speeches, broadcasts, takes part in public discussions. I can't for the life of me see why she should be all strung up about this Field affair."

Inspector Colt suggested that great ladies sometimes took a fancy to a good-looking young man.

Frank Abbott shook his head.

"Oh, no, she's not that sort. Besides, I don't get at all the impression that she's plunged in grief, or that there is any reason why she should be. It is just a general feeling of tension. Of course being mixed up in a murder would get her quite the wrong kind of publicity—it might be that. Or she might have something else on her mind. She seems to have been having headaches and taking something to get her off to sleep. Well, then there's Mrs. Maybury—pretty, flighty creature, and apt to take things very much as they come. I've got a cousin married into the same regiment as Bill Maybury, and I've heard quite a lot of chat about Pippa. She's a good-time girl with a solid husband who lets her have her head. She looks as if she'd had a pretty bad shock. May not be anything in it, but I shouldn't expect her to be a sensitive plant. Now Mrs. Hardwick is, and she was brought up with Alan Field and came within an ace of marrying him, but she doesn't look as strained as Pippa Maybury."

When they had finished discussing the people at Cliff Edge, Inspector Colt had a contribution to make.

"We've got some evidence about the number of that car," he said—"the one the foreigner got into at the Jolly Fisherman. The fellow who saw him was with a girl. He didn't say so at first, but I got hold of him last night and he gave me her address. She says the man was certainly a foreigner, because she heard him speak, and the girl he had with him looked like one, but she didn't hear her say anything. They went past close to her to get into their car, and she noticed the number. There were three threes in a row, and another figure she wasn't sure about because of being taken up with the threes. And she isn't sure of the letters, but she thinks one of them was an O. I thought you could get your people to find out whether this chap Cardozo has a car, and what the number is."

Frank considered for a moment. Quite possible that Ernest Pearson might know whether José Cardozo ran to a car. He had the type of mind which would automatically register a number, and it was possible that he might be available at his agency.

The luck was in, for the call came through quickly and a girl's voice informed him that she was speaking from Blake's agency, and that she believed that Mr. Pearson was on the premises. With the slightest of delays Pearson's rather deprecating voice announced his presence.

"Hullo, Pearson—Inspector Abbott speaking. Look here, can you tell me, has Cardozo got a car?"

"Oh, yes, sir, a small Ford. It was parked outside when I went to take his instructions."

"I suppose you didn't happened to notice the number?"

"Oh, yes, Inspector. A dark green car with a narrow black line—OX.3339."

Frank said, "Thank you very much, Pearson," and rang off. He repeated the information to Inspector Colt.

"Well, that's that. Did your girl say anything about the colour of the car she saw?"

"She and the chap both say it was a small dark car. They don't go beyond that, and they don't specify the make. But it looks as if Cardozo would have something to explain."

"We can get him down and see whether these two people identify him. Who are they, by the way?"

"The man is a young chap—porter on the railway—keen on darts. Name of Hosken. And the girl is Doris Hale—works in the Sea Bleach Laundry.

Frank glanced at his wrist-watch.

"When is the next train to town? I'd better take it. As you say, José Cardozo will have quite a lot to explain."

CHAPTER XXI

José Cardozo in the Superintendent's office at Cliffton threw up his hands in protest. He had been brought down here upon an accusation that was no accusation at all. If they did not accuse him, then why did they bring him here? And if they accused him, where in the name of all the saints was their evidence?

Superintendent Phelps said weightily,

"Miss Doris Hale and the young chap Hosken have both identified you as the foreigner they saw come out of the Jolly Fisherman on Wednesday night at ten o'clock. The girl gave us practically the whole number of your car. I have now to tell you that the girl who was with you has also been identified. As Marie Bonnet. Domestic help at the boarding-house where Mr. Field was staying. She has made a statement."

Cardozo sprang to his feet. Then sat down again.

"But if she has made a statement, it will prove that I am innocent! She will say that she was with me! Is there any harm in that?" The greenish grey of his skin was giving way to a more natural colour. "Look, I will tell you the whole truth. I did not wish to do so, because I could see that the affair would be an embarrassment, and why should one plunge oneself into embarrassments? You have a proverb, 'Silence is gold'. It is a good one. I have the idea that I will keep my golden silence. But if I cannot do so, then I will keep nothing back—I will tell all the truth."

The Superintendent remarked that it would be just as well if he did.

Inspector Colt looked down at the papers in front of him— statement of Doris Hale—statement of S. Hosken—statement of Marie Bonnet.

Inspector Abbott's pose was an easier one. He regarded José Cardozo with a steady meditative gaze. If José were contemplating any departure from the truth, it was the sort of gaze that might cause him discomfort.

Cardozo went on with his story. He had done his duty as a brother and as a citizen. Felipe had disappeared. Had he not done all he could to trace him? Had he not been to Scotland Yard? When he was shown a body which resembled that of his brother, was he not to say what he most truly thought? And when he afterwards remembered a thing which put the identification in doubt, was he not to go to the police and tell them that he must now have his doubts? Where in all this was there anything wrong?

This being taken as a rhetorical question, he received no answer to it. Frank Abbott said,

"Better get on to why you came down here. We know that you had suspicions that Field had something to do with your brother's disappearance, and that you had put Pearson on to trace him. We know that Pearson was able to furnish you with his address down here by lunch-time on Wednesday. You therefore had plenty of time to reach Cliffton by Wednesday evening. I take it you now admit that this is what you did. Suppose you go on from there. What time did you get here?"

"It was a little after nine. I leave my car at the end of the road. I walk along and look for the address I have been given. There is a girl who has come out of one of the houses. I ask her if she knows which is Sea View, and she points to the house from which she has come. I ask about Alan Field, and she says he has gone out. I ask when he will be back, and she says, 'Who knows?' Then I ask will she take a note to make an appointment for the morning, and she says yes, when she is ready to go in, but that will not be just yet. So I say what about a little friendly drink together, and she says it will be nice, so we go down to the Jolly Fisherman. And that is how your Miss Hale and Mr. Hosken see us there!" He beamed and spread out his hands. "Not a very criminal affair, I think!"

Frank Abbott leaned sideways and picked up Marie Bonnet's statement.

"Not so far," he said, "but the night is young. Alan Field would still be alive, both according to the medical evidence and the probabilities. Even though the stretch of beach below the cliff walk is a fairly sheltered one, it does not seem very likely that anyone would stab him there in daylight, but by the time you came out of the Fisherman it would be dark enough. Where did you go from there?"

José's alarm returned. He had been getting along so well. He had a sanguine nature, and he had begun to feel that he was well on the way to being out of the wood. But now there was the question of this girl's statement. What had she said? If she had been foolish enough to lie, to say that he had driven her back to Sea View and she had said good-night to him and gone in, then he would be left without an alibi—his position would be very dangerous indeed. But if she had told the truth, or at any rate part of it, how was he to know how much or what part she had told? He must play for safety. But which way did safety lie? He said in a jerky voice,

"How do I know if this girl has told the truth? I can tell you what we did, but I cannot make you believe me."

Frank Abbott went on looking at him in that cool, rather quizzical way.

"Well, and what did you do?"

"We drove back to the end of the road where the house is, and we went for a walk along the cliff—and that is the truth."

Frank Abbott glanced at the sheet in his hand.

"So Marie Bonnet says."

José's confidence came again with a rush.

"It is the truth, as I told you. But sometimes a girl is afraid she will get into trouble."

"For taking a walk?"

Cardozo threw up his hands.

"Her employer is strict—she told me so. She must be in before eleven."

"And wasn't she?"

José looked knowing.

"There is a trick about that. She is not the only girl to use it. Before we go for our walk she returns to the house. Miss Anning lets her in and locks the door."

"And what does Marie do?"

"She goes to her room and she waits until Miss Anning comes upstairs. Then she gets out of the dining-room window."

"I see. And you go for your walk. What time does she really get in?"

Cardozo smiled.

"That I do not know. We are not in a hurry. It is fine, it is warm, we are pleased with one another's company. One does not keep the eye upon the clock."

Frank Abbott looked at the end of Marie Bonnet's statement—"It was fine, it was warm. I do not know what time it was when we came back. Why should one always trouble oneself about the time?"

CHAPTER XXII

MRS. ROGERS got down on her hands and knees at Cliff Edge and started to do the stairs. Properly ashamed she'd be if anyone took a good look at them, for they hadn't been done all the week, and no good saying there wasn't sand brought in off the beach, because there was. It just wasn't possible to get round to doing them every day, not with all the extra work there was in the house, but Monday, Wednesday and Friday she did reckon to do them regular. Well, Monday was all right, and she was all set to get on with them on Wednesday, only Mrs. Beeston called her off to give Major Hardwick's dressing-room a thorough turn-out, and then it was one thing after another, and the day so hot you couldn't rightly be expected to hurry, so she left the stairs to the last, and blessed if Mrs. Beeston didn't go and call her off again—Lady Castleton's white shoes to be cleaned, "And very particular about them she is too." So the stairs were left till Thursday morning.

And come Thursday morning, Mr. Alan Field had been murdered, and there was the police all over the place. It was as much as you could do to get into the bedrooms, what with poor Mrs. Field crying in hers, and Lady Castleton's head that bad she wanted the curtains drawn and a tray brought up. Properly upset, the whole lot of them, and no wonder, for if he wasn't murdered in the house, their own beach hut was as near as makes no difference. And how he got the key, seeing it was kept locked—could anyone tell her that? And what did he want with it anyway? Looked as if he was going to meet someone there to her way of thinking, and if she had her guess who it would be, well, she knew the name that would come into her mind. Married or single, you could pick out the flighty ones, and flighty was what that Mrs. Maybury was, you couldn't get from it.

The stairs didn't get done on the Friday neither. She was all set to do them, when that London police officer come along with his B.B.C. voice and the kind of way with him you'd think he was someone. And then it was Thursday all over again. He'd got to see everyone, and not what she was accustomed to, being interviewed by the police about a murder and lucky if you didn't get your name in the papers, and Major Hardwick saying perhaps better keep off the stairs while there's all this coming and going. Well, you can't keep off stairs and do them at the same time, so they just hadn't got done. But she was going to do them now. No matter what anyone said or did—and it looked as if there was a regular spite against it—she wasn't going to let them go dirty over the week-end. A fair disgrace, that's what they were. She'd be ashamed for anyone to see them and know she worked here.

She went down on her knees and began to brush. Dust swished into the pan. And then she saw the stain. The stair carpet was a handsome one. It had a fawn and blue pattern on a deep crimson ground. What caught Mrs. Rogers' eye was a piece of tread where it looked as if the pattern had slipped.

There was an extra patch of the dark red. She looked at it, frowning, and brushed again. The colour stayed. She went, down a step. All right there. She brushed with vigour and went down again, and there was another of those dark brownish marks. Something came over her, she didn't quite know what. She had had a herring for her breakfast, and she had a feeling that perhaps it wasn't going to agree with her. She got to her feet and fetched a wet cloth from the housemaid's cupboard, and as she went and came again she took care that she didn't step upon the carpet. She hadn't begun to think why she was doing any of these things, she just did them.

When she came back to where she had left her dustpan and brush she didn't kneel down. She bent over and rubbed at the brownish mark with the cloth which she had in her hand, and when she saw the stain which came away on the wet linen she let out a scream which was heard by everyone in the house.

The time being round about half-past-eight in the morning, most of them were not yet fully dressed. Colonel Trevor put his head round the bathroom door. He had been towelling his hair and it stood wildly on end. Pippa Maybury ran out to the middle of the landing in one of those filmy undergarments which emphasize rather than conceal. Adela Castleton was wearing a chinstrap and a kind of mask of some cosmetic preparation which gave her a horrid resemblance to a corpse. James Hardwick was half way through his shaving. Esther Field had snatched up her dressing-gown, but she had not put it on. Cami-knickers of a solid character fitted closely over stays that were doing their best. Her hair was in curlers. She clutched the voluminous blue draperies which she made no attempt to draw round her. Carmona came out of her room, slipping her dress over her head.

Since the hall door stood wide to air the house and the whole of the stair was plainly visible from the threshold, it was this astonishing scene which met the eyes of Colonel Anthony.

As Mr. and Mrs. Beeston came running from the baize door which led from the back premises, Mrs. Rogers screamed again. She stared at the reddened cloth in her hand and went on screaming.

Colonel Anthony said, "God bless my soul!" and stepped

briskly into the hall. He might be an old man, but he hoped he could still tackle an emergency. A corpse at cockcrow in a neighbour's beach hut, a charwoman in hysterics on a neighbour's stair—he could take them all in his stride and be damned to them. He had, as a matter of fact, dropped in to have a word with Hardwick on the subject of the corpse. Very odd thing—very peculiar thing. He felt that they should have a friendly chat about it. Since he was in the habit of rising at six himself, it did not occur to him that the hour was an unseasonable one. Bare-headed, his spare trim figure comfortably arrayed in what survived of a tropical outfit, he strode across the hall and up the stairs. He reached the screaming Mrs. Rogers a bare moment after James Hardwick, who had paused to snatch a towel and wipe some of the lather from his face.

"Mrs. Rogers!" said James. And, "Good God, woman, what's the matter?" said Colonel Anthony.

Mrs. Rogers could find no breath for words. With her left hand she clutched James Hardwick's arm, and with her right she held out the blood-stained cloth. Because there was no doubt now as to the nature of the stain. The red-brown blotches on the carpet, the red-brown streaks on the linen cloth, were quite unmistakeably and dreadfully blood. She was now sobbing continuously, and between her sobs she pointed and stumbled into speech.

"There—on the carpet—there! And I didn't know—I didn't know! I wouldn't have touched it ! It's blood!"

Carmona came down, white-faced, to put a hand upon her shoulder. She couldn't imagine what Colonel Anthony was doing on their stairs, but here he was, and he would have to be reckoned with. She had a dreadful picture in her mind of Pippa coming up from the hall in the middle of Wednesday night; the front of her dress all wet through where she had knelt in Alan's blood.

Mrs. Rogers jerked and heaved under her touch.

"Cold water!" said Colonel Anthony in a loud military voice. "A cold wet spongeful of water! One of you up there—and be quick about it!"

Mrs. Anthony had always responded immediately to cold

water down the back of the neck. During their early married
life she had been regrettably prone to hysterics, but the
persistent application of a cold sponge had brought about a
permanent cure. Mrs. Rogers didn't wait to see if it would
cure her. She wrenched away from his restraining hand and
ran down into the hall, where she cast herself weeping on Mrs.
Beeston and was presently led away to be solaced with cups of
tea.

The remainder of the party stood where they were. They
stood looking at the cloth which Mrs. Rogers had dropped.
Maisie Trevor, in a becoming lace cap and a frilly dressing-
gown which she had waited to put on, now emerged, enquiring
vaguely whether the house was on fire.

"Most inconvenient in such hot weather. Or has that
woman hurt herself? I thought I heard her scream."

Colonel Anthony made a sound which may be written
"Tchah!" and continued the highly unwelcome remarks he
had been making to the Hardwicks.

"You see, my dear fellow, there's no doubt about it—it's
blood. A spot here, and another on this lower step—and oh,
several more lower down. There, Mrs. Hardwick—look for
yourself! A most extraordinary thing, you know—really a most
extraordinary thing. You know, Hardwick, in all the circumstances, and however unpleasant you may feel it, I cannot see
that you have any alternative but to report the matter to the
police."

Carmona turned her head. She was standing on the fifth
or sixth step from the top. She turned her head and looked
up at Pippa Maybury.

Pippa had not moved. She had run out on to the landing
almost as far as the head of the stairs. She had been brushing
her hair. It stood out in clouds about her head, as light as
thistledown and almost as pale. There was no colour in her
face. It was as white as milk—as white as her throat, her
shoulders, as her whole body except where the pale film of
chiffon covered it. Every line of her slim figure showed through
the film. Carmona went to her and touched her on the arm.

"We had all better finish dressing. Come and put something on," she said.

But Pippa didn't move. She looked down over the stairs. She looked at the wet patch on the step which Mrs. Rogers had rubbed. She looked at the stained white cloth which lay there. And she said in a voice which everyone could hear,

"That's blood, isn't it—*blood*? It must have come off my dress when I came upstairs."

Colonel Anthony said, "God bless my soul!"

CHAPTER XXIII

IT was a couple of hours later that Colonel Anthony walked into the police station and demanded to see Inspector Colt. He was not best pleased, because he considered he should have been able to see him before. He had important information to impart, and in his opinion he should not have been told that Colt was engaged. He resented it. He resented being fobbed off with the suggestion that he should see somebody else. He had no desire to see anyone else. He wanted to see Inspector Colt with whom he should have some standing as the person who had originally discovered young Field's body. He could not conceive that Colt could possibly be engaged on anything more important than the really crucial evidence which he was in a position to impart.

And he had been kept waiting for the best part of two hours. He had been present at the discovery of incriminating blood stains. He had heard a young woman make what practically amounted to a confession. And he was kept dangling. He had been extremely military on the telephone. No, he was not prepared to give a message. He would like to know when Inspector Colt would be free . . . Yes, he would hold on whilst the constable enquired . . . Very well, then, he would come round to the police station at ten-thirty precisely.

It was now ten-thirty precisely.

He was shown into a room where Inspector Colt was prepared to cut the interview as short as possible, having just given it as his opinion to Frank Abbott that the old chap had a theory and wanted to ram it down his throat.

He was to change his opinion in time to call Frank back, and after no more than a brief outline of what Colonel Anthony had that morning witnessed at Cliff Edge for the two of them to proceed there with all possible speed.

Colonel Anthony would have liked to accompany them. Or would he? He wasn't sure. He had lived next door to Octavius Hardwick for the best part of twenty years. Having discharged his duty as a citizen, he could remind himself of his duty to his neighbour. Very awkward situation for James Hardwick. Perhaps better to keep out of it. He had seen young James grow up. Painful situation all round. Better keep clear of it as far as he could. He went for his usual morning walk.

At Cliff Edge breakfast, such as it was, had been cleared away. Colonel Trevor ate three fishcakes and his usual four slices of toast and marmalade, but nobody else approached this standard. As far as the women were concerned, tea or coffee was for the most part the beginning and the end of it. Mrs. Rogers broke a coffee-cup, one of the set which Mr. Octavius Hardwick's mother had brought into the family when she married his father in 1859. Informing her of this fact with some severity, Mrs. Beeston remarked that she had better take and pull herself together, because they hadn't got china to break— "And I'd say best go home and have a good lay-down, if it wasn't certain sure the police would be here again and wanting to see you."

Mrs. Rogers gave a rending sniff.

"Do you think she done it, Mrs. Beeston?"

Mrs. Beeston looked very decided.

"It's not my business to think, nor yet yours, Mrs. Rogers, and there's the work to get on with."

Adela Castleton had come down to breakfast after all. She ate some fruit and she drank a cup of tea, and she looked very handsome and self-possessed.

Pippa stayed in her room.

Going upstairs when the rather ghastly meal was over, Carmona found the fruit and toast she had sent up untasted, though the cup of coffee had been drained. Beyond stretching out her hand for the cup and setting it down again Pippa did not seem to have moved. She sat there in her transparent undergarment, her hair still floating wild.

Carmona made herself speak as firmly as she could.

"Pippa, you must dress—you really must! And you must do something to your hair!"

"Why?"

"The police—they will be coming up."

"Will they?"

"Pippa, they are bound to."

"You mean—that horrible old man—will tell them?"

She spoke in a flat expressionless voice, and she did not look at Carmona. If she had looked up she would have seen her own reflection in the mirror on the wide Victorian dressing-table. But she looked no higher than the china tray which lay there. It had a pale green edge and a pattern of primroses on it. She had been counting the primroses. If she counted them from left to right she made them seven, but if she counted them from right to left she made them nine.

Carmona stood silent. Whichever way she looked, there was trouble. She had not thought whether she believed Pippa's story. She must believe it, because she couldn't believe that Pippa had killed. People don't—not the people you know—not the girl you were at school with. It must be somebody from quite outside, someone from the world in which Alan had been living for the last three years. It couldn't be anyone they knew. But when she thought about James her heart shuddered and was afraid. Why had he gone out in the middle of the night? It was after twelve when Pippa had gone to meet Alan. Where was James when she went? Carmona herself was asleep. James had not come to bed. His coming would have waked her. He had not come. Where was he? When she waked to hear Pippa's footsteps, to see her come slowly up the stairs with that dreadful stain on her dress, it must have been something not far short of half-past-twelve, because later when she looked at the clock in Pippa's room the hands were standing at twenty-to-one. Half an hour later, when they had finished all they had to do and had gone back to their rooms, James was in bed and asleep.

Something checked in her mind. Was he asleep? Or did

he only mean her to think so? The time that had passed since then was the time between Wednesday and Saturday morning, and neither had asked the other, "Where were you?" She had waked and found him gone. He had returned and found her empty place. Neither of them had said, "Where were you?" The days had been full of the comings and goings of the police, of making statements, of the watchful guarding of tongue and eye. Even when they were alone they kept guard. You never knew when someone might be listening, you never knew if someone might come by, you never knew whether you were really alone. They had kept close council.

Carmona stood there with these thoughts in her mind. And then they were startled out of her, because Pippa whirled round upon her suddenly. All the deadness, the dullness, the flatness was gone. Her eyes were bright and her cheeks flamed.

"What's the good of our sitting here like this? We've got to do something! I've been like a rabbit caught in a headlight, just scared stiff and waiting to be run over! And if we wait long enough, I shall be! Only I'm not going to! I know exactly what we've got to do, and we're going to do it at once! We've got to call in Miss Silver!"

"Miss Silver?" Carmona's blank dismay showed in her voice.

Pippa had jumped up. She was opening a cupboard, pulling on a dress, slipping her feet into beach shoes, and talking, talking, talking all the time.

"Yes, yes, yes—Miss Silver! Don't you know who she is? I didn't at first, because you'd never think it to look at her! But then I remembered that is just what Stacy said she looked like—a little old-maid governess, but frightfully, frightfully on the spot!"

"Pippa, what are you talking about?"

"Stacy Mainwaring,* darling. At least she is really Stacy Forrest, because she married Charles all over again, but she sticks to Mainwaring for her miniatures."

"Pippa, I still do *not* know what you are talking about." Pippa stopped winding a bright red scarf about her head. "That's because you're not trying," she said. "Stacy Forrest

* The Brading Collection.

painted a miniature of me for Bill—he simply adores it.
And she told me all about Miss Silver to keep me quiet whilst
I was sitting. And at first I didn't think it was the same,
and then I did, because I said something about Stacy, and she
fairly beamed over her and Charles—who really is a lamb,
and how Stacy ever thought she could get on without him, I
don't know, but anyhow they are madly happy now."

"Pippa do come to the point! What did Stacy Forrest tell
you about Miss Silver?"

Pippa stared.

"You haven't been listening, and we've got to do something
quickly. Stacy and Charles got caught up in that jewel murder
—you know, the Brading Collection. It was dreadful for them,
because they thought Charles had done it, and it was Miss Silver
who found out he hadn't. Stacy says she's marvellous. And
Minx Raeburn was in a most awful flap because her mother in
law had lent her some frightfully historic jewelry and it had got
stolen. Minx said she nearly died, because Lady Dalrae is
the world's grimmest Gorgon. But Miss Silver got it back for
her, and the police never came into it at all."

Carmona assembled these disjointed facts.

"You mean she is a detective?"

Pippa nodded vigorously.

"And we must get her to come here at once. That London
policeman is the one who was on the Brading Case. He is the
new Police College sort. Stacy says he more or less eats out
of Miss Silver's hand. I can't think why I didn't get hold of
her straight away—I must have been asleep or something."
She was tucking in the ends of the red scarf.

"But Pippa—what do you want to do?"

"Get hold of Miss Silver—at once, before the police get
here. You do think they'll really come?"

Carmona, unfortunately, had no doubts about it.

"Colonel Anthony went off to tell them. He said it was
his duty."

"Don't you hate people who say that? It just means they
are going to be unpleasant." She had begun to do her face—
lacquer-red lipstick——

Carmona said,

"Pippa, I wouldn't."

"Wouldn't what, darling?"

Carmona indicated the lipstick.

"I really wouldn't—it's too bright. And that headscarf—I don't think it's a good idea."

Pippa stared.

"Because it's red? Darling, you're not suggesting I should go into mourning for Alan, are you?"

Carmona shook her head.

"Just not red. There's the one you had on yesterday—that shaded blue one."

Pippa changed the scarf, but refused to give up the lipstick.

"And I've got to hurry—because of the police! If I can get away before they come I'll have a chance of talking to Miss Silver before they start asking all their frightful questions!"

Carmona said,

"Pippa, the person you ought to be talking to is Bill. Have you sent for him? Because I think you ought to."

"Bill? No, of course not! You don't listen when I tell you things! He's over in Germany giving evidence at some dreary trial! I don't suppose I could get hold of him if I wanted to!"

"It will be in the papers."

"Do they get them over there? Well, it doesn't really matter, because it's all about Alan and his being Penderel Field's son, and bits about you, and Esther, and James. And as Bill doesn't even know I'm here——"

"Oh, Pippa—doesn't he?"

"No, darling. He thinks I'm staying with his Aunt Muriel—the world's completest dreep. I rang you up instead."

She laid down the lipstick, used her powder-puff in an expert manner, and turned from the glass with an encouraged expression.

"There, darling—I must fly! Keep your fingers crossed!"

CHAPTER XXIV

"You wish to consult me professionally?"

"Oh, yes, I do!"

Miss Silver gazed thoughtfully at the girl in the flowered beach-dress with its pattern of cherry and blue and the blue head-scarf which bound the lint-white hair. Pippa Maybury was all talk, all animation. The high, rippling voice carried a flood of irrelevant chatter about Charles Forrest—about Stacy—about the only too appropriately nicknamed Minx Raeburn. This girl had much the same voice and manner. Girls all wore lipstick nowadays, but in the circumstances Miss Silver considered that something less noticeable would have been in better taste. After all, Alan Field had been stabbed to death at very close quarters to Cliff Edge, and poor Mrs. Field was actually staying in the house. Something more subdued both in dress and in make-up would have shown consideration for her feelings. She checked herself. These were outmoded standards. People no longer thought about such things, and perhaps it was all to the good. Mourning and its observances had certainly been carried to exaggerated lengths under the shadow of Queen Victoria's widowhood. One could no longer judge by appearances. One must look below the surface.

With this in mind, Miss Silver continued to gaze. Beneath vanishing-cream and powder she was able to detect unmistakable marks of strain. But she looked deeper than this. The bright talk was too bright, the light laugh too rippling, the whole performance too taut, the tempo just a shade too quick. She was reminded of a gramophone record put on at an exaggerated rate of speed. She said, herself speaking a little more slowly than usual,

"You wish to consult me. Will you tell me why?"

bit her lip. She had thought about going to Miss Silver and asking for her help, but she hadn't thought about what she was going to say when she got there. All that seemed to matter was that she should get out of the house and reach

Miss Silver before the police arrived to stop her. Well, she had got out of the house and reached Miss Silver.

They sat facing each other in the pleasant bedroom, part of what had once been Mrs. Anning's big spare room, and she didn't know what to say. Miss Silver sat in the chintz-covered chair by the window, and Pippa on what had been a music-stool but now served the dressing-table. As the girl stared at her blankly, Miss Silver picked up the ball of pink wool into which her needles had been thrust and began to knit.

Perhaps it was the homely action, perhaps it was the kind yet searching look which accompanied it that prompted Pippa to a childish gesture and to childish speech. She put out her hands in what was an oddly natural way and said in a trembling voice,

"I'm so frightened——"

Miss Silver continued to look at her. She also continued to knit.

"Will you tell me why?"

"The police—Carmona said they would come——"

"The police were coming to question you—was that what you were afraid of?"

"Because of the blood on the stairs. It must have dripped off my dress that night. You see, I knelt in it and all the front was soaked." A quick shudder went over her. She said, "Mrs. Rogers was doing the stairs. Nobody knew it was there—but her cloth was stained and she screamed. Everyone came out of their rooms, and I said it was blood and it must have come off my dress because of its being soaked. At least I think that was what I said—I don't really know, and I don't know why I said it. But Carmona said the police would come. Colonel Anthony was there, and he heard me—everyone heard me—and Carmona said Colonel Anthony would go to the police."

When she stopped Miss Silver said in her gravest voice,

"Mrs. Maybury, do you really wish to tell me all this? I think you should realize that you are making admissions of a very compromising nature, and that there might be circumstances in which I would not feel justified in keeping them to myself."

Pippa's eyes widened.

"What—what circumstances?"

"If someone else were accused——"

She was interrupted with vehemence.

"But that is just what I want you to do! Minx said you were so marvellous! I want you to find out who did it! Because somebody must have done it—mustn't they? And if you find out who it was, everything will be all right, and—Bill needn't know!" The last words came out with an anguished gasp.

Miss Silver contemplated her with new attention.

"Your husband?"

"Oh, *yes*!"

"There is something you do not wish him to find out?"

Pippa gazed imploringly. Two large round tears rolled slowly down her cheeks.

"You see—he thinks—I'm good."

Miss Silver laid down her knitting for a moment.

"Before we go any farther, Mrs. Maybury, will you listen very carefully to what I am going to say? There is something you are anxious to hide—something that you hope your husband need not know. I do not ask you what it is. It might very easily be something that I do not wish to know. If it concerns the death of Alan Field, I think that you should see a solicitor without delay. You have made a very serious admission in the presence of a number of witnesses, and it will not be possible to hush it up."

Pippa looked startled.

"But it hasn't got anything to do with Alan, except that he was being a beast about it. I wouldn't ever have gone to meet him if he hadn't said he would tell Bill. I would have done anything in the world to stop him doing that. Because, you see, Bill is *good*, and he thinks I am, and if he found out I wasn't it would do something to him, and nothing would ever be the same again. So what did my pearls matter, or anything!"

From these obscure and fragmentary remarks Miss Silver began to perceive the emergence of a pattern. As if her admission that she had been on the scene of the murder was not enough, Mrs. Maybury appeared to be bent upon supplying herself with a motive.

"Mr. Field was blackmailing you?"

"Oh, *yes!*"

Miss Silver was knitting again, but her eyes never left Pippa's face.

"That would give you a motive for the murder."

Pippa said, "Oh!" Her mouth remained a little open red circle, but under the lipstick all the natural colour had drained away. She leaned forward with a jerk. It was like seeing a marionette move.

"But you don't think I *did* it? I wouldn't have come to you if I had! You can't possibly think—why, he was dead when I got there! That was what was so horrid. It was all dark, and I didn't want to use my torch, because of anyone seeing me. I could just make out the beach hut—the door was open. I stumbled over something—and came down. It was Alan—he was dead. There was such a lot of blood. My dress was all wet—and my hands. That's how the stain came on the stairs. It was a long dress, and it was all wet."

Miss Silver said in her quiet voice,

"What did you do after that?"

Pippa told her.

"Carmona helped me. She came out of her room and saw me coming up the stairs. I told her about finding Alan, and we burned my dress in the kitchen fire."

"That was a very foolish and a very wrong thing to do."

"Carmona said we ought to call the police, but I told her I would rather kill myself. Because of Bill. You do see that, don't you? I was meeting Alan in that beach hut in the middle of the night, and they were either going to think he was my lover, or I should have to tell them he was blackmailing me about someone else, and I should have to give evidence, and Bill would know. I simply couldn't let her call the police."

Miss Silver shook her head.

"You should have done so. A prolonged course of deception is extremely difficult to sustain. You were ill-advised to embark upon it. We have now to consider what is best for you to do. If you wish me to be of any assistance to you, you must make up your mind to be perfectly frank."

"You are going to help me?"

Miss Silver coughed.

"I will do my best to discover the truth. I cannot go into any case with the intention of helping this or that person. I can have but one motive, the bringing of the truth to light. If you are sure that that will help you, I shall be willing to take the case."

Pippa stared.

"But that is just what I want you to do! Somebody killed Alan, and if you can find out who it was, the police won't bother about me any more—will they?"

Miss Silver made no reply to this. She began, instead, to ask a great many questions, to all of which Pippa replied in a perfectly open and natural manner. She hadn't met anyone on her way to the beach hut or on her way back—not to say meet. But just when she got to the top of the path she had had a kind of frightening feeling. No, she didn't know what she meant by that—it was just a feeling. She had come running up the steep path and she was trying to get her breath. She wouldn't have heard if there was anyone there. All she wanted was to get back into the house—and all the more when she had that horrid feeling that there might be someone looking at her and listening.

Miss Silver put that away to think about. She said,

"Mrs. Maybury—you say when you put your torch on in the hut you saw that Alan Field had been stabbed."

"Oh, yes, I did."

"Will you tell me just how he was lying?"

Pippa shuddered.

"On his face—one arm flung out."

"How did you know who it was?"

"His hair. The light shone on it."

"And what made you sure he had been stabbed?"

"The knife—it was sticking in his back."

"Did you touch it?"

"Oh, no!"

"You are quite sure about that?"

"Oh, no—I *wouldn't*!"

Miss Silver said gravely,

"No weapon was found by the police. Are you really quite

sure that you saw a knife, and that you did not touch it or take it away?"

"But of course I'm sure! I keep telling you so! The knife was there, sticking up under his shoulder, and I wouldn't have touched it for anything—*anything* in the world!"

After a slight pause Miss Silver said,

"If you saw this knife you can describe it. What was it like?"

Pippa had no hesitation.

"It was Mrs. Field's paper-knife. Her husband gave it to her, and she was very fond of it—one of those sort of dagger things with a lot of gilt on the handle and some little coloured stones. It was quite sharp. She had it down on the beach that day, because she was by way of reading one of old Mr. Hardwick's books—sort of memoirs—and he couldn't have really bothered to read it himself because the leaves had never been cut."

"Mrs. Maybury, will you think very carefully. Where was that dagger kept?"

Pippa didn't need any time to think at all.

"Whenever I saw it, it was sticking in the book. Esther just took it out to show it to me, and then she stuck it back again."

"What was the title of the book?"

This did appear to call for consideration.

"Well, I don't know—'Pages from the Lives of Great Victorians', or something like that—*too* dreary."

"And was it brought up to the house on Wednesday night?"

Pippa's lips parted on a sharp breath.

"Oh—no—it wasn't—"

"What makes you think so?"

"Because I saw it—down there—when I put on my torch. I saw Alan—and the blood—and the knife in his back. And the book—was lying there—on the floor—close to his hand—as if he had pulled it down."

CHAPTER XXV

IN the morning-room at Cliff Edge, so restful, so delight-fully cool, Miss Silver sat knitting. She had chosen one of those low armless chairs produced by the Victorian age in which needlework was considered a woman's most necessary accom-plishment. Miss Silver's own needles were of a composition then undreamed of, but she found the same comfort as the ladies of that generation in the low seat, the dumpy back, and the absence of restraining arms. She had a chair of this type in her own flat, the legacy of an aunt, and she valued it highly. The heat outside was at its most extreme, but in this north room the temperature was really pleasant, very pleasant indeed.

She was not alone. For the time being at anyrate, police interviews with members of the household were over. Inspector Colt had departed. But Inspector Abbott stood with his back to the carved overmantel and addressed himself to his "revered preceptress".

"You are actually staying in the house?"

"Mrs. Hardwick has most kindly invited me to do so."

He exclaimed, "Well, I don't know how you pull it off!" His tone was half affectionate, half exasperated.

Miss Silver permitted herself a slight reproving cough.

"My dear Frank! As I have already informed you, Mrs. Maybury has asked for my professional assistance. I have ex-plained to her the terms on which it can be given, and Mrs. Hardwick has suggested that I should transfer my things from Sea View. Proximity with the members of the house-party and the opportunity which this will give for a more intimate observation than can be afforded by any casual meetings——"

He threw up his hands.

"Oh, yes—you will see them all from the inside! Which is just what we poor policemen never do. What we get is a carefully decorated outside with all the garbage tidied out of the way."

Miss Silver allowed it to appear that she considered this metaphor to be lacking in refinement. Without a spoken word,

Inspector Abbott stood rebuked. After a brief but impressive pause she said,

"There are certainly great advantages in being within the family circle. No one is always on his guard, or if he is observed to be so, it would in itself be a highly suspicious circumstance."

He nodded.

"And that, as I said, is where you have the pull. Now will you tell me just what you make of Pippa Maybury's story?"

Miss Silver dipped into her gaily flowered knitting-bag and produced a fresh ball of wool. She had hoped to finish this little pink coatee for her niece Dorothy's expected baby from the one at present reposing in her lap, but since it was now reduced to a few filmy strands, she would have regretfully to break into a new ball. This would leave her with just too little for another coatee, but perhaps some small white stripes could be introduced. Her attention had not really wandered, but she now brought it fully back to the question she had been asked.

"What do you think of it yourself?"

One of the colourless eyebrows lifted slightly.

"Well, she is either such a natural born liar that she can reel it off without so much as having to stop and think, or— she is telling the truth."

"Yes, I think so."

"You think she is telling the truth?"

"Yes, Frank."

"Would you mind telling me why?"

The pale grey needles clicked.

"She made no attempt to impress me. There were many points in her story where a very slight alteration of the facts would have shown her in a more favourable light, but I could detect no tendency in this direction. In the second place, she was shocked, upset, and frightened, but her chief preoccupation was not lest she should be arrested for murder, but whether her husband would come to know that she had once put herself in a very false position."

"Well, I noticed that myself. We didn't press her as to just what she had done, but it was plain that it had given Alan

Field a hold over her. And that supplies her with a pretty strong motive for the murder."

Miss Silver inclined her head.

"On the surface, yes. But actually I do not think so. She told me the whole story, which she need not have done, and the preoccupation of which I spoke was very noticeable. It was her husband of whom she was thinking. She really did not seem to notice that she was furnishing evidence which might deepen the suspicion against her. I should like to say that she did not carry her foolish behaviour to its logical conclusion— her real feelings for her husband stopped her in time. But she had placed herself in a position which could have been exploited by Alan Field."

Frank whistled.

"He really had something on her then, and he was black-mailing her! She was terrified that he was going to tell her husband. She had an assignation with him at twenty-past-twelve in the beach hut where he was murdered, and she comes in some time after that with her dress soaked and drips blood all up the stairs. You know, my dear ma'am, it's quite a formidable case."

Miss Silver smiled.

"I do not need to point out to you that it would be extremely difficult to prove the blackmail."

He laughed.

"As always, you touch the spot! Now let us for the moment adopt your view of the engaging Pippa and review the alternatives. This evidence about Mrs. Field's paper-knife, which at first sight appears to fasten the crime upon someone in this house, quite fails to do so if we are to accept Pippa Maybury's further evidence—and I'm afraid we've got to accept it, because it has quite a lot of backing. She says the dagger was sticking in the book Mrs. Field had down on the beach on Wednesday, 'Pages from the Lives of Great Victorians'. This is corro-borated by Mrs. Hardwick, Lady Castleton, Mrs. Trevor and by Mrs. Field herself."

"As far as the morning is concerned, I can add my own testimony."

"When it comes to the late afternoon, Mrs. Hardwick says

the book was still there, and so does Mrs. Field. They left all their things there and locked the hut. Pippa Maybury says she saw the dagger there after midnight when she stumbled over Field's body, and she also says that the book was there on the floor beside his outstretched hand. Which is perfectly true, because that is where it was when Colt arrived on the scene after being rung up by Colonel Anthony. So I think we have got to accept her evidence as to the dagger and the book. Which means that the dagger was there in the hut and could have been used by absolutely anyone who came along. Let us now see who that someone might have been."

Miss Silver coughed.

"You are not, I suppose, forgetting Mr. Cardozo?"

"Certainly not. He shall be Provisional Suspect Number One. He could have done it of course. There was plenty of time between his leaving the Jolly Fisherman and midnight. He says, and Marie Bonnet says, that he spent the time in her company, but I don't think it would be at all difficult to persuade Marie to say anything that was made really worth her while. The weak part of the alibi is, of course, that it places him entirely in her power. If she thinks she is running too much risk, or that he isn't paying enough, she has only to go to the police and his number will be up. He might have stumbled into such a situation, but I doubt whether he would have planned it."

Miss Silver gazed at him in a meditative manner.

"It would have been quite possible for him to be aware of Alan Field's presence at the hut. He states that Marie returned to Sea View, remained there long enough for Miss Anning to lock up, and then slipped out again. I think it is very probable that Mr. Field followed the same course. Miss Anning says he came in, and that she did not know he had gone out again. But he did go. Marie could have seen him, and so could Mr. Cardozo, who on his own statement was waiting for her. There would have been no difficulty about following him to the hut. He may not have intended the use of violence."

"Yes, that's possible. But how are we going to prove it if the girl sticks to her story?"

"I do not know."

"Nor I. Let me offer you another suspect. What do you say to James Hardwick?"

"Dear me—you surprise me!"

"Well, I don't often do that, so I had better make the most of it. Just take a look at him. Mrs. Hardwick was brought up with Field, and they were going to be married. He walked out on what was to have been their wedding day and went off in a hurry to South America, leaving quite a dust behind him. When Cardozo told me the name of the man he was after, I had heard it before. A couple of drinks with the biggest gossip of my acquaintance, and I knew a lot more. He was full of information about Alan Field. Had actually run into him on the eve of his departure. Said he was jingling with money and standing drinks all round. As the evening wore on, he got very chatty indeed and practically told my friend that it was being made well worth his while to clear out. George inferred that someone thought Carmona Leigh would be better off without him, and when she married James Hardwick three months later he came to the conclusion that he knew who that someone was. Now, do you see, if all that is true—and George really has got a knack of picking things up—Hardwick might not be altogether pleased to find that the prodigal had returned. He comes back on the Wednesday and finds Field actually in the house. There are indications that he was, well, let us say restrained in his greeting, and that Field left almost at once. The butler's evidence is that Mrs. Hardwick had quite a colour, but was quiet at dinner. Mrs. Trevor, who is a silly chatterbox of a woman, said she thought Carmona had a headache—such a pity when James had just come home, but such a hot sun, quite like India, and Lady Castleton had felt it too. Everyone else very firm about dear Carmona being just as usual. Well, we don't know what may have taken place between the Hardwicks, but you will admit that there was quite a situation, and that there may have been words. I think there are definite indications that the reunion wasn't being a great success. Beyond that we can't really go, but it is fascinating to speculate. Suppose Field had been upsetting Carmona by (a) making love to her, (b) trying on a spot of blackmail, or (c) letting cats out of bags, there would be all the material for a tense connubial scene. Leaving the first two on one side, and speaking as one to whom girls are an open book, what would you say Carmona's reactions would have been to hearing that she was the subject of a financial transaction, and that Field had in effect been bought off marrying her?"

The pink coatee revolved. Miss Silver said,

"She would be deeply humiliated, and in all probability extremely angry."

Frank nodded.

"Exactly. And in any of the three cases James might easily be left in a fairly maddened state and quite under the impression that she was regretting her precious Alan. Now suppose he saw Pippa Maybury go down the garden and took her for Carmona—he could have done, you know—his dressing-room windows look that way. I don't suppose the difference in the colour of the hair would show. It was after midnight, and anyhow a jealous man doesn't always stop to think. Well, he could have followed her—no, that won't do, because he would have had to get there first, and a good bit first, in order to have a row and leave Field stabbed before Pippa arrived. A pity, because it was coming out rather well that way."

Miss Silver looked meditatively at a particularly hideous piece of Indian brass which cumbered the mantelpiece to Frank Abbott's right. She might have been thinking how distressingly it went with the black marble clock in the middle and the bronze horses on either side, but she was not. She was, as a matter of fact, debating in her mind whether or not to put forward a speculation of her own. In the end she considered that she might as well do so. Turning towards him, and with a slight introductory cough, she said,

"Has it not occurred to you that Alan Field could have had an earlier appointment than the one with Mrs. Maybury? If her story is true—and I believe that it is—someone had been there before her. This person, whom we must suppose to be the murderer, may or may not have had such an appointment. He, or she, may have noticed a light in the hut and gone down to see who was there, or Mr. Field may have been followed."

Frank gave her a quick look.

"Have you any reason to suppose that he was? Because

that brings me to the third of my suspects, Miss Darsie Anning. When we were talking about Cardozo it emerged that Alan Field must have slipped out of the house in some way, as Marie Bonnet did, since Miss Anning had locked the front door and was under the impression that all her guests were in. If she had been looking out of her window she could have seen him leave and she could have decided to follow him. I wonder whether she did, and whether anyone saw her. You know, Marie Bonnet said a curious thing when we were questioning her. Colt had been pressing her about this alibi which she was giving Cardozo. Did she really come out and rejoin him after she had gone into Sea View? Had he offered her any inducement to say that she did? Didn't she risk losing her place by admitting to it? Well, she was all innocence. Was it not her duty to be frank with the police? And besides, her services were valuable—Miss Anning would not be in a hurry to dispense with them. Oh, no, she wasn't afraid that she would lose her place. It doesn't sound anything when you repeat it, but she had a sort of look—assured, sly, confident—I can't get the right word for it, but it was something like that. I didn't think so much of it at the time—the girl is always putting on an act of some kind—but whenever it comes back to me I find myself wondering whether she thinks she has some kind of a hold over Miss Anning—something over and above what she told us before about hearing her say to Field, 'I could kill you for that!' I should rather have expected her to bring the incident up, but she didn't, and I thought it odd."

Miss Silver made no comment. She continued to knit. After a slight pause she remarked that he had now presented a choice of four suspects, and all that seemed to be lacking was the evidence necessary for an arrest.

Frank Abbott gave her a shrewd look.

"Do you really consider that there is such a lack of evidence in Pippa Maybury's case?"

CHAPTER XXVI

Two things happened after lunch. Miss Silver went down to Sea View to retrieve a missing skein of wool, and James Hardwick took his wife out in the car. Carmona had found him at the writing-table in the study. Looking up as she came in he noticed how pale she was. How very, very pale. And not with the clear translucent pallor which he had noticed the first time he saw her. This was a drained, exhausted look, and the marks under her eyes were like bruises. She shut the door behind her, leaned against it, and said in a low, steady voice,

"James, we can't go on like this. I must speak to you."

He laid down his pen.

"Some things are better left unsaid, don't you think? The less you know, the less I know, the less we talk about whatever we know, or don't know, or guess, or suspect, or imagine, the better."

For a moment she thought—she did not know what. That he had made, or that he was going to make some movement in her direction—she didn't know——

James Hardwick checked himself. He could snatch her into his arms and say, "Why do you look like this? Has the bottom dropped out of everything because Alan Field is dead? Does he matter to you so much?"

He said nothing.

If she had had a vague hope that he would say something that would make her feel less frightened, less urged by a dread she could no longer escape, the hope failed her. His look was stern, and there was no comfort in it. She said, her voice almost gone,

"But I must—I really must—I can't go on——"

He considered her in a frowning silence. If she must— well, then he supposed she must, and better to him than to anyone else. Only not here in this house where there were too many eyes and ears, too much concern, compunction, and all the other sensibilities—too many people noticing too many things and talking them over in too many words. He pushed back his chair and got up.

"All right, if you must. I think much better not, but if you feel you've got to talk to someone, it had better be to me. Only not here, with people popping in and out like a warren, and the police on the doorstep every half hour or so. I'll get the car, and we'll drive out along the coast road. Damnably hot, but no eavesdroppers. You'd better get a hat."

It certainly was hot—no shade, and the sun pouring down. When they were clear of the houses and the small bungaloid growths which had fastened upon what had once been the pleasant outskirts of Cliffton, he said,

"If I keep her at forty, we shall get some air."

"But I couldn't talk," said Carmona—"not really."

He gave her a sudden smile.

"Not very modern, are you? Forty is a mere crawl, you know. I believe what you would really like is somewhere between fifteen and twenty."

She felt a very slight easing of the tension in her mind. The needle of the speedometer went back to twenty-five. The sun was scorching hot, but there was still a little breeze. She said,

"James, I've really got to know. It gets worse and worse, and I can't bear it any longer. You've got to tell me. Where were you on Wednesday night?"

"I?"

"Yes."

"What do you mean?"

"I woke up, and you weren't there. I felt as if something dreadful was going to happen. Someone was running—up from the cliff. I went and looked in your dressing-room, and you weren't there. Then I went out on the landing, and Pippa was there by the newel. The front of her dress was all soaked with blood. We went into her room. Alan had been blackmailing her. She went down to the beach hut to give him her pearls, and she stumbled over his body and came down. That is how the blood got on her dress. He had been stabbed."

"Yes, I understand from the police that that is her story. Do you believe it?"

"Yes, I do. She wasn't in the sort of state when you can make anything up. If she had stabbed him she would have told me. Please let me go on. We burned her dress and her stockings.

She had on beach shoes—they washed. We didn't know about the marks on the stair carpet. We thought we had got everything cleared up—we took about half an hour. When I got back to my room you were in bed and asleep. At least I don't know—perhaps you only wanted me to think you were asleep."

She didn't look at him. She looked at his hands, which were steady on the wheel, and waited for him to speak. When he said nothing, words came from her with a violence which he had never known her use.

"Where had you been? And what did you think had become of me? You were not in your room, or in mine. Where were you when I was asleep? And afterwards, when I was in Pippa's room? We were there—and we went down to the kitchen to burn her dress. Where were you, and where did you think I was? I've got to know!"

He said without any expression at all,

"It is sometimes better to know too little than too much."

The thing that frightened her, the thing she wouldn't look at, came nearer. Through all the heat of the day she felt the cold of it. The force went out of her voice. She said in a whisper,

"What do you mean? James—*please*——"

He laughed.

"Just exactly what I say. When one is being asked a great many questions by people like the police it is sometimes quite useful to be able to tell the truth and shame the devil by saying you just don't know."

Carmona said, "I've got to know."

"All right, I'll tell you. When I put out the dressing-room light I drew back the curtains and looked out. Someone was going down the garden in the direction of the cliff path. It was about a quarter-past-twelve. I thought it was an odd time for anyone to be going for a walk. I also thought it might be someone who hadn't any business to be there, so I went down to have a look, and found the glass door of the drawing-room ajar. Poor old Beeston would have had a fit. I couldn't very well lock it again, and I didn't much care about leaving it as it was, so I went out to have a look round."

Carmona drew a long breath.

"Pippa said she had a feeling there was someone watching her—after she had run back up the path. Was it you?"

"I expect so."

"Did you know it was Pippa?"

"I thought it might be. She was in a very considerable state—sobbing and catching her breath."

"Why didn't you speak to her?"

"I didn't know what she had been up to, and I didn't really want to know."

The cold fear had not left Carmona. This was a story that didn't fit in. If James had followed Pippa, where had he been whilst she went down the steep path to the beach? If he had gone down there too, she would have heard him on the shingle. Nobody can walk on shingle without being heard. And if he had stayed on the narrow path, Pippa would have run into him when she came flying back. She said,

"What did you do? She went down to the beach. Did you go down too? You couldn't have done that—she would have heard you."

He was silent for a minute. Then he said.

"When I opened the gate from the garden I couldn't see anyone on the cliff walk. I had a torch, but I didn't want to put it on. I walked along until I came to the path to the beach. Someone was there, going down. I couldn't say who it was, or even if it was man or woman. I went a little way along the cliff walk and came back. As I was coming back, someone came up from the beach. That is all I can tell you."

She had a feeling of something withheld, but her own relief prevented her from dwelling on it. Her hand went out to touch him. She said,

"Oh, James!"

"Satisfied? Or have you still got a lurking suspicion that I somehow managed to reach the hut and murder Field before Pippa got there?"

"James!"

"That is what you have been thinking, isn't it?"

"Not *thinking*——"

"Well, being afraid of—getting cold feet about. That is what you have been doing, isn't it? I can't say I'm flattered, you know. Stabbing in the back isn't really in my line—at least I hope it isn't. A bit medieval, don't you think?"

Carmona wasn't thinking. She was feeling a warm rush of emotion. The tears began to run down her face.

James Hardwick stopped the car.

CHAPTER XXVII

MISS SILVER put on her hat and the open-work gloves—such a kind present from her niece Dorothy, and so suitable to the weather—and then discovered that the pair of light summer shoes which she would have preferred to wear had been abstracted by Mrs. Rogers, no doubt with the laudable intention of cleaning them. Since all her outdoor shoes were made to lace primly to the ankle, a stranger might have seen no difference between the pair at which she was looking with disfavour and that which now presumably reposed in the scullery, but to Miss Silver the absent pair was suitable and this was not, being stronger, thicker, and altogether less in keeping with the really almost tropical weather. With a slight shake of the head she went down the stairs, crossed the hall, and opened the door which led to the back premises. Always considerate of others, and anxious to avoid giving unnecessary trouble, it was her design to listen for some indication that the staff had finished their midday meal, and if she found Mrs. Rogers disengaged to ask for her shoes.

She became aware that the meal was certainly over as soon as she opened the door. It gave upon a short length of passage. Other doors stood wide. There was a clatter of china. There was the sound of running taps and of a conversation which sometimes rose above the noise, and was sometimes obscured by it. The participants were Mrs. Beeston who was going to and fro between the kitchen and the pantry, and Mrs. Rogers who was washing up, whilst Beeston, who was engaged upon the glass and silver, enlivened the proceedings with occasional snatches of song.

"Properly got her head turned, if you ask me," said Mrs. Rogers at the sink.

Beeston had time to come in with the last line of *The Lily of Laguna* before his wife could reply that she hadn't anything against the French herself.

It was at this point that Miss Silver decided that it was her professional duty to listen. As a gentlewoman she deplored the necessity, but if, as she supposed, it was Marie Bonnet who was under discussion, what these women had to say about her might be of value. She stood with the door in her hand and heard Mrs. Rogers say,

"That's as may be. And I've nothing against anyone myself so long as they behave themselves, but when it comes to that Marie giving herself the airs she does, why, you'd think she'd bought the place and was only waiting for it to be wrapped up in a parcel and handed over."

Mrs. Beeston's reply being lost in a great splashing of water and a fresh burst of humming from her husband, the next thing that was heard distinctly was Mrs. Rogers' remark that she didn't hold with getting mixed up with the police and didn't consider it was what a person had a call to be proud of, not if they had any refined feelings—"And so I said to her this morning. She was outside doing the step as I came along, and 'I shan't be doing this much longer,' she says. So I said, 'Going off on your holidays, are you?' And she tosses her head and says she's through with working her fingers to the bone. Well, we all know what happens to girls who think they can do better for themselves than work, so I said, 'You be careful, Marie, or you'll be getting yourself into trouble.' And she laughs and says, '*Out* of it, you mean!' "

Beeston had stopped his humming. He repeated the last words with emphasis,

"*Out* of it. Now that's a thing that you can take two ways, isn't it? Speaking humorously, you might say Marie was getting out of it because of what she was getting out of it, if you take my meaning."

"Well then, I don't," said Mrs. Beeston with a shade of asperity.

Beeston laughed.

"If that girl isn't getting something handsome out of keeping her mouth shut, I'm a Dutchman!"

Mrs. Rogers had turned off the taps in order to listen. The voices were admirably clear. When Mrs. Beeston said, "What's she got to hold her tongue about?" Beeston laughed again.

"No use asking me that! Ask the girl, or ask that Mr. Cardozo that she says she was out half the night with on Wednesday! Why, if it wasn't for that, he'd have been arrested by now. Everyone in the police don't hold his tongue, and you can take it from me that's a fact. And no use telling me the girl is doing it for nothing."

It was at this moment that Miss Silver decided to wear her thicker shoes. She closed the door softly upon Beeston instructing Mrs. Rogers that she was not to repeat what he had said and went back to her room. As she tied her shoe-laces she considered Beeston's words. They assumed no more than she already suspected, but that Marie should be behaving in a manner to augment this suspicion certainly gave food for thought. If the girl had set out, or was setting out, to blackmail the murderer of Alan Field, she was embarking upon a very dangerous course.

She emerged from the front door and walked the short distance to Sea View without giving a single thought to the fact that she was wearing the heavier shoes.

Arriving, she was informed by Marie Bonnet that Miss Anning had gone down to the shops.

"I have told her that she would be better to take a little repose in this heat. What she goes for, it will do just as well later on. Apples, they do not take long to cook, but will she listen! *Jamais de la vie!* She is not one of those who can be still—she must be here, she must be there, she must be everywhere at once! For me, I would not trouble myself to have a house like this! One goes out, one comes in, one does not rest! I do not find that amusing!"

Miss Silver observed Marie with attention. There was a flush upon her cheeks and a sparkle in her eyes. The usual discretion of her manner had given place to a familiarity which might at any moment become impertinent. There was no one better qualified to check such a trend than Miss Maud Silver. Not only the pupils who had passed through her schoolroom in the days when she was engaged in what she herself invariably alluded to as the scholastic profession, but many older and wiser persons—even Chief Inspector Lamb himself—had been known to feel themselves exceedingly ill at ease under her reproving eye. But on this occasion the eye did not reprove. It regarded Marie Bonnet in a questioning manner.

"No, it would not be at all amusing—for you. You are planning to leave Cliffton?"

Marie tossed her head.

"What is there to stay for? When I see a chance I take it!"

"And such a chance has come your way?"

The trend towards impertinence became more definite.

"That is my affair!"

The point was conceded.

"Yes, that is true. But there are chances which may lead into dangerous places. To make an advantage for oneself out of something one knows or guesses—that may be a very dangerous thing to attempt."

There was a spark of anger in the dark eyes, but the lashes came down and veiled it.

"I do not know what you mean, ma'mselle."

Miss Silver regarded her gravely. The air of excitement, of independence, the whole circumstances surrounding her association with José Cardozo, prompted suspicions which were deepening rapidly. She said.

"If you know what is embarrassing to someone else, it may easily become a danger to yourself. If you ask a reward for your silence you are breaking the law, and the punishment may be severe. So there is danger in two directions. You have been in England for a good many years—perhaps you know the meaning of blackmail. In your own language the word is, I believe, *chantage*."

Marie Bonnet looked up innocently. If her fingers tingled to be at Miss Silver's throat, no one must know it. This pious lecturing old maid, this friend of the police, she must be persuaded that she was mistaken. They were sharp, these old maids, and had a finger in everybody's business. If Miss Silver had not come just then when she was in the middle of picturing what she would do with the money José had promised her——

She lifted her lashes and said in a bewildered voice,

"But, ma'mselle——"

Miss Silver's suspicions were confirmed. If there had been no foundation for them, Marie would certainly have lost her temper. That she was taking a good deal of trouble to control it could only mean one thing. She said,

"That is all, Marie. I do not suppose that Miss Anning will be long. I will wait for her." She made a move towards the stairs. "And while I do so, I will pay a little visit to Mrs. Anning. It is a day or two since I have seen her."

It was, to be correct, two whole days and the greater part of a third since Miss Silver had paid her usual visit—not in fact since the Wednesday evening when Alan Field was still alive and Mrs. Anning had declared in a very excitable way that he ought to be punished. He had been wrong to go away and leave Darsie, and people who did wrong ought to be punished. It said so in the Bible.

Marie hesitated, but only for the moment. She knew very well that Miss Anning would not have permitted Miss Silver to visit her mother. Since Wednesday night she had not permitted anyone to visit her. She had even taken in the meals herself, and she had stayed in the room whilst the bed was made and the dusting and tidying were done. To everyone she had said that Mr. Field's death was a great shock to her mother, and that it must on no account be mentioned. Very well, then, but it would not be Marie who would be mentioning it. As for standing in the way of that Miss Silver—no, no, Marie knew better than that. She was too well in with the police, that one. It would not be prudent to oppose her.

Miss Silver entered Mrs. Anning's pleasant bedroom to find her in her usual chair with her embroidery frame in her lap. There was a needle threaded with a strand of pale green silk in her hand, and she was taking a stitch with it. She had the air of someone who walked among her own thoughts and found them sufficient company. When Miss Silver spoke, she started slightly, and said,

"You don't come and see me any more."

Miss Silver smiled.

"I am paying a short visit at Cliff Edge."

"To Esther Field? No, it is not her house, is it—it is

Carmona's. She is Carmona Hardwick now. Darsie says I forget things, but I haven't forgotten that. We knew them so well in the old days, and she was engaged to Alan too. That was after he went away and left Darsie and everything went wrong—quite a long time afterwards. But he left Carmona too. He was like that, you know—he made them care, and then he went away." The straying voice became suddenly hard and angry. "He was wicked! Girls don't know enough—they ought to know more. He was wicked, and that is why he had to be punished! Wickedness always has to be punished!" She had become very much flushed and was speaking rapidly. "He has been punished, you know—somebody stabbed him, and he is dead. The knife was sticking up out of his back—he was quite dead. He won't make love to any more girls and leave them. It was a wicked thing to do, and he has been punished for it. You would never think how pretty Darsie was—and such high spirits too——"

The door opened and Miss Anning came in. There was no colour under the brown of her skin. The deep marks beneath her eyes were ghastly. Her lips were tight, her whole face rigid. When she spoke her voice was tense.

"My mother is not well enough to see visitors, Miss Silver. I must ask you to go. Marie should have known better than to let you in."

Miss Silver rose to her feet. She showed no sign of offence as she said,

"Pray do not blame her. I am afraid I just walked in. Let us leave Mrs. Anning to rest. It was you whom I came to see, and if you can spare me a few minutes of your time——"

There was a moment before Darsie Anning turned and led the way to the door. They went down the stair together in silence.

In the study Miss Anning walked to the window and stood there looking out. Heaven knows what she saw. Not the gravelled path with its edging of evergreens. Not the staring sunlight. She saw her own thoughts. They were bitter ones. She turned and said,

"Why did you come?"

"Miss Anning, will you not sit down?"

"Thank you, I would rather stand. Why did you come here?"

"I wished to see you."

"Well, I'm here. What do you want?"

There was no pretence that this was an ordinary conversation. Look and voice were keyed to some desperate strain. Miss Silver said gently,

"I have felt obliged to come. I had no wish to do so, but I believe the police to be on the verge of arresting Mrs. Maybury. If it is possible to prevent this, it is my duty to do so."

Darsie Anning kept that rigid look.

"Why should they arrest her?"

"I cannot go into that. There is—some evidence."

"Then why should she not be arrested? If she did it——"

"I do not believe that she did it. I believe that you may have evidence which could help to clear the matter up."

"I have no evidence."

"Miss Anning——"

"I have no evidence, I tell you."

There was a pause. Miss Silver looked at her compassionately. At last she said,

"It is no use, Miss Anning. I appreciate your feelings, but you cannot allow an innocent person to be arrested. Will you let me tell you what I myself saw and heard on Wednesday night?"

"You?"

Miss Silver made a slight inclination of the head.

"The night, as you will remember, was extremely warm. I found myself unable to sleep. I got up and sat by the open window. There was a breeze from the sea which I found refreshing, and the view over the dark bay with the star-lit sky above it most uplifting. I was enjoying the prospect, when I heard footsteps coming up the garden. There was first the sound of a gate being closed or latched, and I was then aware that two persons had entered the garden by way of the gate from the cliff, and that they were now approaching the house. A moment later I heard your mother speak, and I heard you answer her. You were then immediately below my window, and I heard every word distinctly. Your mother said, 'People who do wrong should be punished. I always said he would be punished some day.' And you said, 'Mother, for God's sake, hush!' "

There was a pause. At the end of it Darsie Anning said, "Well?"

"You passed on and came in by the glass door to the drawing-room. I heard you both come upstairs. I could not fail to be aware that Mrs. Anning was restless and excited, or that it was at least one hour before you came out of her room."

"I suppose you listened!"

Miss Silver looked extremely shocked.

"I hope you do not suppose anything of the kind, Miss Anning. I could not avoid hearing the words beneath my window, nor recognizing the voices on the stairs, but it was not my business to listen to what was said."

"My mother was restless—you have said so. She wandered out into the garden, and she did not wish to come in. When she is in one of these moods she talks—at random. Her mind goes back into the past. What she says often has no connection with things that are happening now."

"But that is not always the case. What I heard Mrs. Anning say on Wednesday night referred, I believe, to Mr. Alan Field."

Darsie Anning laughed, if so harsh and bitter a sound can be called laughter.

"What rubbish!"

"I think not. It was in just such terms that Mrs. Anning had referred to Mr. Field upon more than one previous occasion."

"And what business was it of yours to question her?"

"I had none then. And I can assure you that I did not do so. She spoke of his being wicked and deserving of punishment, and I endeavoured to turn her thoughts into pleasanter channels."

Darsie Anning was not listening. She had heard no more than the initial sentence. She broke out almost with violence.

"What do you mean by *then*—you had no business *then*? What business have you now—or what business do you think you have?"

When Miss Anning had refused to be seated, Miss Silver had remained standing. She repeated her former suggestion now.

"Pray, will you not sit down? It will be best if we can talk this over quietly."

"I have nothing to say."

"But you asked me a question, did you not?"

With an impatient movement Darsie Anning reached for the chair at her writing-table, jerking it back. If she could have gone on standing she would have done so, but the room had begun to waver before her eyes. It was not possible for her to relax, but the chair would at least hold her up. She felt the hard seat under her, leaned her arm along the rail, and said,

"What do you want to say?"

Miss Silver had seated herself also. She spoke in a grave, steady voice.

"Just this, Miss Anning—what was not then my business has now become so. In case my professional activities are not known to you, I must inform you that I am a private enquiry agent, and that I am engaged upon the Field case in that capacity."

Through the rushing sound that was in her ears Darsie said, "Then I have nothing to say to you."

Miss Silver coughed.

"You will, I think, be well advised if you will listen to me. I have spoken to no one of what I heard from my window on Wednesday night, but I do not think that I can preserve this silence to the point of allowing Mrs. Maybury to be arrested."

Darsie Anning stared.

"Pippa Maybury?"

"There is a case against her. She had an appointment with Alan Field in the beach hut at a little after midnight. He was blackmailing her, and she was to bring him her pearls. She states that she kept the appointment, but found him lying there dead. You must see that any evidence—any evidence at all—which corroborates her statement, or which serves to narrow down the time at which the murder must have taken place, is of such grave importance that it is not possible to neglect it."

"Blackmail——" The word was barely audible. And then, with the extreme of bitterness, "Why not?"

Miss Silver said.

"You will see that I can no longer undertake to be silent. I must tell you that the police already know from Marie Bonnet that you were overheard to say to Mr. Field in a very vehement manner, 'I could kill you for that!' "

"*Marie!*"

"It was on the Tuesday. She was passing through the hall when my niece opened the door. They both heard what you said, and if called upon to do so, Ethel will be obliged to corroborate Marie Bonnet's statement. The police are also aware that you were once engaged to Mr. Field, and that it was considered that he had not conducted himself at all well in the matter. I am very far from wishing to distress you, but your mother has talked quite freely upon more than one occasion of how badly he had behaved, and of her conviction that he would be punished for it. You must see that this exposes you to some suspicion in the matter of his death. When it is learned that Mrs. Anning was out on the cliff that night, and that you either followed or preceded her there——"

Darsie Anning lifted her head.

"There is no question of either of us being out on the cliff. It was a hot night, and my mother went into the garden for a breath of air. She often sits up late in her room, and when she found she could not sleep she went into the garden. I heard her, and I went after her to persuade her to come back. You are making a mountain out of a molehill. Now will you please go."

Miss Silver's small neat features were composed and stern.

"In a moment, Miss Anning. I have something else to tell you first. Just before you came into your mother's room she was speaking of Mr. Field. I would like you to believe that I had not so much as mentioned his name. I had only told her that I was staying at Cliff Edge. She mentioned Mrs. Hardwick and passed at once to speaking of Mr. Field. She said Carmona Hardwick was engaged to him, and that he left her too. After that she went off into saying he was wicked, and that was why he had to be punished. She became very much excited and went on to say, 'He *has* been punished, you know! Somebody stabbed him, and he is dead! The knife was sticking up out of his back!'"

Darsie Anning began to lift her hand from where it lay. It moved a little and fell again, as if she lacked the power to raise it. She did not speak.

After a moment Miss Silver said,

"You must see what this means. No description of the wound has appeared in the press. Mrs. Anning was describing something that she had seen."

Darsie made the kind of effort which it is painful to watch.

"My mother lives—in a dream. She describes what she sees there. No importance—can be—attached——" Her voice just faded out.

CHAPTER XXVIII

THE two young people who stood hesitating outside the police station appeared to be a good deal on edge. Frank Abbott observed them because the girl was rather out of the way graceful and well put on. She was, as a matter of fact, Miss Myrtle Page, and she worked in the local beauty parlour. Her companion, Norman Evans, was a clerk in the solicitor's office over the way. They were in the middle of an argument, and as Frank approached he heard the girl say, "I said I'd meet you here, but I didn't say I'd go in." To which Mr. Evans replied that she ought to make up her mind and not keep chopping and changing.

"Well then, I have made it up! Let the police find out about their own murders! It's no business of ours!"

Frank slackened his pace.

"But Myrtle——"

"I don't care what we heard her say! We didn't see her do anything, did we? And he wasn't pushed over the cliff either! If he had been, perhaps you'd have had something to come bullying me about! Yes, I did say bullying, and I meant it! And of all things I do hate a bully, so you had better have a good think over that!"

Frank Abbott came up with them and addressed himself to Mr. Evans.

As it happened, he had an assignation with Miss Silver a little later on. She was at once aware that he had something to tell her. He lost no time in letting her know what it was.

"I am afraid the scales are being weighed down against Pippa Maybury," he said.

The heat was dropping out of the day. Miss Silver had spread out a rug and had spent the hour before he joined her with a book, her knitting, and her thoughts. She was serious, though not unduly disturbed, as she enquired,

"Pray, what makes you think so?"

He sat down on the sand beside her.

"Just a little piece of corroborative evidence. Two young people who were walking on the cliff on Tuesday night overheard part of what was probably Alan Field's blackmailing interview with Pippa Maybury. Anyhow they heard her say, 'I can't think why someone hasn't murdered you, Alan.' To which he replied 'My dear Pippa, you surprise me.' And then, 'Look out—someone is coming!'"

She maintained what appeared to be a placid silence for a moment or two before she said,

"Has it not occurred to you to wonder how often such things are said? They pass unnoticed, and are, in fact, just a part of the exaggerated style of speaking common to the young and sometimes persisting into later life. They have no real significance, and it is very improbable that they would be employed by anyone who was seriously contemplating the crime of murder."

He ran his hand over hair already immaculately smooth. "In general I will agree. In this case I don't know. Here are two stubborn facts. On Tuesday night Pippa Maybury is heard to wonder why no one has murdered Alan Field, and on Wednesday night he is murdered. Since there is already a good deal of evidence against her, this certainly does add some corroborative detail, and I must warn you that her arrest is not likely to be long delayed."

Miss Silver opened her lips to speak. She closed them again as he forestalled her.

"You will, of course, remind me that Darsie Anning went a step farther on Monday when she was heard to say, 'I could kill you for that!' but we have no evidence to show that she took any steps to carry this sentiment farther than words."

The little pink coatee was now almost completed. Another

row and she would be casting off. Miss Silver laid the knitting down upon her knee and said in a reluctant voice,

"I am afraid, my dear Frank, you may feel that I owe you an apology."

"Now what have you been up to?"

Her glance reproved this levity.

"There is something which you will feel I should have communicated to you before."

"And are you going to communicate it to me now?"

"I do not feel justified in withholding it any longer."

With careful accuracy she repeated her conversations with Mrs. and Miss Anning, and proceeded.

"She had on several previous occasions referred to what she called Alan Field's wickedness and the fact that he ought to be punished. This afternoon she used these words, 'He *has* been punished, you know! Somebody stabbed him, and he is dead! The knife was sticking up out of his back!'"

Those rather pale eyes of Frank Abbott's had become intent. He said quickly.

"The knife—you're sure she mentioned the knife?"

"Yes, Frank. I found the inference quite inescapable."

"That she had seen the body?"

"I feel sure that she had done so."

He whistled softly.

"That looks like throwing a spanner into the works! You don't think she—Look here, how mad is she?"

Miss Silver contemplated him and the question in a very thoughtful manner.

"I am not, of course, qualified to give you an opinion, but I would not like to say that Mrs. Anning was out of her mind. She has seemed to me to be suffering from the effects of some shock or strain too great for her to bear. They have robbed her of initiative and kept her thoughts imprisoned in the past. The return of Alan Field revived some very painful memories, and if I may so express it, the barrier between past and present was broken down."

"You think she may have killed him?"

"I believe she saw him lying dead. I do not know who killed him."

He was sitting up straight, his arms clasped about his knees.

"I should say it was much more likely to have been Darsie. Look here, what time was it when you were at your window and saw them come up the garden?"

"I cannot say."

"You must have some idea."

Miss Silver shook her head.

"I could not put a time to it. There was no reason to suppose that the incident had any importance. I found myself unable to sleep. My room had become very much heated by the afternoon sun, and I got up to enjoy the breeze at the window, but I did not put on the light or look at my watch. In such circumstances one's sense of time can be very misleading, and I should not care to hazard a guess."

"Well, that's unfortunate, because it all turns on the time. Pippa Maybury's appointment was at twenty past twelve. She says someone had been there before her, and Field was already dead. If it was the Annings, then the odds are one of them killed him, but if they came along after Pippa ran away, then all they did was to find the body. Now what are the probabilities at the Sea View end? Field could have gone along to the hut at any time before, let us say, five or ten past twelve. There doesn't seem to be any reason for Mrs. Anning to go there unless she followed him—or her daughter. Look here, what about this? Field has another appointment at the hut— an earlier one with Darsie Anning. She keeps it, and her mother follows her. There is another bitter quarrel and one of them stabs him. That's the most likely way of it, you know." He glanced at his wrist-watch. " 'Brief are the moments of repose which duty's day affords,' as Lord Tennyson would doubtless have said if he had thought of it. I must now go and hunt the wretched Colt, who will be very far from pleased. You haven't any more evidence up your sleeve, I take it?"

"I have no more evidence, Frank."

He went away over the shingle, and she watched him go. Surmise and suspicion were not evidence. After a brief pause she picked up the little pink coatee, knitted the last row and cast off.

CHAPTER XXIX

MARIE BONNET was in two minds. One had to make the best
bargain for oneself, naturally. If one neglected to do so one
was a fool and had no one to blame but oneself. On the other
hand it is sometimes extremely difficult when two bargains
present themselves to decide on which will suit one best.
As far as Cardozo went she knew pretty well where she was.
He would have to dance to her tune, or he would find himself in a very uncomfortable place. She had only to waver,
to weep, to say to the police, yes it was true they were together but it was also true that she had dropped asleep for a
little there on the grass. She could not say for how long.
Perhaps there would have been time for Cardozo to slip down to
the beach and return again. She had only to say that and he
would be lucky if they did not arrest him for the murder.
No, he must give her what she asked, but the question was just
how much could she ask? He had got the paper he wanted—
the paper which he swore had been stolen from his brother by
Alan Field. In that moment of triumph and terror when he
stood up from searching the body with the wallet in his hand
he had not been able to contain himself. He had told her it was
a fortune for both of them and the proof that it was Alan who
had murdered Felipe Cardozo. He was, in effect, in so great a
transport of emotion that she had had her work cut out to get
him away before anyone came. But this paper which he had
recovered, and the fortune which it was to bring him, they
were at the moment very much in the air. Before the one
could produce the other, José must go to South America—that
he had been obliged to confess. And once he was a few thousand
miles away . . . Contemplating her chances of getting anything
out of a José on the other side of the Atlantic, she thought
very little of them.

To come down to hard facts—what could she get from him
here and now? Perhaps fifty pounds—perhaps a hundred. He
would need all the money he could raise if he was to get hold
of the fortune. A hundred pounds was not enough. What else

could she get out of him? Marriage perhaps. But suppose he did not get hold of the fortune after all . . . She would have to think very seriously before she took a step like that.

She would have to think very carefully about the other bargain which presented itself. She had not taken any steps in the matter as yet. It required to be handled with the greatest delicacy, and she had needed time to consider the matter. In the beginning it had seemed to her that there was a choice to be made, and that it would be a hard one. Now it came to her that there was, after all, no need of any choice. She would get what she could from José, and from the other as well. Faced with such evidence as she could produce, there could be no refusal.

She had been walking slowly along the hot street, stopping to look in at a shop window here and there, remaining apparently entranced in front of a display of beach-suits. Now she made her way to the call-box at the corner.

Her conversation was a short one. She had to wait whilst the person for whom she asked came to the telephone, after which there were very few words. She said,

"I saw you on Wednesday night. I can tell you where you were and what you were doing. I have not told anyone yet, but my conscience is troubling me."

To this there was no reply at all. With an impatient jerk of her shoulder Marie Bonnet said,

"It will be better if we meet."

This time there was a single word, spoken low. The word was "Yes."

Marie said, "Where?" And then, quickly and before there could be any answer, "Upon the cliff or on the beach I do not go! From the house I do not go! It must be there."

There was a little silence that seemed long. Then the voice said,

"Why not?"

The appointment was made.

CHAPTER XXX

"AND where do you think that gets us?" said Inspector Abbott. After a couple of hours at Sea View, Inspector Colt opined that he was damned if he knew.

Frank nodded.

"Somewhere—anywhere—nowhere—you pay your money and you take your choice. But better hold off the Maybury girl. I don't think she did it, you know."

Colt looked glum. He considered that they had had a very promising case against Mrs. Maybury.

"I expect nine juries out of ten would say she did."

"Oh, juries—we haven't got as far as that yet. Suspects —that's what we're dealing with at the moment. Baa, baa, blacksheep, have you any wool? Yes, sir, yes, sir, three bags full. In other words, have we a bagful of suspects or haven't we? And too many of them spoil the broth quite as fatally as too few. Just take a look at them! There's Cardozo, who could have done it on his head if Marie is lying about his alibi—and if ever I came across a natural born liar, it is Mlle. Bonnet. There's Pippa Maybury, who has an assignation with Field and comes back from it dripping blood all over Cliff Edge. And there's Mrs. Anning, who sticks to it that she always said he would be punished and he has been punished, and who certainly saw him after he had been stabbed."

"You think she really saw him with the knife in his back?"

"I don't see what else you're to make of what she said to Miss Silver. Field went off to keep his appointment, or an earlier one, and she followed him. She rambles a lot, but I think that's clear enough. Darsie wouldn't let her see him, and she wanted to tell him how wicked he was. She may have knifed him herself by way of bringing the punishment home, or she may have seen somebody else knife him."

"The somebody else could have been Miss Anning."

"In that case it would be her daughter whom she followed, and not Field. Yes, I'm inclined to think that is the more likely way of it. She sees Field go out, and she sees Darsie follow him, so she follows Darsie all the way to the hut. There is a quarrel and she sees him stabbed But I don't see how anyone is going to prove it. What a rambling old woman may have said to Miss Silver isn't evidence. And as to putting her in the box—well, I ask you!"

Inspector Colt was understood to agree that Mrs. Anning would hardly make a reliable witness. "And as far as the daughter is concerned—well, I should say she would stick to her story."

"Which is just what she produced to Miss Silver. Her mother couldn't sleep. She went out into the garden for a breath of air, and Darsie heard her, followed her, and brought her back. Neither of them left the garden or went out on the cliff, let alone down the steep path to the beach. Her 'My mother is an invalid, Inspector,' was quite effective. Also the matter-of-fact manner in which she explained her mother's resentment—'You see, I was once engaged to Alan Field, and my mother blamed him when it was broken off. As a matter of fact it came to an end by mutual consent, and for the simple reason that neither of us had any money.' And then all that piece about there being no reason for any resentment, but that Mrs. Anning had a severe illness about that time and it had all got muddled up in her mind. Quite a plausible explanation, you know, Colt."

"Show me something in this case that isn't plausible!" said Inspector Colt bitterly.

Miss Silver was devoting what remained of the day to the art of conversation. Mrs Field had joined her on the beach after Frank Abbott left her, and appeared to derive a good deal of relief and comfort from talking about her husband and stepson.

"In some ways I think they were very much alike," she said. "I don't mean in the wrong things that Alan did—you won't misunderstand me about that, will you? I mean in their dispositions. They both liked things to be beautiful and pleasant. In Alan's case I think it led him into doing wrong. He had not his father's artistic gifts, but he had the artistic temperament, and of course that does make people unpractical and careless about money. That is why I did not think it right to lend him any. And then he could not bear to say no. Pen couldn't bear to either—my husband, you know. It was rather awkward sometimes, because women really were very silly about him. He was as good-looking as Alan, and so gifted. And he didn't like having to snub them, so it was sometimes just a little awkward. That was what upset me so much when Alan spoke of having his father's letters published."

Miss Silver was putting the little pink coatee together. She looked up from it to say,

"Did he talk of doing so?"

"It upset me very much," said Esther Field. "I was ill, you know, and so he had all the papers to go through. There were some letters—from a very foolish girl. I am afraid she may have fancied herself in love with Pen, and he would be too kind to snub her. He always said it was like measles—it ran its course and they got over it."

"It happened on more than one occasion, then?"

"Oh, yes," said Esther Field comfortably. "It was just a kind of hero-worship. But I couldn't get Alan to see how cruel it would be to publish the letters. People are so ready to believe the worst. And in this case—well, Alan didn't tell me, but I can guess who the girl may have been, and it would have been very, very unkind indeed. Pen ought not to have kept the letters. I didn't know that he had. How could I? It was very careless of him. It would have given dreadful pain to—to her family if they had been published—*terrible* pain."

Miss Silver regarded her gravely.

"You say, 'to her family'. But what about herself?"

"That is just it," said Esther Field. "She is dead. She died ten years ago. It was a terrible shock to Pen."

"An accident?" enquired Miss Silver.

Esther Field gazed at her doubtfully.

"Oh, I don't know—I hope so—I do hope so. Oh, yes, it must have been. She was bathing, and she swam out too far. She must have got cramp, and she was drowned. Such a tragedy!"

Miss Silver said, "Yes indeed."

Mrs. Field sighed.

"It doesn't do to think of these old sad things, does it? One needs all one's courage for the present. Poor, poor Alan!"

They went back to the house almost immediately. Miss

Silver having changed into the dark blue artificial silk which
Ethel Burkett had persuaded her to buy at Wildings—"Such
good style, Auntie, and it will last you for years"—descended
to the drawing-room, still shaded by sun-blinds but now
admitting a pleasant breeze. She was, as always, meticulously
neat—her hair with its deep Edwardian fringe in front, close
coils behind, and an overall restraining net; the locket in
massive gold with the raised and intertwined initials of her
parents and the treasured locks of their hair; the black lisle
stockings of her invariable summer wear, and the glacé shoes
with their beaded toes. That the whole effect was that of someone who had stepped out of an album of family photographs,
she was naturally unaware.

In the drawing-room she found only Mrs. Trevor, turning
the leaves of a book in which she did not appear to take any
interest. No one could have presented a greater contrast—
her hair compelled into the latest style, her dress as near to
the last vagary of fashion as collaboration with a local dress-
maker could contrive. The result, if not altogether successful, undoubtedly ministered to her morale. Since Miss Silver
would be someone to talk to, she was pleased to see her.

Esther Field had also gone to her room to change. As
she took off her grey linen for the old black crepe-de-chine
which she had put in because it was cool and comfortable, she
was thankful that custom no longer prescribed the mourning of
an older day. She remembered Pen's mother telling her that
when their father died she and her sisters wore black with
crape on it for six months, plain black for another six, after
which a white tucker might be added and a gradual progress
made through black and white to grey, and in the last three
months of the second year to purple, mauve, and heliotrope.
Nowadays people as often as not just wore what they had, not
even avoiding the brighter colours. She had been rather
shocked herself at seeing a young widow in crimson corduroy
slacks. The old observances were oppressive, but there was a
happy mean, and in the case of anything so dreadful as a murder
one neither had the inclination to go shopping nor to wear
anything that would attract attention.

She slipped the old black dress over her head and felt

refreshed. The stuff was cool against her skin. Her talk with Miss Silver had done her good. It had been a relief to speak of the things which had lain so heavily upon her heart. It was sometimes easier to talk to a stranger who brought no emotions of her own to cloud the issue. Looking back, she only hoped she had not said too much. All that about Pen and Irene—she had never spoken of it to anyone before. Not that there had been anything to speak about—just hero-worship on her side and kindness on his. And perhaps the letters Alan wanted to publish were from someone quite different. Pen was always getting letters from women, and they meant so little, so very little—she knew that. She hadn't thought about Irene—not at first—but now she couldn't get away from her. It was almost as if she were there in the room, or as if at any moment a door might open and let her through. There was nothing frightening in the thought, only the gentle sadness into which all grief must turn as time goes by. She stood for a while by the window with the breeze coming in and let the gentle sadness have its way. Poor, poor Irene, so lovely, so young, and so tragically dead. Whatever foolish things she had written, no one would ever read them now. As soon as all this dreadful business about Alan was over she would go through the papers herself and see that the letters were burned.

Downstairs in the shaded drawing-room Maisie Trevor was indulging in her favourite occupation. Give her a receptive and sympathetic listener and she could be perfectly happy. This she now enjoyed in Miss Silver, and the stream of anecdote and reminiscence never flagged.

Miss Silver, casting on stitches for the first of a pair of bootees to match the little pink coat, was most gratifyingly attentive. Her original remark of "You and Mrs. Field and Lady Castleton are such very old freinds," had, as it were, released the waters, and they now flowed without pause or stay. Miss Silver was able to count her stiches very comfortably during some recollections of Carmona's parents.

"George Leigh was really the handsomest man! Carmona isn't anything special, but he *was*. All the girls were in love with him." She laughed self-consciously. "I know I was. Now that it's so long ago, I don't mind saying so. But it

was Adela he was in love with—never had eyes for anyone
else until she turned him down for Geoffrey Castleton who was
a much better match and he went off and married Monica on
the rebound. I don't know what he saw in her after Adela.
She was rather sweet of course, but Adela had everything!"

Miss Silver began to knit the first row of the bootee.

"When people have so much, it is sometimes a little over-
powering," she said.

Maisie Trevor's blue eyes widened.

"I don't know that I've ever thought of it like that, but
I suppose it might be. Of course, there *was* something hard
about Adela. Perhaps it was doing so many things and doing
them all so dreadfully well. She did, you know. Dancing,
tennis, swimming, fencing—they all seemed to come to her so
easily. I remember someone saying to me—I don't remember
if it was Jennifer Rae or Mary Bond, or it might have been
Josephine Carstairs, but we were all in the same set and it
might have been any of them—only not Esther, because she
never said anything unkind about anyone—but it would have
been one of the others—Oh, where was I?"

"Something that was said about Lady Castleton."

"Oh, *yes!* And now I am pretty sure it was Jean Elliot—
because she was terribly in love with George Leigh, and
frightfully jealous of Adela. Well, Jean said—I am really
practically sure it was Jean—'You can't do such a lot and do
it all so well and have much time left for the ordinary human
feelings'. And in a way that was true. She didn't get fond
of people, or have crushes, or fall in love like the rest of us
did—she just had a raving success, and then made the most
suitable marriage that came along. Geoffrey was in the Diplo-
matic, you know. He was supposed to have a big future, but
he died young, and she never married again. She didn't really
care for people—only for Causes. She had a very big job in
the war, and she speaks in public, and takes part in debates
on the wireless—all that sort of thing. But as to people, I
believe the only one she was ever really fond of was Irene."

Esther Field came into the room with Lady Castleton just
as Miss Silver enquired,

"Who is Irene?"

CHAPTER XXXI

THERE was one of those silences which bring it home to even the most dull-witted person that something of an unfortunate nature has been said. In this case quite obviously it was the name pronounced by Miss Silver. Seeing no reason to check herself, she had not done so, and Lady Castleton, coming in first, had reached the middle of the room before the sentence was complete.

"Who is Irene?"

Miss Silver's enunciation, always very clear, seemed especially so on this occasion. Had Lady Castleton been nearer the door, had there been any possibility of ignoring what had been said, it is likely enough that she would have done so, but she was so near, so much exposed to the direct impact of the name— She paused for a moment, tall and graceful in her black dress, and said with perfect dignity of voice and manner,

"I think Mrs. Trevor may have been speaking of my sister who died ten years ago." And having spoken, she passed on to join Esther Field where the long windows stood open to the terrace.

Maisie Trevor showed signs of confusion. She said, "We were all so fond of her," and began to talk about something else. But no sooner had Adela Castleton and Esther Field stepped across the threshold and moved slowly out of sight than Miss Silver, usually so full of tact, returned to the subject. Leaning a little nearer, she said,

"I hope I did not embarrass Lady Castleton just now."

Mrs. Trevor bridled.

"It's not easy to embarrass Adela—in fact I shouldn't think it could be done. She just puts on her grand manner and sails past you like she did just now."

Miss Silver paused to contemplate the tiny frill of pink which had begun to show upon her needles. Then she said,

"It is sometimes quite startling to hear the name of someone very near and dear when one is not expecting to do so. I should be sorry to think that I had inadvertently revived a painful memory."

Maisie Trevor dropped her voice.

"Well, of course it was a dreadful tragedy. She was so young, and really more beautiful, I think, than Adela—softer, you know, and not so dreadfully good at everything."

"And she died? How extremely sad."

"She was drowned. She must have swum out too far. They said it was cramp."

Miss Silver was never quite sure whether there was any stress upon the *said*. If so, it was of the slightest.

Mrs. Trevor's tongue ran on. Cramp was such a horrid thing. But perhaps they had better not talk about it in case Lady Castleton came back. She really had been devoted to Irene. "No children of her own, you know—and some women seem to mind about that so much, though I really don't quite see why, and I don't know that Adela *did*. Tom and I never had any, and I've never minded in the least. Babies are so messy, and when they grow up they date you dreadfully. And then look at how some of them turn out! All these divorces, and boys getting mixed up with the most dreadful sorts of politics, or writing the sort of poetry that means they don't wash or shave! Well, I shouldn't have liked it at all—I really shouldn't!"

Miss Silver agreeing that some of these modern trends were indeed to be deprecated, they were able to have a very comfortable talk upon the subject.

Pippa Maybury came down in a scarlet dress with so little top to it that it really might hardly have been there at all. She was made up after a rather startling fashion too, with a good deal of eye-shadow, and mascara, skin of an even pallor, lipstick that matched her dress, and scarlet finger nails. Carmona, overtaking her in the hall, made a sound of dismay.

"Pippa!"

"I know, I know—'Darling do go up and put on something nice and quiet and dowdy'! And I'm not going to—not for you or anyone! If I'm going to be plunged into a prison cell tomorrow, I'm going to have a good last kick tonight—so there!"

James Hardwick came up behind her. Pippa blew him a

kiss and ran on. His eyebrows rose as he looked at Carmona.

"Let us eat and drink, for tomorrow we die?"

Carmona's eyes were full of tears, She said,

"Yes. James, where is Bill? She wants to keep him out of it, and she can't. He ought to be here."

He nodded.

"Come along—we should go in."

"James, if they arrest her——"

"I don't think they will."

"I can't think why they don't."

"Perhaps because she really didn't do it."

She had a sudden startled feeling.

"Why did you say that?"

He said, "Second sight!" and walked away from her into the drawing-room.

CHAPTER XXXII

MISS SILVER found it a very interesting evening. Of those present at least three were the objects of her particular attention. She did not talk much, but she listened a good deal, and her needles were busy. When after dinner Lady Castleton laid out her usual game of patience, she moved her chair close up to the table and became a most interested spectator. Her murmured deprecatory "I hope you do not mind" being dismissed with a brief "Oh, no," she did not speak again. There was the occasional click of a needle, and the pink bootee began to take shape.

Adela Castleton sat there in her filmy black, leaning a little forward over the red and black and white of the cards, her beautiful hand with its ruby ring poised above them, laying down a King here, picking up a Queen, moving diamond and heart, club and spade, bent on the game and ordering it with skill.

Colonel Trevor was reading *The Times*. He never did anything else in the evenings except on the rare occasions when he was dragged into a game of Bridge. Sometimes he went to sleep behind it, when even Maisie had learned that it was better not to wake him. She was herself engaged in turning over the pages of the latest *Vogue*, exclaiming at the more extravagant styles and picturing herself glamorously arrayed in them with the minute waist, the fabulous height, and the last word in hair-does which they demanded.

Esther had discarded her knitting for some fine embroidery. She was working a large ornamental H upon a set of face-towels for Carmona—the material a fine damask, and the design and stitchery really exquisite. She was of the women to whom needlework is a relaxation. Her soft brown eyes dwelt upon it with pleasure. Her mood was quiet and at peace.

The three younger members of the party sat together. James Hardwick had a magazine, Pippa a book which she did not read. When she had fluttered through the pages she let it drop and picked up another, and rapidly, intermittently, she talked to Carmona, to James, to Maisie Trevor, to Miss Silver, to Esther Field—questions that did not wait for an answer, irrelevancies about this and that, startling because they disclosed the painful hurry with which her thoughts ran here and there and found no shelter. And all the time she was lighting one cigarette from another until the stubs were piled high upon the formidable ash-tray which Octavius Hardwick had won in a golf tournament round about the turn of the century.

There was a moment when James laid down his magazine and went out upon the terrace. Miss Silver watching him go, observed that the breeze must be most refreshing.

"Such a wonderful spell of warm weather. I feel that one should make the most of it. Perhaps Major Hardwick will not mind if I join him."

She might have been addressing herself to Carmona, or to the room in general. Carmona murmured, "Oh, yes, of course," and the pink knitting, the ball of wool, and the needles were slipped into a flowered chintz bag.

As Miss Silver crossed to the window she glanced back. Carmona and Pippa were looking in her direction. Esther Field had lifted her eyes from her embroidery. Adela Castleton looked down at the pattern of her game. The hand that was poised above it held the ace of spades.

The air upon the terrace was delightful. Turning at the sound of a footstep, James Hardwick was considerably surprised to see who it was that had followed him. She came up to him and said,

"You would prefer to be alone, but I would very much appreciate a short talk with you. Perhaps we might walk down the garden and out upon the cliff path. The breeze will be most refreshing."

"And we need refreshing?"

"I think we do."

They walked down the cement path between Uncle Octavius' figureheads, but until they emerged upon the cliff neither of them spoke. Then James Hardwick said,

"What did you want to speak to me about?"

"About Mrs. Maybury."

"What is there to say?"

"A good deal, I think."

"Well?"

If his words were abrupt, they somehow did not offend. The impression she had been forming was deepened. She said with gravity,

"I do not think that she can stand very much more."

He threw away the cigarette he had been smoking.

"Abbott is a friend of yours. Are they going to arrest her?"

"Not immediately."

"What is holding them off?"

"I believe her story to be true. Truth makes its own impression. And"—she made a slight pause—"there are other avenues to be explored."

"They suspect someone else?"

"It is a disturbing and complicated case. Where is Major Maybury? He should be here."

"He may be at any moment. I got on to him this morning. He is flying over."

"I am glad. The strain is too much for her. One has to think of that. It is not just a matter of whether she can escape arrest. There has been a severe shock and a prolonged strain. I think you must consider that."

"I?"

"You, Major Hardwick."

They had been strolling along the cliff path. He stopped now and turned to face her.

"And just what do you mean by that?"

"I think you know."

"I assure you that I do not."

"Then there is no more to be said."

"But I should like to know what you meant."

"Something very simple. You know something that you have not told to the police, and I think the time has come when you have no right to withhold it."

"That is quite a large assumption on your part, isn't it?"

"But it is true, is it not?"

"What makes you think so? I should really like to know."

She was silent for a moment. Then she said,

"You are, of course, acquainted with the process by which a coral reef is formed. Infinitesimal living particles combine in it. You ask me how I have arrived at a certain conclusion, and this simile presents itself. I do not think I can give you a better answer. An infinite number of small things combine, and an opinion is formed. Since I have undertaken to give Mrs. Maybury my professional help, it has become my duty to observe the other people in the house."

"And you have been observing me?"

"Yes, Major Hardwick."

"And where did your observations lead you?"

"I could see that you were profoundly disturbed."

"You think that strange, when a man has been murdered practically on my doorstep?"

"Oh, no. There would have been nothing strange about the disturbance." There was some slight emphasis on the word. "Mrs. Field was under your roof. Mrs. Hardwick and Mr. Field had been very closely connected——"

"Then may I ask——"

"Certainly you may. It was not that you were disturbed, but that this disturbance was producing a conflict in your mind which struck me. I had to consider what this conflict might be. There could be but one answer—you had seen or heard something which you must either disclose to the police or withhold from them. For a time I had to consider whether you yourself were involved. Your wife was obviously under a considerable strain, not only on account of her friend Pippa, but also on your account. I was aware of this continually, until her return from the drive which she took with you this afternoon, when it was apparent that a weight had been lifted from her mind. It was plain that whatever her misgivings had been, you had succeeded in removing them. Yet you yourself showed no sign of relief."

He said drily,

"I cannot, of course, prevent you from exercising your imagination in my direction, or in that of anyone else, but do you really believe that by doing so you will be helping Pippa Maybury?"

"I hope that I may do so."

Her tone at this point arrested his attention. He had been prepared for offence, anger, justification—for anything but the deep, almost sad gravity with which she spoke. It was in the same vein that she now continued

"Major Hardwick, will you listen to me, and as far as possible without resentment? You ask me why I should think you have some knowledge which you have not shared with the police. I should like to answer that question in some detail. On that Wednesday night when Mrs. Maybury went to keep her appointment with Alan Field she did so by way of the path we have used tonight. Your dressing-room overlooks the garden and commands a view of the path. The same applies to the adjoining bedroom. Upon so hot a night all the windows would be open."

"My dear Miss Silver, I had been travelling all day. Do you imagine that I spent the night looking out of the window?"

"You are quick to perceive the point. I will not labour it. You could have seen, or heard, Mrs. Maybury as she went down the garden. She tells me that she heard what might have been a footstep on the terrace as she turned to close the garden door behind her. It startled her very much, and she ran the rest of the way to the path that goes down to the beach. When she was returning in a terrible state of distress after seeing

Alan Field lying dead she had the very strong impression that there was someone not very far from the top of the path, and that this someone was watching her. She thought it was the murderer, and again she ran in terror."

"And can you supply any reason why this 'murderer' should hang about on the cliff path instead of getting away?"

"I was about to raise that point, Major Hardwick. I am quite certain that the person on the cliff path was not the murderer—and for the reason which you have just put forward. Whoever killed Alan Field would be under the necessity of getting away as quickly as possible. The only thing which would oblige this person to remain in the vicinity would be the descent of the path to the beach by someone else before he or she had time to get away. This might render it necessary to remain at the foot of the cliff until the coast was clear. I am unable to see that it could compel the murderer to run the risk of loitering at the top of the cliff. I have, therefore, some grounds for supposing that it was you who stood there watching. If you did so, your evidence must be of the very highest importance."

"Miss Silver, you have a very vivid imagination."

"I am telling you what I think. Pray allow me to proceed. I think you followed Pippa Maybury when she left the house. When she went down to the beach you did not like to go after her lest you should seem to be intruding upon her private affairs, but on the other hand, neither did you like to go in and leave her there. She has a volatile character and is capable of very foolish actions. She is an old friend of your wife's. I think you felt a certain responsibility."

James Hardwick was experiencing what clients of Miss Silver not infrequently did experience—surprise, anger, respect, and the odd sensation of being exposed to an observation so acute that it was useless to put up any defence against it. She had described not only his actions but the motives which had prompted them. He found himself without anything to say, but continuing to listen.

After a momentary pause she went on.

"The crucial importance of any evidence you may have to give comes from the fact of your position at the junction of the two paths. The person who was watching on the cliff commanded the approach from the beach. If you were that person—and I believe you were—you and you alone can say whether more than one person came up that way. It is clear from the state of Pippa Maybury's dress and from her other evidence that the murder had only just taken place. It is possible that the murderer had not had time to get away before she could be heard descending the path. A person with so strong a reason for haste would lose no time once the way was clear. Pippa Maybury went down the path and over the beach to the hut. I believe that you were waiting up here. Did anyone else come up the path before her return?"

He had no refuge but silence. It was some little time before he said,

"This is all the purest conjecture."

"Major Hardwick, if you did not follow Pippa Maybury, where were you? I do not think that you were in the house. Your wife was out of her room for a considerable time. She and Mrs. Maybury were backwards and forwards—to the bathroom, to the kitchen. During all this time your wife never mentioned you. She neither suggested asking for your help nor expressed any fear lest you should wake. I think she already knew that you were not in her room."

"The house was full of people who did not wake."

"The Trevors are down the passage on the left of the main landing, Mrs. Field in the corresponding room on the right. Lady Castleton, whose room was next to Mrs. Maybury's, had taken a sleeping-draught."

"Had she?"

"She had been complaining of a headache. Your wife went up with her and saw her take a couple of tablets. She also looked in later on when the others came up in order to make sure that they had had the desired effect."

He had no comment to make. Miss Silver said,

"I will not press you any farther now. Whatever your motive for silence may be, I ask you to weigh it against these facts. Pippa Maybury would have been arrested tonight if it had not been for a piece of evidence which the police have felt obliged to investigate. But unless there is some further development I am afraid that the arrest may take place. I ask you to consider the consequences. Even if it were not she but some other innocent person who was arrested, what must the effect be? Unhappiness—ruin! And in the end you would be forced to speak. There is also another aspect of which you probably do not know. Alan Field was, I believe, murdered because he was blackmailing a person who was prepared to go to any length to protect the secret which he threatened. I have some reason to suppose that this person is being blackmailed again. Do you imagine that someone already proved to be ruthless would hesitate at a second crime? Pray think of what I have said."

As she spoke she turned and began to walk towards the house. The interview was over.

James Hardwick found himself a little dazed. Frank Abbott had once remarked that as far as Miss Maud Silver was concerned the human race, was glass-fronted. To find one's thoughts and actions suddenly laid bare to a probing eye is a good deal too like the Day of Judgment to be a comfortable experience. When, as in this case, the experience is quite unexpected, and the things revealed not such as one would wish to have exposed to view, the result is apt to be confounding.

They walked in silence until they reached the garden door. Here Miss Silver turned to him.

"Are you by any chance an admirer of Lord Tennyson?"

He considered this to be a social digression. He hastened to respond.

"I think I am. He has had quite a vogue again lately, you know." Miss Silver coughed.

"A great man, too much neglected. May I for a moment quote from one of his poems?

'. . . . . to live by law,
Acting the law we live by without fear;
And, because right is right, to follow right
Were wisdom in the scorn of consequence'."

Once more James Hardwick found that he had nothing to say. Fortunately, it did not appear that he was expected to say anything. Alfred, Lord Tennyson was to have the last word. They went up the garden together in silence.

When they had come to the glass door, they stood for a moment looking in upon the lighted room. They might hardly have left it. Nothing had changed. And to James Hardwick there seemed to be a strangeness about this. When thought has been strongly moved, there is an instinctive feeling that the world about us should also have suffered change. But this room and its occupants might have been here for time indefinite. The light from an overhead chandelier shone down with a mellow glow. Behind *The Times* Colonel Trevor was undoubtedly asleep. Over her magazine Maisie Trevor yawned. Lady Castleton was still at her game—or it might be that one had been swept away and another begun. Esther Field took the fine stitches of her embroidery. And on the stiff Victorian sofa the two girls sat together, the scarlet of Pippa's dress, her floating ash-blonde hair, in vivid contrast with Carmona's dark waves and flowing white.

And then all in a moment the scene broke up. Beeston opened the door on the farther side and a man came past him into the room—a strongly built man, square-faced, sunburnt, and in a hurry—"Never gave me time to announce him nor anything—just said, 'My name's Maybury—I think my wife's staying here,' and walked right past."

Pippa looked up and caught her breath. Then she was on her feet, gasping his name and running down the room to throw herself into his arms.

"Oh, Bill! Oh, Bill—Bill—*Bill*!"

CHAPTER XXXIII

THE night closed down. The earth gave out its heat. The water lay dark under a sky which never quite lost a faint mysterious light. In the houses there were some that slept, and some who could not sleep because of the weight upon the heart or the restless procession of thoughts which passed ceaselessly before the tired mind. There were some who could have slept if they had dared, but did not dare because of what might wait for them in dreams. There were some who waked because they had that to do which could not be done in the day.

Marie Bonnet had very little difficulty in keeping herself awake. She was in a complacent and confident frame of mind, and in a state of great satisfaction with the cleverness, the competence, the efficiency, and the prudence of Marie Bonnet. It was, of course, to be seen at a glance that the affair must be conducted in a private manner. Such things could not be discussed in the street, upon the beach, or in a tea-shop. It was of the first importance that the two persons concerned should not be seen to meet at all. If the matter was to be safe, it must be private. With José she was on a different footing. A girl may meet a lover and incur no more than a little scandal, but with this one it was different. There could be no meeting that would not set every tongue in Cliffton asking why.

So the meeting must be private. But if that one had had the idea that Marie Bonnet, prudent Marie Bonnet, would come to a meeting on the cliff, for example, where a push would be enough to send one over, or on the beach—perhaps even in the very hut where a man had died already . . . No, no, no—she was not born yesterday! She knew how to look after herself, and from this house she did not go! They could talk through the window, and after all, what was there to be said? She had seen what she had seen, and the money must be paid, or she would go to the police. One-pound notes, and within the week. Just how and where, was one of the things to be arranged at the meeting.

The clock of St. Mark's struck twelve. Another half hour and there would be a tap on the dining-room window. Marie would open it. Not wide, it is understood—there would be no need for that, since there would be neither going out nor coming in. A little pushing up of the old-fashioned sash, a few minutes whispered talk, and the whole thing would be settled. Mrs. Anning's room looked out to the sea, Miss Anning's to the side of the house. On this side only one bedroom occupied for the moment, and by old Miss Crouch who would not hear if the house fell down.

At five minutes to the half hour Marie went down the stairs in her stocking feet. The curtains in the dining-room had not been drawn, and the two big windows showed up against the darkness of the room. She skirted the table, made her way to the one on the left, and pushed back the catch. She had done it often enough before to be assured that there would be no sound. No sound from the catch, no sound from the cords of the big sash window as she lifted it. It ran up a little over a foot from the bottom and stopped there. She took her hands away. The space would be enough. They could talk through it very well, but if anyone had the idea that they could get in, it would be easy enough to push the window down. Marie Bonnet knew how to look after herself.

The air from outside came in, cooler and fresher than the air in the house. Kneeling in front of the window, Marie's head came just about level with the open space. With the person she was expecting kneeling or stooping on the other side, they would be able to converse very well, and there would be no noise—no noise at all. No need to waste time. She would say what she must have, and what could the other do except agree? Whatever she liked to ask, it must be paid, because it was the price of the murderer's life, and what is the use of money when you are dead? One must be practical.

She began to wonder whether she was going to ask enough. But if one put the price too high, there might be at least delay, perhaps even danger. The movement of a too large sum of money—it might occasion suspicion. No, better to take what she had fixed in her own mind, and then see what could be done when one came back again. Because naturally one would come back again. When a dish is so tempting, it is to be expected that the plate will return for more than one helping.

Clear and sharp upon the soft air came the two strokes of the half hour from the church of St. Mark. The bell was always a loud one. Now it sounded as if it must wake everyone in the house. Before the air had ceased to tingle a voice spoke from the other side of the window. In a deep quiet monotone it said,

"Are you there?"

Involuntarily Marie drew back. The striking of the clock had made her start, but the quiet voice startled her more sharply still. Because there had been no warning of it. She had been listening for a footstep upon the road, upon the path

—for the groping of a hand, the catch of a hurrying breath. And there had been nothing—nothing at all—but quite suddenly out of nowhere the sound of that quiet voice.

It spoke again, repeating the same words, and in a moment she was herself, and angry because she had allowed herself to behave like a child that is scared at the dark. She said,

"Yes, I am here. And we must be quick. It will not suit either of us if someone should come."

The voice said, "No." And then, "You are asking me for money. Why?"

"I have told you. I saw you on the Wednesday night."

"I don't know what you mean."

"You know, or you would not be here. I saw you in the hut."

"I do not know what you mean."

"You know very well. You were there in the corner when José came in. He went down on his knees with his torch in his hand. When he put it on, the light went over your face as you stood in the corner where the towels hung to dry. You did not see me because I was behind him—I was still outside. And you did not think he saw you—you thought that you were hidden."

"He did not see me."

"Perhaps. But I saw you—and my conscience troubles me that I have not told the police."

The voice said, "I think we will leave your conscience out of it. I am willing to pay you. How much do you want?"

Marie had one moment to make up her mind. In that moment she doubled the amount for which she had meant to ask. She had not expected so easy a victory. She would be a fool if she did not take the most that she could get. She said, "A thousand pounds" and waited to hear the voice demur.

Instead, it spoke as smoothly as if she had asked no more than a bus fare.

"Very well, you shall have it. I want to close the matter now and for always. This is to be a final settlement."

Final! Well, they would see about that! Marie smiled in the dark. She said,

"That is understood."

The voice spoke again.

"Then we can finish the matter now. I have brought the money with me. There must be no more meetings."

"You have brought it with you? But it must be in one-pound notes—that goes without saying."

"That is what I have brought—it would not suit either of us to have them traced. But you will want to count them."

"Assuredly."

"It will take a little time. I have the notes here in a bag. They are in bundles of twenty-five. If I push the bag up on to the windowsill, you can take them out for yourself. They are quite heavy."

Yes, a thousand pounds would be heavy. Paper money—not so heavy as metal. A thousand pounds . . . Now, why hadn't she asked for more? *Ça ne fait rien*—there is always another day!

As the thought went through her mind, there was the shape of the bag at the window. The person who knelt there lifted it to the outer sill and Marie reached for it from the opposite side. It slid away from her, tilting, slipping—smooth, shiny stuff and nothing to take hold of. Instinctively she leaned forward, catching at it. It fell, but the sound of its fall never reached her. As she leaned out over the sill, two strong hands closed about her throat.

CHAPTER XXXIV

DARSIE ANNING woke to heaviness. It was a long time since deep sleep had been hers, but last night she had gone down into a sort of stunned unconsciousness. Emerging from it now, the insupportable burden of the day came on her again. She braced herself to carry it. There could be no proof. The ramblings of an invalid could carry no serious danger. Only there must be no more of them—there must be no more. And how was that to be ensured? She would have to speak very plainly indeed, and perhaps defeat her own ends by frightening her mother out of all control. To say enough but not too much. To alarm her to the point of caution but not past it to where she would babble all she knew. As she dressed, it seemed that this must be her immediate task. She had slept beyond her usual hour. The clock of St. Mark's was striking half-past-six. As she opened her door and went down, the silence of the house surprised her. Marie was an early riser, and at this hour she should have been up and busy.

But Marie was neither in the hall nor in the drawing-room. Miss Anning set the windows wide and came back across the hall to the dining-room. Here too the windows were still closed. This was her thought as she opened the door—closed windows and a heavy air, instead of the fresh morning breeze blowing in. Then, as she moved from the threshold, she saw.

Marie Bonnet lay in a heap at the foot of the left-hand window. Darsie Anning had only to look at her once to know that she was dead. She went and looked at her with a cold sickness at her heart. She bent and touched the wrist in which no pulse had beat for many hours. She looked at the window. It was shut but the catch had been pushed back. It was shut now, but there had been a time in the night when it had been opened from within. It must have been Marie herself who had pushed back the catch and pulled the heavy window up. It must have been that way, and she had let murder in. But it was not Marie who had pulled it down again, because Marie was lying dead—Marie was lying there dead.

Miss Anning walked stiffly back to the hall and across it to her office. The telephone was on the table there. She sat down in her office chair and rang up the police.

It was nearly two hours later that Miss Silver was called to the telephone. Since Mr. Octavius Hardwick had never anticipated the use of such an instrument on the bedroom floor, she was obliged to descend to the study, but as she was already up and dressed she found this no hardship.

Frank Abbott's voice came to her along the wire.

"Is that you?"

His tone was not quite so nonchalant as usual. Her face took on a grave expression.

"Yes, Frank."

"I am speaking from Sea View. Do you think you could come down here?"

"Certainly. I will come at once."

Without further enquiry, she hung up the receiver and went back to her room, where she put on hat and gloves. Proceeding on her way, she encountered Major Hardwick in the hall, and informed him that she was obliged to go out— "To Sea View. I think perhaps Mrs. Anning is not very well. I shall be glad to be of any use I can."

He looked at her hard for a moment before he said,

"May I ask who rang you up?"

She shook her head.

"I think not, Major Hardwick."

But she had hardly gone down the road before Beeston came to him, looking grey about the corners of the mouth.

"If I might have a word with you, Mr. James——" He indicated the study, and James followed him there.

"What's up, Beeston?"

"You may well ask, sir! There's been another murder!"

"Who?"

"That maid of Miss Anning's—the French girl. Found strangled this morning, and the police in the house. The paper-boy's just been along with the news. And it's right enough, for I stepped into the road to see for myself, and there was. a police car outside, and the ambulance and all."

James recalled the paper boy. Red hair and freckles, and a kind of streaked-lightning technique with a bicycle. He said,

"Trust that young devil to pick up anything that's going!"

"Asking for it, she was, if you ask *me*," said Beeston with gloomy pride. "No longer ago than yesterday I remarked on it to Mrs. Beeston. It's my belief she knew something, and thought she was going to make money out of it. Very full of herself according to Mrs. Rogers, and talking high. And Mrs. Rogers told her she'd be getting into trouble if she didn't watch it. And she couldn't have spoken a truer word, as it's turned out."

James nodded.

"Look here," he said, "I think we'll get breakfast over before we tell the ladies."

Miss Silver found the front door at Sea View open, and a constable in the hall. The ambulance was just driving away.

As she stepped across the threshold, Frank Abbott came out of the dining-room to meet her. He took her back there and shut the door upon them.

"Marie Bonnet has been murdered. Strangled here in this room—over by that left-hand window. They've just taken her away."

Miss Silver said, "Dear me!"—that being the strongest exclamation she permitted herself.

"'Dear me!' it is, with a vengeance! Colt swears Miss Anning did it, and he wants her arrested out of hand. Says we've had two murders and we can't afford another. Well, it looks as if he might be right."

"On what grounds?"

"Come over to the window. That's where she was found—slumped down right under the sill. The catch of the window was drawn back, but the window itself was shut. In fact everything as it is now."

"The curtains?"

"Open, as you see them. They had not been drawn."

"And Inspector Colt's theory is?"

"That Marie came down in the night—the body was found at six-thirty, and she had been dead for some hours then—she came down in the night and drew back the catch to let herself out of this window, just as she did when she joined Cardozo on Wednesday night. She got the catch drawn back, but she hadn't time to get the window open because, according to Colt, Miss Anning came down and caught her. He says she probably slanged the girl, who retaliated by accusing her of the murder of Alan Field. I've always had an idea that she knew more than she had told. It looks as if it was something so damning that Miss Anning killed her for it."

Miss Silver coughed.

"Who found the body?"

"According to her own statement, Miss Anning. At six-thirty—her usual hour for getting up, or so she says. The girl ought to have been up too. She came down to look for her, found her lying under the window, and rang up the station. The front door was bolted and all the ground-floor windows latched."

"Except this one."

"Except this one—which has Marie's fingerprints upon the catch and upon the window-frame."

"Not Miss Anning's?"

"An old print or two—nothing relevant. Marie's are all over the place."

"Not anyone else's?"

"No. Well, there it is. Officially, you are here because, if Miss Anning is arrested, something will have to be done about her mother. I thought perhaps——"

Miss Silver inclined her head.

"Presently, Frank. There is something I have to say to you first. I have reason to believe that Marie Bonnet was engaged in blackmailing the murderer of Alan Field."

"What makes you think so?"

"There have been a number of small indications. I overheard a conversation between the Beestons and Mrs. Rogers." She repeated it with her usual meticulous accuracy. "Later, when I had the opportunity of warning Marie as to the danger of such a course, her manner convinced me that there had been no mistake."

"She was angry?"

"No, Frank. She put on an innocent air and could not imagine what I meant. If she had been really innocent she would have resented my caution with a good deal of vehemence and have told me to mind my own business. The fact that she took the trouble to control this natural impulse convinced me that she had something to conceal."

Frank Abbott made a slight impatient movement.

"If you are by any chance advancing this as a defence of Miss Anning, it seems to me that it points the other way. There is no one on whom she would be more likely to have a hold than Miss Anning—no one about whom she would be more likely to know something of a compromising nature, except perhaps Cardozo, and he's out. Had business in London yesterday, and we let him go, but they put a tail on him at the other end, and you can take it from me that he didn't come back here last night and kill Marie Bonnet."

"You are sure about that?"

"Oh, yes. He went back to his rooms, dined with another

man at a café in Soho, went with him to a cinema, and on to a night club. Didn't get back till three in the morning. It just couldn't have been done."

Miss Silver coughed.

"I thought you said he went up to town on business."

Frank Abbott laughed.

"It may have been the kind that is done at night clubs— I wouldn't know. The one he went to has quite a South American flavour. He may have wanted to see a man about a deal, or he may have left his business till the morning. He was out by ten o'clock—went to see a solicitor and one or two other people. But wherever he went, he didn't come down here and kill Marie. And that puts the odds on Miss Anning."

She looked at him.

"Do you really think so?"

"It looks like it."

"Does it?"

"You don't think so?"

"Why should Miss Anning make an appointment with Marie Bonnet down here in her own dining-room in the middle of the night?"

"How do you know that it was an appointment?"

"If, as I believe, it was a question of blackmail—and that is the only conceivable motive for this murder—Marie would have to meet the person she was blackmailing in order to drive her bargain. If the person was Miss Anning, nothing could be easier. She could see her privately at any time of the day—in her bedroom, in the office. There would be no need for an appointment in the night. But if it was not Miss Anning—if it was someone from outside—it would be a different matter. Where and how could these two people meet without arousing comment? The days are long and light. Any meeting would be remarked and would cause talk. You see, it is not so easy. But Marie would have some prudence. She would not go out on the cliffs in the middle of the night or down on to the beach to meet someone who had killed already. She might have thought it would be safe to talk from the window. She would, I think, have thought that."

"But the window was shut."

Miss Silver turned towards it.

"They have finished with the fingerprints?"

"Oh, yes."

"Then will you raise the sash from the bottom?"

He did so. When it stood about eighteen inches above the sill she stopped him.

"Now will you go round and come up on the outside?"

She stood waiting until he appeared, her face composed and rather stern. As he bent to the open space between them, she knelt down on the polished boards. Her head was now very much on a level with his.

"You see, Frank, two people could talk like this, and if I were so incautious as to lean forward, you would not, I believe, find it difficult to strangle me."

He bent lower to examine the ground.

"There is no sign that anyone has been here."

"Would you expect there to be? The cement of the drive comes right up to the wall, and in this heat there is no dew. The nights are as dry as the days."

He stared.

"But the window was shut."

"I think you will find that you can close it from where you are."

"From the outside? There were no fingerprints."

"Do you suppose that the person who planned this murder would be so careless as to leave any?"

CHAPTER XXXV

HE came back into the house and joined her in the dining-room. When he had shut the door he said,

"You speak of the person who planned this murder. You maintain that it was not Miss Anning. I have given you proof that it could not have been Cardozo. If Marie was killed in the way that you suggest by someone who reached in at the bottom of that window and took her by the throat, the person who did it must have had very strong hands. I suppose you are not suggesting that Pippa Maybury could have done it?"

"Oh, no, I am not suggesting that."

"James Hardwick? Is that what is in your mind?"

"I would prefer not to say. There is a point we have not touched on, and it is, I think, important. Marie was a strong, active girl. When she felt hands at her throat she would have fought desperately to release herself. Has Miss Anning any scratches or bruises about the wrists or arms?"

He gave her rather an odd glance.

"No, she hasn't. Do you know of anyone who has?"

"No, Frank. But if, as I believe, the murder was very carefully planned, this would have been guarded against. Gloves would have been worn, or the wrists and arms padded in some way."

He nodded.

"A man's coat sleeves would protect him. But if, as you say, the whole thing was planned, a woman could guard against being scratched or bruised—Darsie Anning could guard against it."

She said mildly but firmly,

"I do not believe that it was Miss Anning."

He raised his eyebrows.

"Can you produce an alternative? There is a good deal of *prima facie* evidence—motive and opportunity—bad blood between her and Field—the old business of his jilting her. And Colt tells me there was quite a lot of talk about that. She was away for months and came back very much changed. Local gossip believed the worst—and sometimes local gossip gets hold of the right end of the stick. Marie may have got something there. She disliked the Annings and would have enjoyed tormenting them, especially if it meant money in her pocket. On the psychological side it all adds up, you know. And I must say that if I had to pick a probable murderer out of our set of suspects I think I would go for Darsie Anning. She is an embittered, frustrated creature and obviously strung up very nearly to breaking point."

Miss Silver said in a tone of deep compassion,

"She has been very unhappy. If you arrest her, what will happen to Mrs. Anning?"

"Are there any relatives? If not, I suppose a nursing home."

She said,

"That is why you sent for me, is it not? And if you proceed with this arrest, I will do what I can. But if you could see your way to staving it off, even for a few hours——"

"We can't risk another death."

"No, I realize that. But pray consider, if Miss Anning is arrested, her business here will be ruined, and the effect upon her mother may be very serious indeed. If she is guilty, all this goes for nothing, but if she is innocent, irreparable harm will have been done, and for the want of perhaps only a few hours delay."

He looked at her intently.

"Do you seriously believe that you can produce the murderer in those few hours?"

"I believe evidence can be produced which will point to someone else as the guilty person."

He said,

"Well, you've never let me down yet. You can have until tomorrow. I'm not in charge, you know, only assisting—Cardozo is really my pigeon—but I think I can stall the local people off until then. Do you want to see either of the Annings?"

"No, Frank, I think not. I believe I should return to Cliff Edge. Later on I shall appreciate the opportunity, but at the moment I think I should go back."

Darsie Anning never knew just how near she had been to arrest. She had been interrogated endlessly. But everything did at last come to an end, and now they had all gone—the police surgeon, the fingerprint man, the photographer, the two Inspectors, and the Superintendent, a big blunt person who came in after the others and went away before they did. Now they were all gone, except for Sid Palmer whom she had known since he was a shy little boy hanging on to his mother's skirts when she brought their washing home. She was a very good laundress, but nobody did that kind of private work now. Sid must be twenty-five. He was long and lanky, and as shy as ever. He turned the colour of a beetroot when she spoke to him, and never got beyond "Yes, miss" and "No, miss" in his mumbled replies.

Presently he was giving her a hand in the kitchen. Not that there was so much to do. A murder in the house had sent the old ladies scuttling like rabbits. The big house held no one but the Annings and Sid Palmer. Mrs. Anning was fretful, and wanted to know what was going on. The information that some of the boarders were leaving did very little to soothe her.

"And how are we going to pay the bills if everybody goes? Is there anybody else coming in? You don't tell me that. You don't tell me anything—you never do!"

As Darsie went out of the room, it came to her with surprise that she could not remember her mother having ever made any reference before as to how the bills were to be paid. Not since her illness, she thought. She had sat in her room with her unfinished embroidery in her lap, or walked a little in the garden, on the cliff, or down into the town, and never spoken of anything except the merest surface trivialities—"It is very hot today, Darsie," or, "It is a little colder," "There are not so many visitors as there used to be." It was as if all this turmoil of thought about her was breaking in upon the dead secluded place in which she had lived so long.

Miss Silver went back to Cliff Edge, and found, as she had expected, that the news of the murder was there before her. Since her avowed errand to Sea View had been a visit to Mrs. Anning, it was not altogether easy to answer Esther Field's concerned enquiries, or to take a natural share in the general conversation. She avoided prevarication, and maintained a discreet reserve by offering the simple fact that it had been thought wiser to put off telling Mrs. Anning of Marie Bonnet's death until the police had completed their investigations.

"Miss Anning has naturally had a great deal on her hands, and since Mrs. Anning does not as a rule leave her room except occasionally to take a turn in the cool of the day, it has been quite possible to keep the tragedy from her for the present. I will go down there again later on, when I may perhaps be of use."

Lady Castleton observed that according to all accounts Mrs. Anning was very little likely to be disturbed by the death of a maid in the house.

"Even in the old days she was always inclined to be wrapped up in herself and her family. Didn't you think so, Esther?"

"She was very fond of them," said Esther Field in a troubled voice.

Adela Castleton sketched a slight but perfectly graceful shrug.

"One of the women to whom the domestic hearth is not only the centre but the boundary of their interests," she said, and walked towards the door. "I think I shall go down on to the beach. The tide won't be right for bathing until later on, but the water will be delicious then. Are you coming, Esther?"

"Yes, I think so—presently."

"Then, my dear, do us all a favour and leave that hot knitting of yours behind. It is really quite unendurable to see you martyrizing yourself with that conflagration of crimson wool." She looked back with the flashing smile which was one of her beauties and went out, shutting the door behind her.

Esther Field said in what sounded like a tone of apology,

"She didn't really know the Annings at all *well*—she just knew them."

Pippa's light nervous laugh floated out.

"Oh, Aunt Esther, *darling*!"

Esther looked up, puzzled.

"Why, my dear——"

"She just doesn't care a rap for anyone except herself— but you'd find excuses for anyone. Well, I'm off to get into a bathing-dress. I don't care how low the tide is, Bill and I are going to walk out in it for miles. I adore catching those little squirly crabs with my toes, and if it never gets deep enough to swim, we can paddle and look for odd creatures in the pools—Bill knows quite a lot about them. And we'll forget there's ever been such a thing as a policeman or a murder——" The carefully made-up features dissolved suddenly into the face of a child who is going to cry.

As she ran out of the room, Miss Silver rose and followed her. Behind her, before she had time to close the door, she heard Maisie Trevor say with something very like a sniff,

"Really—that girl! How uncomfortable it all is! And Tom says we can't go away until after the inquest!"

Miss Silver did not follow Pippa in her flight upstairs.

The scarlet beach-shoes were, as a matter of fact, already taking the last two steps in a flying leap. As she emerged into the hall, Colonel Trevor was coming out of the study. Looking, not at her, but back over his shoulder, he said,

"All right then, James, I'll see about it."

Miss Silver let him go by and up the stairs, after which she opened the study door and went in.

CHAPTER XXXVI

JAMES HARDWICK was sitting at the writing-table with a pen in his hand, but he was not writing. His face was hard and set. He certainly wasn't thinking about the reinvestment of some shares of Carmona's which Tom Trevor had been talking over with him. He looked at Miss Silver with acceptance. After what had passed between them last night it was inevitable that she should return to the charge. Better get it over.

She came right up to the table before she said,

"I think you must have been expecting me. I was detained at Sea View, and on my return I met Mrs. Field and Lady Castleton on their way to the morning-room. It seemed best to give a little time to answering their very natural enquiries."

"Yes?"

She said, "I should like to feel that we shall not be interrupted."

"Colonel Trevor won't come back. Carmona is the only other person who might look for me here. You want to speak to me?"

"Yes, Major Hardwick."

The chair which Colonel Trevor had been using stood at a convenient angle to the table. She seated herself. James, who had risen, sat down again. The room had a faint smell of leather and old books. Green and white sun-blinds shaded it, giving a twilight effect. There was no breeze, and the air was hot. Miss Silver said,

"You will have heard of Marie Bonnet's death. She ran a more immediate risk than I expected. I feel that we are both of us to blame."

"You don't expect me to agree about that?"

She said,

"I blame myself. If she was blackmailing a murderer, I knew that she must be in danger. I warned her, but I did not anticipate that the murderer would strike again so soon. I should have reflected that every moment Marie Bonnet continued to live was a moment of danger to a person who had killed once already—skilfully, ruthlessly, and without warning. Major Hardwick, you will not, I suppose, regard this, but if you know something about that person I have to warn you that you are not only making yourself an accessory after the fact, but you are taking a very considerable risk. If your knowledge is suspected—and I think it may be—the person who has already killed twice will not hesitate at another crime."

They sat looking at one another across the rubbed green leather and shining mahogany of the late Mr. Octavius Hardwick's writing-table. There it was, a symbol of the solid Victorian age when a gentleman had everything handsome about him and as much elbow-room as he wanted. A massive silver inkstand with an inscription bore witness to an earlier Hardwick with forty years service on the Bench. He had been Nathaniel James, and the great grandson to whom this trophy had descended was wont to feel some gratitude that he had been spared the Nathaniel. His glance left Miss Silver and dropped to the inscription. Against this background of respectability and worth the conversation in which he was now taking part appeared fantastic.

But there had been two murders, and he was being seriously warned that he might be the subject of a third. He spoke as much in protest against his own thoughts as against anything she had said.

"I think we need not exaggerate. And I think you are assuming a good deal. For one thing, I haven't admitted to any special knowledge, and I don't see that you have any grounds for imputing it. I have made a statement to the police. I have nothing to add to that statement."

He heard his own words, and was aware that they received no credence. Abruptly, and with complete irrelevance, he was reminded of an examination taken when he was rising twelve. There was a *viva*, and he had gone in feeling quite all right, and then all at once his inside was shaking like a jelly and he got his very first answer wrong. He knew it was wrong because of the look in the examiner's eye. At this moment Miss Silver had that identical look. He had made the wrong answer, and she was, not angry, but rather sorry about it. She said,

"Major Hardwick, I said last night that I would not press you then, but there has been another murder, and I feel obliged to do so now. I will tell you in confidence that the local police have made up their minds that Miss Anning is in this case the murderer, and since it is accepted that the motive is to be found in an attempt by Marie to blackmail the person who committed the earlier crime, this would also involve her in that. Mr. Cardozo is out of it. He had gone to London, and very fortunately for himself he was being shadowed by the police. It is not possible that he can have killed Marie. That leaves Mrs. Maybury and Miss Anning, and the circumstances of this second crime are such that they are considered to point strongly to Miss Anning. If you do not speak, she will be arrested in the morning. An accusation of this sort once brought is never wholly forgotten. Apart from the damage to her business, Mrs. Anning's health would almost certainly be seriously affected. I believe that you are in a painful and difficult position, but I urge you to tell what you know."

She was aware of a change in him. The antagonism between them was gone. His eyes were candid and serious.

"It might make very little difference."

"You did not see the murder committed?"

"No—no—of course not!"

Something that was not quite a smile just touched her gravity. She said,

"I did not think you had. I believe you would not in that case have remained silent. What did you see?"

He threw out a hand.

"Just someone coming up from the beach."

"After Mrs. Maybury went down?"

"Immediately after. Pippa was still crossing the shingle in the direction of the hut. Someone came up the path from the beach and went past me. That is all. You see how little it is."

"But you know who it was?"

He remained silent.

"This person passed you, and went where? In the direction of Cliff Edge?"

"And of Sea View, and the town."

"Was it Miss Anning?"

"I can't tell you anything more."

"Not even that?"

"No—not now—not yet."

Miss Silver coughed with a slight note of reproof. If she pushed him too far she might get nothing more. There were other points. She said,

"Very well, we will leave it. What did you do after this person had passed you?"

"You know that already. I waited for Pippa Maybury to come back. She wasn't very long—seven or eight minutes from start to finish—perhaps ten—certainly not more than three or four in the hut."

"Not long enough for anything like a quarrel?"

"Oh, no."

"And she came back in a very considerable state of distress?"

"Very considerable."

"You didn't speak to her?"

"I didn't know what had happened. I didn't think she would want to know she had been seen."

"And for the same reason you did not follow her back to the house?"

"Well—yes."

Where was this taking them? He was to know immediately.

"Instead, you went down to the beach hut yourself."

It was not a question, it was a calm and positive statement. He could find nothing better than,

"What makes you think so?"

She said,

"How could it be otherwise? If you did not follow Mrs. Maybury, you would certainly have gone down to the hut. It was plain that she had been greatly disturbed and upset, and I am quite sure you would have felt yourself bound to investigate. Will you now tell me what you found when you reached the hut?"

"Just what Pippa has described. Field had been stabbed. He was lying on his face with one arm thrown out. He was dead."

"Did you see the dagger?"

"Mrs. Field's paper-knife? Oh, yes—it was sticking in his back."

"You recognized it. And you decided that it would be better out of the way."

"I?"

"I think so, Major Hardwick. It linked the crime with your household. I suppose you threw it into the sea?"

He nodded.

"It seemed the best thing to do at the time."

She shook her head in reproof.

"It was extremely wrong. Major Hardwick—did you at any time believe that it was Pippa Maybury who had stabbed Alan Field?"

"I knew she hadn't."

"How?"

"I suppose I might as well tell you. I could hear Pippa on the shingle. I knew when she reached the hut. Well, she cried out—I heard her. It must have been when she stumbled over the body and came down. It wasn't a scream, you know, just a sort of gasping cry. I waited a minute and listened. Then I started to go down the path, but before I got half way she came out, running across the shingle. I only just had time to get back to the upper path and out of her way before she passed me."

She was silent for a few moments. Then she said,

"You have made up your mind to tell me no more than this?"

"For the moment."

She said in a reflective tone,

"You want time— —"

It was what she had wanted herself and what Frank Abbott had given her—time to bring pressure to bear upon James Hardwick, time to test his reactions to that pressure. And now it was he who wanted time. It was not hard to guess that it would be for the same reasons as her own. There was pressure to be brought, perhaps a warning to be given. But in this case at what a risk! Would the double murderer submit to pressure, accept the warning, and with it the label of guilt? Or would there be a third and most disastrous attempt to find a violent solution? She said,

"I can give you a little time, but not much. After that I shall have to go to the police with what you have told me. If I do not go immediately, it is because I very much hope that you will take this course yourself. And meanwhile I beg of you to remember that you are in danger. If your knowledge is suspected, the danger may be grave. I beg you to put aside all preconceived ideas and to remember only this, that with each crime a killer becomes bolder and more ruthless. Pray do not neglect this warning."

Going from the study to her bedroom, she encountered Carmona on the landing, bathing-dress, towel and bathrobe over her arm, and made trite comment.

"You are going to bathe——"

"Presently, when the tide is right. I think we all are. Pippa and Bill have gone on. They say they don't mind walking about half a mile to get out of their depth, but as far as the rest of us are concerned, we would rather wait for the sea to come to us. I'm going to see if I can get out to the Black Rock. I've never managed it yet, but I don't mind trying if James is going to be there."

"He is a good swimmer?"

"Oh, yes. He and Lady Castleton are our star performers. Esther is quite good too. She and Adela were at school by the sea, and swimming was *the* thing. Colonel Trevor isn't bad either."

"And Mrs. Trevor?"

Carmona laughed.

"Oh, she doesn't go in! She says it upsets her waves!"

A little later as she was coming downstairs Miss Silver met Carmona again, coming up. She was still carrying towel, robe, and bathing-suit. Miss Silver stopped to admire.

"Such a pretty green. It should be most becoming. I shall look forward to seeing you swim out to the Rock in it."

As she spoke, it struck her that Carmona's expression had altered. She was paler, and she had lost the look of pleasurable anticipation which had been noticeable when they had met so short a time ago. Her smile was a little forced as she said,

"Well, I don't think I'm bathing after all. I find the others are going to race each other to the Rock, and I should be in the way. I'm not in that class at all, you know. I should just be left behind, and then James would feel that he had to come back for me. It's quite a long way out to the Black Rock, and I should be on his mind. He wouldn't like me to do it alone."

It seemed to Miss Silver that she was putting forward all these reasons in order to convince herself, and that in spite of them her spirits were a good deal dashed. They parted with no more said, Carmona continuing on her way upstairs, and Miss Silver descending to the hall.

The two older ladies were just going out. They carried towels and bathing-suits, and were proposing to change later on in the hut. To their enquiries she replied that she would join them presently.

Colonel Trevor, it appeared, had letters to write, and Mrs. Trevor was going down into the town to have her hair washed and set.

Miss Silver passed on into the morning-room, where she left the door ajar and waited.

After a little while Mrs. Trevor went down the stairs and out by the front door, which stood open to take the breeze. Then the house fell silent again until James Hardwick emerged from the study. He went upstairs and out of sight and hearing. Miss Silver judged that it would not be long before he was down again. Since there was only the one instrument in the house, she could not prudently use the telephone until she could reasonably count on being safe from interruption. She set the door a little wider and waited.

Carmona and James came down together, she in a flowered beach-suit, bright green sandals and shady hat, and he bareheaded in a dark-blue regulation swimming-suit, with a gaily patterned bath-robe draped across his shoulders and a towel over his arm. Snatches of what they said came through the partly open door.

"Don't be disappointed, darling. I just want to have this

talk. Esther never sits about after swimming, and it seems such a good opportunity. We can go any other time."

He had an arm about her shoulders, and Carmona laughed a little and said,

"Oh, yes, of course we can. It wouldn't be any fun in a crowd."

They went through the drawing-room and out by the door to the terrace. Miss Silver came from the morning-room to watch them go. Carmona was happy again.

They went down the hot cement path and through the gate at the bottom of the garden. When it had closed behind them, Miss Silver went to the study and shut herself in.

Inspector Abbott had left Sea View.

No, he was not at the police station.

Inspector Abbott? The receptionist at the George would see if he was in the hotel.

She stood at the writing-table and waited through some very long minutes until the line came alive and Frank Abbott was saying,

"Miss Silver?"

"Yes, Frank."

"What is it?"

"I am not at all easy."

"What can I do for you?"

"You are a good swimmer?"

"Well, I rather flatter myself——"

"Then——" She spoke rapidly for a minute or two. He received his instructions. Even if the weather had not rendered them extremely agreeable, there was an urgency in voice and manner which he would have hesitated to neglect. As it was, it was easy and pleasant enough. He had not been fool enough to come down to the sea in this heat without providing for at least a swim before breakfast, and the George on the sea front was no more than an easy distance from the private beach which served the houses on the cliff.

At her end Miss Silver rang off, and with her mind somewhat relieved picked up her knitting-bag and went to join the others.

CHAPTER XXXVII

LADY CASTLETON and Mrs. Field were in their accustomed place. Since there was at this hour nothing to be gained by such close proximity to the beach hut, the sun being now directly overhead and no shade obtainable, Miss Silver found herself a little surprised that they should not have preferred to be at a greater distance from the scene of Wednesday's crime. The surprise deepened when she learned that both ladies intended retiring into the hut in order to change. Some of this surprise must have been apparent, as Esther Field remarked,

"You think that strange. But isn't it really better that we should just go on using everything before there are any foolish stories? They start so easily, and are so hard to get rid of. A friend of mine found that to her cost. There was a violent death in the house—a relative committed suicide there. She had a feeling about using the room, and in less than no time people were saying it was haunted and no one would sleep there. It was very inconvenient, as it left them a room short, and in the end she had to give up her own bedroom and move into it. But it was quite a long time before the talk died down. So we thought——"

Miss Silver measured the foot of her little pink bootee.

"Yes, that was wise of you. Especially as Mrs. Hardwick tells me they are anxious to sell the house."

Esther Field tilted the large sun-umbrella which shaded her. Having never been able to acquire a fondness for glare, she had been delighted to discover this antique object in a corner of the hall amongst a collection of sticks which had belonged to Octavius Hardwick. She found the holland cover and green lining a very comfortable protection from the heat. But Adela Castleton sat in the eye of the sun and looked out over the bright water which reflected it.

With a slight preliminary cough Miss Silver ventured a remark on this. She did not herself feel the heat—the English summer was so sadly short that it was a pity not to take advantage of it—but she was not averse from the protection of an old black umbrella so much more often in use against the rain. She said,

"You do not feel the sun, Lady Castleton?"

"Oh, no."

There was a hint of surprise that the question should have been put—almost of surprise that Miss Silver should have addressed her at all. There was certainly nothing to encourage a continuance of the conversation. Yet Miss Silver continued it.

"You do not find that it gives you a headache?"

"No, I do not."

Miss Silver went on knitting.

"Mrs Hardwick mentioned that you had been suffering from headaches, and I wondered whether it was really prudent to expose yourself so freely to this heat."

Adela Castleton looked out over the sand to that bright stretch of sea. The shingle ended, the sand ran out, the tide was coming in. The Black Rock showed like a distant speck. Without taking any notice of what Miss Silver had said or so much as looking at her she got to her feet.

"Well, I think I shall go in," she said, and strolled towards the hut. "Are you coming, Esther? James and Carmona are down by the pools, but she isn't going to swim. It's a pity you never had her taught properly."

She raised her voice to carry the last few words, and so came to the beach hut and went in. The door stood open to the sun and to the air. The floor had been scrubbed. A new gay strip of matting lay across it. Under it, stubborn and enduring, the stain of Alan's blood.

As she watched, Miss Silver could not see that there was either hesitancy or avoidance. Lady Castleton crossed the threshold with an even step and shut out the sun.

Turning her head again, she saw that Esther Field was folding her white embroidery and wrapping it in an old soft handkerchief.

"I don't really care to walk so far down the beach, but Adela never can bear to wait. If she wants a thing, it has to happen at once. But I'm not like that. I don't mind how long I wait if there is something worth while at the end of it."

She too went up the beach, and she too was watched. But

at the closed door there was again no hesitation. Her hand came up and knocked. Then she lifted the latch and went in.

Lady Castleton was the first to come out—black bathing-suit modelling the perfect figure, black and emerald scarf hiding the close-bound hair, a bright green towelling robe across her arm. She went down the beach without looking back, passed Miss Silver without a glance or a word, and so down to the water's edge, where she stood talking to James and Carmona.

Esther Field followed her. She too wore a plain black suit, but, conscious that she no longer had a figure slim enough to display, she hugged her robe about her and only handed it to Carmona at the water's edge.

Carmona came up with it over her arm. She looked relaxed and happy. Her brief sun-bathing suit was splashed and wet. Its colours contrasted gaily with the bare brown of her skin. She slipped into the matching overdress and buttoned it. Then she sat down to watch the three swimmers who were making for the Rock. The hot, lazy time went by.

Frank Abbott was finding his assignment a pleasant one. The temperature was probably climbing towards the nineties. Colt and the Superintendent were stewing in it, and the hotter it got, the more passionately would they feel about arresting Miss Anning. And here he was, in the water where they couldn't get at him. He had now for many years considered Miss Silver to be unique, but seldom had he experienced such a glow of admiration as when he reflected that it was her beneficent hand which had plucked him from being a fellow sufferer with the Superintendent and Colt and plunged him into this cool buoyancy. He began to assemble a suitable tribute, enhanced by quotation from Alfred, Lord Tennyson:

"Break, break, break,
At the foot of thy cliffs, O Sea (or was it crags?)
And I would that my heart could utter
The thoughts that arise in me."

After which he would, of course, do his best to utter them.

As he rounded the point, the Black Rock came into view, looking small and far away. It would take him another quarter of an hour, he judged. Having all but reached it early yesterday morning, he had been near enough to identify it as one of those chimneys which rise up suddenly in prolongation of a headland. On the landward side it rose sheer from the water, but towards the sea where the tides had fretted it there was a series of ledges, accessible to swimmers at any but the highest of the spring tides and a pleasant basking-ground in weather like this.

As he drew nearer, someone dived from the rock and began to swim towards the shore—a woman in a black bathing-suit. She swam strongly and without turning her head. There was no reason to suppose that she had seen him.

He came to the shoreward side of the rock and skirted it, paddling gently. He might be too early, or too late. There might have been no need for him to have come at all. Miss Silver had not really told him very much. He was to swim out to the Black Rock, and he was to avoid being seen. There might be two people there. What passed between them could be of vital importance.

He paddled slowly. So far only one person had shown up, and she was making for the shore. Then, as the thought passed through his mind, the sound of voices came to him, a man's first, and then a woman's. That was all for the moment. He must come nearer if he was to hear what was being said. Another silent stroke or two and the sound carried words. It was the man speaking, and he was James Hardwick. He said,

"I don't see that I can do anything else."

The woman laughed.

"You can hold your tongue."

"Not if they arrest Miss Anning."

"And why not?"

"I tell you, I saw you. I followed Pippa, and I saw her go down to the hut. She must have given you the fright of your life, but she didn't see you. I suppose you were close up against the cliff where the path comes down. As soon as she had passed you and got on to the shingle you came up the path, running."

She laughed again.

"Oh, not I! I was in bed and asleep—I just don't qualify. You see, I went up early with a headache and took a couple of sleeping-tablets. Carmona was there. And when you all came up to bed she looked in just to make sure that I was really asleep—as of course I was."

James Hardwick said,

"Carmona brought you the tablets and saw you drink something out of a tumbler. She came into your room somewhere after half-past-ten and heard you breathing as if you were asleep. There was still plenty of time for you to keep your appointment at the hut—perhaps an hour, perhaps even longer. You had all the time you needed, but you overran it. Of course you didn't know that Pippa had an appointment too. A minute or two earlier and she might have been a very inconvenient witness."

Her voice hardened.

"This is all quite absurd. You cannot seriously suppose that I went to the hut at midnight to meet Alan Field. That sort of thing is hardly in my line. *Really*!"

He said,

"No of course not. I didn't mean anything like that."

"Then what did you mean?"

"I think he was probably blackmailing you."

"I can assure you that there is nothing in my life which would give him the opportunity."

"There are things that can be twisted—there are things which affect other people. All I know is that you came up from the beach on Wednesday night just after Pippa went down. She cried out when she came to the hut, and I started to go down after her. Then I heard you running. I only just managed to get out of your way before you passed me."

"It was not I who passed you."

He was silent. Her voice came again with an edge to it.

"It was the middle of the night. How can you pretend that you could recognize anyone in the dark like that?"

"I did recognize you."

She drew a sharp breath.

"How?"

"How does one recognize anyone? By your height? By the way you walked?—no, I should have said by the way you ran. And that is a more individual thing than a walk, especially in a woman. So few women run well."

"And when have you seen me run?"

"Last year, when we stayed with Esther at Woolacombe. The very first day—you came running down over those sands. I thought then that I had never seen a woman run so well. And on Wednesday night you came up that path at the same smooth pace, where Pippa was stumbling and choking for breath. Besides, these summer nights are not really dark, you know—I recognized you as you went by. Afterwards, when I had been down to the hut and found that Field had been stabbed—"

She broke in, still with that edge to her voice.

"It seems to me that you will have something to explain to the police yourself!"

"I suppose so. I should, of course, have rung them up at once."

"They will want to know why you did not."

"Yes."

After a moment's silence he went on.

"I didn't know why you stabbed him—I didn't want to know. I thought there might have been—well, pardonable circumstances. You were a guest in my house. I made up my mind that I would hold my tongue unless someone else was arrested—I didn't see how I could go farther than that. And then you killed the girl."

She laughed.

"Are you wasting pity over her? How like a man! She was a cheap blackmailer concerned with nothing but making a good purse for herself. She came to the hut with that foreign man whom the police had up for questioning. I heard them on the shingle and hadn't time to get away. I stood behind the towels that were hanging to dry at the back. If they were going to give the alarm, I thought I could get away whilst they went to telephone. But they had business of their own. The man bent over the body and began to search it. He was looking for some paper, and when he had found it, that was all he seemed to care about. But once the torch tilted, the beam struck me full across the face. The towel had slipped, and that girl saw me. Of course I didn't know it at the time. She didn't call out, or say anything to the man. When he stood up, she said they must find a pool, and he must wash, and not risk

going up the same path again in case there was anyone about.
The tide was low enough for them to get round the next point,
and they could take another way up. So I waited until they were
gone. And then, before I could get away up the path, I heard
Pippa coming down."

She might have been talking of the most everyday occurrence
—so tiresome to have missed the bus, or have failed to fit in
some casual appointment. But Frank Abbott, listening to the
easy cultured voice, was aware that it sounded a warning note.
Not in itself, but just because it had fallen on this easy tone.
He began to move round to the seaward side of the Rock with
the echo of an old tag sounding in his mind—"Dead men tell
no tales." Were you quite as frank as all that came to if there
was going to be any risk of the tale being told again?

On the other side of the rock Adela Castleton and James
Hardwick sat side by side on a ledge that was just above water.
The sun shone down on them, and a slow ripple lapped their
feet.

"Well," she said, "that is really all. You can now go and find
the police and do the thing handsomely. I think, perhaps, I
won't come with you." There was a faintly mocking inflection
on the words.

James looked down, frowning. Yes, it was over—or would
be soon, and the sooner the better. He did not see Adela
Castleton's hand go up to the green and emerald scarf which
was bound about her head. It came away with the small heavy
spanner which had been hidden under the bow. He did not see
it come down hard and strong. He felt the blow, but not the
deep cool plunge into green water.

And Adela Castleton laughed—not loudly, but with a
singular note of triumph. There had been three dangers in her
path, and this was the third and last. Two men and a woman,
all quite sure of their own safety and of their power to injure
her, each eliminated after a separate and careful plan. And
now it was she who would be safe. As she let herself down
into the water after James Hardwick she had it all mapped out.
How he had slipped climbing on the Rock, how he had fallen
and struck his head, how she had dived in after him and done
all she could to save his life. Presently she would swim round to

the other side of the Rock and try desperately to attract attention. It was a completely foolproof plan. All these thoughts were exultantly present as she watched James Hardwick slide down off the rock into the sea. The sun was so hot that it would be pleasant to be in the water again. She let herself down off the ledge, dipped under, and came up to see Frank Abbott no more than a couple of yards away.

It was a shocking blow, but she had her part all ready to step into. She gasped and said,

"Major Hardwick—he fell! I'm afraid he hit his head! Oh, Inspector Abbott, it is you! He went down—I am afraid he is hurt!"

For the next few moments Frank had not even time to think that he had probably failed to save James Hardwick's life. He went down, and did not think until afterwards that he might be intended to stay there. But before he could clear his eyes or see what was happening he bumped into James coming up, grabbed him, and got a kick for his pains. They broke surface together, James with a gasping for breath and a wild flailing of the arms, Frank letting go and sheering off, since it was obvious that James was a good deal less dead than dangerous— muzzy in the head and fighting mad. Life-saving courses taught you how to knock the other fellow out when he tried to drown you, but in this case perhaps better not. Frank had seen that something bright in Adela Castleton's hand as it fell. He thought James had probably been hit enough already, and just as well that he should be capable of self-defence in case there were any more tricks up the murderer's sleeve.

But Adela Castleton was too intelligent not to know when she was beaten. She could have coped with one man half drowned and half stunned and have carried her plan through to the end, but not with this policeman, fit and strong, and as good a swimmer as herself. And even if she could have out-witted them both and eliminated them both, there was no way in which two such deaths could be explained. No, it was over. She had played, and she had lost. She told herself that it had been a good game and worth playing. She had nothing to regret.

By the time that James had stopped choking and Frank had helped him up on to the ledge from which he had fallen, Adela

Castleton's black and green scarf was a hundred yards away. The water was perfectly calm and clear, and she was heading out to sea.

CHAPTER XXXVIII

THE person least surprised was Esther Field.

"You see, I have known Adela for so long, and she has always been the same—if she wanted something she wouldn't let anyone or anything stand in the way. It always frightened me a little. Geoffrey Castleton was engaged to someone else before she married him, but she didn't let it stand in her way. The other girl never had a chance—I don't suppose Geoffrey had either. But he wasn't really happy with her, you know, and he died young. I remember his saying to me once that after you were thirty there really wasn't anything very much to look forward to."

Miss Silver coughed.

"A tragic thing to say."

Esther put her handkerchief to eyes already red.

"I couldn't get it out of my mind. And he was considered such a rising man. I said something about that, and he said, 'My dear Esther, one can't live on a career.' It was all very sad. And lately—lately I have been frightened. Not all the time, you know, but sometimes when it came over me. Because— well, you guessed, didn't you, that Alan was trying to get money out of me. Those foolish letters that Irene wrote to Pen . . . People wouldn't have understood them, or his answers. It just wasn't in him not to be kind when a woman said she cared. But if they had been published it would all have been shockingly misunderstood. And if Alan had been trying to get money out of me—and he was—it seemed dreadfully likely that he was doing the same thing with Adela, and when he was stabbed—I couldn't help—being afraid——" Her voice broke, and it was some moments before she could go on.

Miss Silver's sympathetic attention helped her back to self-control.

"You are so kind," she said. "It has always helped me to talk to you. It does help when things you hardly dare to think about——" She pressed her handkerchief to her eyes again. "That poor girl Marie—I didn't like her very much, and I suppose she was trying to get money out of Adela too. But it was a fearful thing to do, and when everyone kept saying that it must have been a man, because no woman would have had the strength to choke anyone like that, I couldn't help remembering how strong Adela was——" Her voice tripped and fell to a stumbling whisper. "She did—choke—a dog once. One of those big farm animals. It attacked her, and she got it by the throat—and choked it. I couldn't help—remembering. But I didn't think—she would try—and harm James——"

"He could not allow Miss Anning to be arrested."

"No, no—of course not. The poor Annings—did you see them when you went down there just now? I ought to have asked before, but I somehow couldn't think of anyone but Adela—only I must, mustn't I? How are they?"

"Yes, I saw them. Miss Anning has been under a great strain, but her mother is surprisingly well. She has, in fact, to a great extent come out of the vague state in which she has been for so long."

"I always liked her," said Esther Field. "She wasn't clever, you know—but don't you think one gets a little tired of clever people? She was kind, and so fond of her family. I shall be so glad if she can be more like she used to be. It must have been very hard for Darsie. And then all these terrible things happening."

It was some time before Inspector Abbott was free. He accompanied the motor launch which put out in search of Adela Castleton, and the search could not be given up in a hurry. She was a strong swimmer, and there was more than one possibility. It might have been her intention to swim out to sea until she could swim no more, or there might have been a moment when she turned shorewards again to make for another part of the beach. When at length the launch put back, he took time to change, have something to eat, and call in at the police station before responding to the message which awaited him there.

"It's Miss Silver," he told Inspector Colt. "She says Mrs. Anning has a statement to make."

"Mrs. Anning!" His tone was one of protest. "Is she fit to make one?"

"Miss Silver says so. You had better come along and judge for yourself."

Colt nodded.

"You'll have to give me about twenty minutes before I can get away. We can meet at Sea View."

Up at Cliff Edge there was much that Miss Silver was anxious to hear. The bare facts reluctantly imparted by James Hardwick had left her uncertain as to just how much Frank had overheard, and to what extent the police would now be satisfied as to the murderer's identity.

When he had given her a lively account of what had happened, he said,

"And now perhaps you'll tell me whether it was second sight, or witchcraft, or what-have-you that made you send me off to the Rock in the nick of time."

The morning-room was an ugly room, but it was cool, and the chairs were comfortable. Frank's slim length was stretched out in the largest of them. His fair hair shone. Suit and socks were a delicate study in grey. With eyes half shut and a teasing gleam between the lashes, he looked as if he had never exerted himself in his life.

Miss Silver, in a small upright chair, was engaged upon a crochet edging to one of the pink bootees. She thought it right to administer a mild reproof.

"My dear Frank, you should not use such exaggerated language."

"The Chief definitely suspects you of knowing more than you ought to. He has a secret fund of country superstitions tucked away in the back of his mind, and there are times when you set them buzzing."

The crochet-hook went in and out.

"Chief Inspector Lamb is a most worthy man. As to my suggestion that you should swim out to the Black Rock, I had already warned Major Hardwick that in my opinion he might be in considerable danger until he had told the police what he knew. I did not share that knowledge—I could only guess at it. And until it was shared, I felt sure that he would be in danger. It was, of course, plain to me that he could not allow Miss Anning's arrest to take place, and that he intended to warn Lady Castleton before giving his information to the police. When, therefore, I learned that he was proposing to allow this conversation to take place at so dangerous and lonely a spot as the Black Rock, I began to feel extremely anxious."

He cocked an eyebrow.

"You are not going to ask me to believe that Hardwick told you he was going to swim out to the Rock for the express purpose of warning Lady Castleton!"

"It was perfectly apparent that that was his intention."

"Do you mind telling me how? On the face of it, nothing could have looked less like anything of the sort, since Mrs. Field was one of the party."

"Mrs. Field does not care to sit about in a wet bathing-dress. When she has had her swim she prefers to come out of the water and change into ordinary clothes. I discovered this from overhearing a short conversation between Major and Mrs. Hardwick. I was waiting in the morning-room with the door open, and they were coming down the stairs. He then implied that he wanted to have a talk with Lady Castleton."

Frank burst out laughing.

"How simple it always is when you know how!"

She inclined her head.

"As soon as they had left the house I went into the study and rang you up."

"Thank goodness you did!"

She withdrew the crochet-hook for the last time.

"It was indeed providential," she said.

CHAPTER XXXIX

Miss Anning received Miss Silver and the two Inspectors with an air of protest quite stiff enough to stand alone. She had done her best to keep them out, and she had failed. Since Dr. Adamson, called in as a reinforcement, had declared that the improvement in Mrs. Anning's condition was really quite staggering, and that as far as he could see anything that continued to rouse her and take her out of herself would be all to the good, there was no more to be said. She led the way in silence, and when they were all seated took her place upon a hard bedroom stool.

The first thing that Frank Abbott noticed was that Mrs. Anning's embroidery had made considerable progress. She no longer drew a knotless thread through canvas upon which it left no mark. Two flowers and a leaf had been completed since he had had his last brief interview with her. Her appearance too had changed. The eyes were no longer blank, the pose no longer that of a person sunk in dreams. She greeted them quietly but with some obvious pleasure, especially in the case of Miss Silver, to whom she observed.

"Darsie thinks it does me harm to talk, but she is quite mistaken. I have been ill, but I am much better now. And though Alan behaved very badly and I never did like that French girl, people ought not to be murdered. And I would not like any innocent person to be suspected." She was making her neat, even stitches as she spoke,

Frank Abbott said,

"That is why we hoped that you would help us, Mrs. Anning."

His quiet cultured voice gave her confidence. She laid down her embroidery frame.

"What do you want me to say?"

"We want you to tell us just what you remember about Wednesday night."

She was sitting in a rather upright chair. Her grey hair had been fluffed out and made the most of, and there was a faint flush on her cheeks. Darsie's dark colouring must have come from the other side of the family. Mrs. Anning's skin was fair, and her eyes blue. She said.

"Oh, I remember everything."

"Then will you tell us just what happened?"

She closed her eyes for a moment, then opened them again with a wondering expression.

"Oh, yes—I went out—I don't remember why—I sometimes do when it has been hot ... No, that wasn't the reason! I remember now, I was looking out of the window and I saw Alan going down the garden."

"What time was this?"

"I don't know—it was late. I couldn't sleep, and when I saw Alan I thought I would go after him."

"What made you think of doing that?"

She said in a pettish tone,

"Darsie wouldn't let me see him, and there were things I wanted to say, so I thought it would be a good opportunity."

"Were you dressed?"

"Oh, no. But I put on my nice dark blue dressing-gown, and I had my bedroom slippers—they are so comfortable."

"And you followed Alan Field?"

"Oh, yes, I followed him. Not too close, you know. It was very pleasant on the cliff path, and I wanted to see where he was going. When he went down the path to the beach I went after him. When I got to the bottom he was over by the Cliff Edge hut with his torch on, opening the door. I waited until he had gone inside, and then I went there too. I thought perhaps he would hear me on the shingle and come out again, but he didn't—and I really made very little noise in those soft slippers. Or perhaps he thought I was someone else, because of course he was expecting someone."

She paused with a small complacent smile and looked about her. Miss Silver who had been so kind—this nice policeman who reminded her of the young fellows who used to come about the house in the old happy days—the other Inspector, writing down what she said—they were all pleased with her. She could feel them being pleased. But not Darsie—oh no, not Darsie. She gave a small defiant shrug and turned away from the rigid disapproval of Darsie's face and figure.

Miss Silver sat in one of the small straight chairs which she preferred. She wore a dress of grey artificial silk with a pattern which reminded Frank of black and white tadpoles. On her head the black straw hat from which she had judged it seemly to remove a bunch of coloured flowers. Her hands in Dorothy's cream net gloves were folded in her lap. She had heard Mrs. Anning's tale before, and she listened to it now with the approval due to a pupil who is acquitting herself well.

"And then?" said Frank Abbott.

"I heard someone else on the shingle. She made a great deal more noise than I did—but then of course she hadn't got nice soft slippers like mine. I stood up against the back of the hut, and with the dark scarf I had put over my hair she didn't see me at all. She went round to the front, and I heard her speaking to Alan."

"Could you hear what they said?"

She gave a curious little laugh, like a child who feels it is being clever.

"They were quarrelling—dreadfully. Not loud, you know, but she sounded as if she hated him."

"Mrs. Anning—did you know who it was?"

She looked at him with surprise.

"But of course I did! We all knew each other so well in the old days. It was Adela Castleton."

Inspector Colt wrote the name down.

Frank Abbott said, "What were they quarrelling about?"

"Letters," said Mrs. Anning. "He wanted to publish them, and she didn't want him to. They weren't hers—Adela wasn't like that. They were her sister's. It was all a long time ago, and she was only a young girl. And young girls do very foolish things, because they think they know everything and they don't."

The tears came up into her eyes and brimmed over. To Darsie Anning they seemed to fall in scalding drops upon her very heart. She set herself to endure.

Mrs. Anning was speaking again.

"He wanted her to give him money, and she said she would. They talked about how much it was to be. They had stopped quarrelling. It didn't seem like Adela any more."

"Do you mean you were not sure that it was Lady Castleton?"

"Oh no, it was Adela. But it wasn't like her to give way like that—it frightened me. And she said, 'You can have it now—I've got my cheque-book with me. Just give me that book of Esther's to write on.' And then all at once he gave a kind of a groan and fell down, and she laughed. I didn't know what had happened—I don't see how I could. When you know people, you don't think about them stabbing anyone. I just thought he must have tripped over something, and however badly he had behaved, I didn't think Adela Castleton ought to have laughed. And then, before I had time to think anything more, I heard someone else coming across the shingle."

"Mrs. Maybury?"

Mrs. Anning looked mildly astonished.

"Oh, no—not then. It was two people. One of them was that French girl whom I never liked, Marie Bonnet—and I suppose I ought not to say so now, because Darsie tells me she has been murdered too. Only you can't really like people just because they have got themselves murdered trying to blackmail someone—for of course that is what she must have been trying to do."

"Please go on, Mrs. Anning. One of the people who was coming down to the hut was Marie Bonnet. Who was the other?"

"It was a man—a foreign man. It is curious that foreigners never really lose their accent, isn't it? I could hear it when he spoke to Marie. He said, 'I will control myself—I will control myself. But I must see whether he has the paper. If he has, then he is my brother's murderer, for only with his life would Felipe have parted with it.' 'Now,' I thought, 'what will Adela Castleton do? If she comes out they will see her, and if they go in they will see her, and that will look very odd.' And I thought it very odd that there wasn't any sound from inside the hut—nothing from Adela, and nothing from Alan. It really did seem very strange."

"Yes—go on."

She looked from one to another of them like a child seeking for reassurance. Miss Silver supplied it.

"You are doing very well indeed, Mrs. Anning. Pray continue."

"The man put on a torch, and they went round to the door of the hut. And then they both called out—not loud, you know but as if there was something dreadful. Marie said, '*O mon dieu! Il est mort!*' and the man said a lot of things that sounded like Spanish or Portugese. My husband and I made a tour in Portugal once at the time of the vintage, such lovely grapes and so cheap, and that is what it sounded like. Only when he was talking to Marie they spoke English. She said, 'Quick, quick—we must come away!' And he said, "No, no, no—not until I see if he has the paper!' She said he was mad, and they would be mixed up in a murder. And he said she didn't understand—it was his uncle's letter telling them where the treasure was, and he would be mad if he let it go. And then, I think, he must have found it, because he began to talk his own language again, all very quick and excited and rather as if he was swearing. Marie went on saying that they must get away, and all at once he was in a hurry too. Then she said they mustn't go back up the path, they must find a pool where he could wash, and on around the next point and up another way. They went away down the beach, and Adela Castleton came out of the hut, but she hadn't got as far as the cliff when we could hear someone else coming down from the cliff path. Adela didn't come back. She must have stood close in under the cliff to hide. I went farther round the hut, and I waited to see who was coming now. There was a sound as if someone had tripped over the threshold and come down. Whoever it was called out, and there was the flicker of a torch. So I looked round the front corner of the hut, and there was a girl with very fair hair and a white dress. She had a torch in her hand and it was shaking. One minute the beam went up in the air and the next minute it shone down on a dagger that was sticking in Alan's back. That was when I knew he must be dead. It didn't seem as if it could be real. He deserved to be punished, you know, but it isn't right to murder people, and I was sorry for the girl, because it wasn't her fault. Of course she ought not to have come there, but it must have been a dreadful shock. She was making little crying noises under her breath, and when she got up the front of her dress was most dreadfully stained. She went away, and I was just thinking of going myself, when a man came down the path. I didn't want to have to wait any longer, but of course I had to. I really did think Darsie would miss me if I didn't get away soon, because sometimes these hot nights she looks in and gets me a drink. She doesn't sleep very well, I'm afraid, and she is always so very good to me."

Darsie Anning felt the hard prick of tears behind eyes which had not wept for years.

"Such a good daughter," said Mrs. Anning's placid voice. "And I thought how anxious she would be if she went into my room and found I wasn't there. But of course I had to wait."

"Did you know who the man was?"

"Oh, yes. It was James Hardwick. I used to see him sometimes when he was a boy, and after his uncle died he came to see Darsie and she thought I would like to see him too. He had a torch, and when he put it on the light caught his signet-ring and I saw the crest—a bird with something in its beak. I have very good sight."

"What did he do?"

"He looked at Alan, and he said, 'Oh, my God!' And then he felt his pulse—only of course there wasn't any. And after that he pulled out the dagger and went away down the beach with it towards the sea, and I thought he wouldn't hear me on the shingle whilst he was walking on it himself, so I got away as fast as I could."

"And that is all?"

"Oh, yes. Except that Darsie had come out to look for me. She went into my room, just as I was afraid she might, and she said I had given her a really terrible fright and I mustn't ever do it again."

There was a little silence when she had finished speaking. Then Frank Abbott said,

"Thank you very much, Mrs. Anning. That is a very clear statement. As far as it concerns Marie Bonnet and José Cardozo, the man who was with her, he will of course be asked to confirm it. As regards Major Hardwick and Mrs. Maybury, it coincides with statements they have made, and in Lady

Castleton's case, both Major Hardwick and I heard her make what amounted to an admission of her guilt."

Mrs. Anning reached for her embroidery frame.

"Adela Castleton was always the same," she said. "She had to have her own way. And it's no use, is it? There are times when you can't."

CHAPTER XL

COLONEL TREVOR had been profoundly shocked. Adela Castleton whom he had known for thirty years! It was the sort of thing you read about in the papers. Not that he read that kind of paper himself, but you couldn't always get away from the headlines. Monstrous! He didn't know what they were coming to! Well connected woman—well brought up—poor Geoffrey Castleton's widow—going about murdering people right and left—trying to murder James! Must have been mad—only possible explanation—stark, staring mad!

Maisie Trevor had already begun to say that she had always thought there was something a little odd about Adela. "And that very hot weather—well, I suppose it just finished her. But I always did think . . ." And presently there would be all sorts of instances of strange behaviour on the part of Adela Castleton.

Pippa wept on Bill Maybury's solid shoulder. She cried until her lovely white skin was blotched and her blue eyes practically invisible between swollen lids. All she wanted was to be able to go on crying with Bill's arm round her, and to know that no one was going to arrest her or take her away to prison. Bill would keep her safe, and even if her eyes swelled right up and she looked a complete mess, he would go on loving her just the same. In her secret mind she promised her own rather vague idea of God that she would never, never, never flirt with anyone again, or let anyone kiss her except Bill. It would be dull, but she wouldn't, she really wouldn't. She clung to Bill and told him so between her sobs. He kissed the top of her head and held her close.

"Won't you, Pippa?" he said.

In the big bedroom which had been Octavius Hardwick's Carmona stood looking down over the garden which grew wooden figureheads instead of flowers—a woman with blank eyes and jutting breast; a Triton with a great carved shell; an Admiral battered by storms and come at last into a quiet haven, and many more. The cement path ran between them to the cliff. Adela Castleton had gone down it to kill in the night, not once but twice—had gone down it again on the morning of that very day with murder in her heart for James. Alan had gone down it on Wednesday not knowing that his death was no more than half a dozen hours away. Pippa Maybury had come up it with the stain of his blood on her dress.

She heard the door open and shut again. James came up behind her, but she did not turn. He stood there, looking out too. Presently she said,

"How soon can we get away?"

"You can go tomorrow if you want to. At least I should think you could."

"No, no, I didn't mean that—I said *we*."

"I shall have to stay for the inquest. I shouldn't think they would want you."

"Of course I won't go!"

"Is it of course?"

"You know it is!"

He put his arms round her and she leaned against him. She thought, "It doesn't really matter as long as we are here together."

Miss Silver talked with Inspector Abbott in the morning-room.

"I shall be off by an early train, so I thought I had better come and pay my respects tonight and let you know how the Cardozo affair has panned out."

Really these modern expressions! Derived, of course, from the gold-mining industry, and in its way expressive, but one could hardly approve it. She said,

"You have interviewed Mr. Cardozo?"

"We have. You will remember that he was trying to trace his brother Felipe. On Wednesday he identified as his a body that had been taken out of the river, which is where I came into the case. On Thursday after the murder of Alan Field had taken place he went back on his identification and produced a yarn about Felipe having had a badly broken leg of which the body furnished no evidence. When it came out, as it did, that he had been on Field's track and had actually been in Cliffton at the time of the murder, it wasn't hard to guess why he had invented that broken leg. Felipe was in possession of a family paper which described the whereabouts of our old friend the Pirates' Hoard. It had been discovered by an uncle, reburied somewhere in his own house or garden, *but* he was himself bumped off before he could turn any of it into cash, and his property was sold to pay his debts. We got all this from Cardozo, who I really do believe is telling the truth. He says every time the property has come into the market the Cardozo family has missed the bus. Either they hadn't got the paper, or they couldn't raise the purchase price, and of course the greatest secrecy was necessary. Now the house is for sale again. Felipe had been foolish enough to confide in Alan Field, who swore he could raise the purchase price over here. Just what happened after that José doesn't know. He had a row with his brother over Field being taken in on the deal, and they shut down on him. He didn't know where they were or what they were doing. And then just the other day he heard that they had been seen over here—together. The man who told him knew Felipe well and gave a very good description of Field. José got the wind up and came bothering the Chief. Coming down to Wednesday—he had identified his brother's body and found out that Field was here. He made up his mind that Field had murdered Felipe and got away with the paper describing the whereabouts of the treasure. And he got into his car and drove away to find him. After that everything happened as already stated. He went to see him at Sea View and missed him, picked up Marie who was more than willing, and went off with her to the Jolly Fisherman. She has agreed to take a note to Field when she goes in, but she isn't in a hurry. They get back about eleven, and she plays Miss Anning a trick, obviously not for the first time. She goes in, the door is locked after her, and as soon as she thinks it safe she comes down again and gets out of the dining-room window. As she observed, it was a fine night for a walk.

"It must by then have been getting on for midnight. They are moving off, when Marie pulls him by the sleeve. She puts her lips to his ear and whispers. Someone else is getting out of that convenient dining-room window. They stand perfectly still, and a man drops to the ground and goes off round the house in the direction of the cliff path. When he has gone, Marie says 'That was Monsieur Field,' and Cardozo is angry. He wishes to follow and have it out with him, and that doesn't suit Marie at all. She tries to persuade him to put it off—to wait till tomorrow. She says he is angry, he will make a scene, she will get into trouble—perhaps even it may be a matter for the police, and what would he say to that? Cardozo admits that he would think very poorly of it, and he cools down. They talk a little longer, and then he says that he will be prudent and control himself, but why should they not walk along the cliff and see what has happened to Alan? Well, they do. Figuring it out, they must have just missed Mrs. Anning, who left by way of the glass door in the drawing-room. She must have been on her way down the path to the beach before they came to the place where it leaves the cliff path. They went on beyond that, and so they did not see Lady Castleton come along from Cliff Edge and go down too. But they didn't go very far. All at once Cardozo saw the flash of a torch on the beach—Field put on his torch when he went into the hut, and so did Lady Castleton. When Cardozo saw the light he took it into his head that Field was down there, and that it was a place where they might talk and no one disturb them. He turned back, went down the path to the beach, and came to the hut just as Mrs. Anning describes. Extraordinary thing, that statement of hers, don't you think? Now you heard it twice. Did she vary it at all?"

"By scarcely a word, Frank. But to me that seems natural. Ever since her illness her mind had remained unoccupied. When, once more startled into action, it began to receive and record impressions, I should expect them to be simple, factual, and enduring. She told her story as a child does or an un-educated person, without the distraction of other and competing thoughts. The result, a clear and truthful narrative."

He said,

"Yes. As usual, you hit the nail on the head. Well, that's all about Cardozo, I think. He got the paper he was looking for of course, just as Mrs. Anning says. And if she hadn't made her simple factual statement, it might have cost him his life. No one—no one would have believed he was innocent if that paper had been found on him actually stained, as it was, with Field's blood. He could wash his hands, as Marie very prudently insisted on his doing, but he could not wash the blood off that piece of paper, and if he had been picked up with it on him——"

"Where was it, Frank?"

He laughed.

"In the heel of his right boot. He must have known he was risking his neck by keeping it on him, but there wasn't a soul in the world he would trust with it. And now he'll be off to collect the treasure—if it really exists. Ill-gotten goods don't seem very lucky to handle. This particular lot has the usual trail of blood and crime."

Miss Silver quoted from a very much older author than her favourite Lord Tennyson:

" 'He that maketh haste to be rich shall not be innocent'."

Frank lifted a hand and let it fall again.

"Well, Solomon knew a thing or two," he said. "And now, what about you? Are you staying on, or are you coming back to town?"

"I shall be returning to Sea View for a few days. Miss Anning has been able to get temporary help, a very nice woman who was with them for some years before her marriage, and she will, I think, be glad to have me there, though now that Mrs. Anning is so much better she will be more of a companion."

"I am afraid this business will have hit her financially."

"To a certain extent that is unavoidable. But she has a number of September bookings which she hopes will not be affected. There are three Miss Margetsons who come down every year for the whole of the month. She has rung them up, and they would not think of altering their arrangements. There are also some friends of theirs, a Mr. and Mrs. Bunting, to whom they had recommended Sea View, and who are most unlikely to change their plans. So I hope that Miss Anning will not be too much inconvenienced."

Frank Abbott, stretched comfortably on the small of his back, remarked that she would be lucky if she got out of it so well.

"I hope she knows that if it hadn't been for you she would have been arrested before Lady Castleton showed her hand. In fact if it hadn't been for you, I suppose the hand just wouldn't have been shown at all. Now, how on earth did you come to suspect her? I've been wondering about that."

"The sleeping-tablets," said Miss Silver. "When I found that she had not only taken them in Mrs. Hardwick's presence, but had asked her to look in again and make sure that she was sleeping, the idea of a carefully prepared alibi suggested itself. The whole thing was out of character in anyone so obviously assured and self-reliant as Lady Castleton. I went on to consider her relation to the other people in the house. She had known them all for a very long time. She was beautiful, gifted, and successful, but she did not seem to inspire affection. She was bound to Mrs. Field by old ties of friendship, but the link appeared to be more one of habit than of anything else. There did not seem to have been any warmth in her marriage. Mrs. Trevor informs me that the only person to whom she had ever been truly attached was her sister Irene, drowned ten years ago. There was, I found, a general feeling that she took her own way and did what she chose. One of those dominant women who do not allow themselves to be deflected from whatever purpose they may have in hand. In fact a very dangerous person to blackmail."

"But you did not know that she was being blackmailed."

She said in her most precise manner,

"It became apparent. Mrs. Field talked to me a good deal. It was clear that her stepson had been trying to get money out of her. She did not say that the letters which he was threatening to publish involved Lady Castleton's young sister. She merely told me that girls always would run after her husband, and that he was too kind-hearted to snub them. She said there was one in particular who had behaved very foolishly, and that it had all been very distressing, because she was drowned whilst bathing, but of course that must have been due to an attack of cramp. It was Mrs. Trevor who supplied the link, when she told me of Lady Castleton's devotion to a sister who had met with this tragic fate. It is difficult in retrospect to reckon up all the small things which confirm suspicion and add to it. If the letters mentioned by Mrs. Field were of equal concern to Lady Castleton, would Alan Field have neglected this farther opportunity of blackmail? Was she the kind of woman who would submit to such pressure or allow her sister's name to be damaged? I am sure that she was not. Continuing my observations, I discerned what interested me very much. Everyone in the house showed signs of increasing strain. Pippa Maybury was very near to breaking-point. But Lady Castleton, described as suffering from severe headaches on Tuesday and Wednesday and being obliged to go off early to bed and take a sleeping-draught, appeared now to be in perfect health. Under a controlled manner I was aware of something to which it is difficult to give a name. Triumph is, perhaps, too strong a word satisfaction not in quite the right vein. Perhaps the nearest I can get to it is accomplishment. It kept on getting stronger all the time, and in the end it alarmed me profoundly——" She broke off with a slight smile, adding, "You see, it is all very simple."

He laughed.

"It always is! As I started off by saying, quite a number of people have cause to be very grateful that you found it so. Hardwick might just have gone on holding his tongue——"

Miss Silver shook her head.

"He would not have allowed an innocent person to be arrested."

"Well, you know, the beautiful Adela had a very strong pull—old family friend—guest in his house—Personage with capital P. And against all that—well, when you come to sort it out, nothing but a fairly strong suspicion. She might have put up the same story as Pippa Maybury—said she had come down to meet him and found him dead. As a matter of fact I can't think why she didn't."

Miss Silver coughed.

"Oh, no, she would not do that."

"And why not?"

"She would never have made such an admission. You must remember that she was, as you have said, a personage. In one way and another her name has been before the public for thirty years, and there has never been a whisper against her character. She had a good deal of aristocratic pride, and she would, I am sure, have preferred her own death, or that of anyone else, to having it supposed that she had made a secret assignation with Mr. Field. I am, in fact, reminded of the well known lines in which Lord Tennyson, speaking of Sir Lancelot, says:

'His honour rooted in dishonour stood
And faith unfaithful kept him falsely true.'

The circumstances, of course, are not the same, but there is a certain similarity which I find suggestive."

He watched her through half closed lids. This was Maudie in essence. The Victorian Standard Applied. The Moral Pointed. Penetrating Analysis of Character. And all served up with the true Tennysonian garnish. His respect for her was immense, his enjoyment perennial. He came reluctantly to his feet and kissed her hand.

"Madam, your most devoted! Till our next crime!"

She looked at him between affection and reproof.

"My dear Frank!"